Time of the
Locust

Time of the
Locust

a novel

MOROWA YEJIDÉ

ATRIA BOOKS

New York   London   Toronto   Sydney   New Delhi

30731439/
C

ATRIA BOOKS
A Division of Simon & Schuster, Inc.
1230 Avenue of the Americas
New York, NY 10020

Copyright © 2014 by Morowa Yejidé

All rights reserved, including the right to reproduce this book or portions thereof in any form whatsoever. For information address Atria Books Subsidiary Rights Department, 1230 Avenue of the Americas, New York, NY 10020.

First Atria Books hardcover edition June 2014

ATRIA BOOKS and colophon are trademarks of Simon & Schuster, Inc.

For information about special discounts for bulk purchases, please contact Simon & Schuster Special Sales at 1-866-506-1949 or business@simonandschuster.com.

The Simon & Schuster Speakers Bureau can bring authors to your live event. For more information or to book an event, contact the Simon & Schuster Speakers Bureau at 1-866-248-3049 or visit our website at www.simonspeakers.com.

Interior design by Kyoko Watanabe

Manufactured in the United States of America

10 9 8 7 6 5 4 3 2 1

Library of Congress Cataloging-in-Publication Data
Yejidé, Morowa.
Time of the locust / Morowa Yejidé.—First Atria books hardcover edition.
    pages cm
1. Autistic children—Family relationships—Fiction. 2. Children of prisoners—Fiction.
3. Fathers and sons—Fiction. 4. Murder—Fiction. 5. Retribution—Fiction.
6. Redemption—Fiction. 7. Psychological fiction.
I. Title.
    PS3625.E432T56 2014
    813'.6—dc23
                                    2013027440
ISBN 978-1-4767-3135-3
ISBN 978-1-4767-3137-7 (ebook)

To my mother, Doris, who showed me how to fly.

To my father, Dr. Everette J. Freeman, who taught me how to stand.

To my husband, Lutalo, who dared me to dream.

To my three sons: Jahi, Kachisicho, and Bailo, who reminded me to smile.

Know this: we continue.

—*Two Thousand Seasons* by Ayi Kwei Armah

Contents

PART I

PART II

PART III

PART I

Locusts

The creatures had been flying in Sephiri's dreams for weeks, and they had even begun to take wing on his waking thoughts. And now, as he sat in the children's playroom, he reached for a crayon and a leaf of construction paper with the gravity of an architect, his smooth, creamed-coffee face immobile, a single mole dotting his cheek. He stared down at the paper through two dark, luminous eyes, in which the sharp and bright edges of things flashed in reflection. He blocked out the mosaic of murals on the walls, the stacks of glossy unopened books, the piles of blocks, and the blank-faced children, each lost in an opaque realm of secret activity.

The gleam from the track lighting glazed everything in the room as if it had all been brushed by a baker's egg white. There was the smell of lemon disinfectant, which he did not like, which hung always in the air like a toxic cloud. There was the flicker from the farthest bulb at the ceiling that caught his eye again, as it had for several weeks, a distracting affront to the even order of light. But Sephiri turned his mind away from all of that now. There was only the sheet of white, the crayon in his hand, the images in his head. He'd had dreams before in his seven years on the earth, terrible visions from the Land of Air. There were the shadows that peeled themselves from the walls in his room and chased him out of his bed. There was the red creature that hid inside his mattress, the impish thing that cut through the springs, its incandescent eyes staring up at him through a dark, gaping hole.

Those dreams were not like the loveliness of his World of Water, the realm of deep blue and luminescence where Sephiri spent much of his time floating. He loved to drift far out to the Obsidians, as his sea friends called them. They were the tips of submerged mountains, enormous peaks that rose from the water like black pyramids from the deep. They marked where the invertebrates and the spiked beasts and the water plants ruled. Sephiri loved them all. He could speak there and be understood. The creatures living there gave him assurance that all he witnessed and heard in that place was real.

He wasn't sure about the creatures flying through his dreams. They weren't anything like the creatures of the Land of Air. The caterpillars he'd squeezed between his fingers in the backyard. The flies on the glass rim of his orange juice. The spiders that hung in corners. They were not like the other things he was able to keep a photograph of in his mind after one look: the number of tiles on a floor, the license plates of cars along their street, the label of ingredients of everything in the medicine cabinet. His mother locked the cabinet, but Sephiri was able to get it open anyway. He adored the Tylenol and cold medication boxes and containers, which he would line up and then line up again. There were lists of active and inactive ingredients, with marvelous arrangements of letters, which he had memorized without understanding how to pronounce any of them: acetaminophen, dextromethorphan, phenylephrine, anhydrous citric acid, potassium sorbate. He loved the sodiums madly: sodium borate, sodium chloride, sodium laurel, sodium laureth, sodium bicarbonate, sodium benzoate, sodium citrate.

When he was finished with the ingredients, he would focus on the letters that spelled *WARNING* on each container. He recognized this word from the order of the letters and knew it was the same word on the big sign above the red emergency door at the Takoma Park Autism Center, where he spent nearly every day. There were other things written next to *WARNING* on the boxes. He didn't know what any of those words meant, but he was sure they were trying to save him from tasting something disgusting. Sephiri thought the words, especially in this case, probably referred to various kinds of foods he hated. Say, squash or chicken, for example. Or nasty sandwiches, which he was sure had to be any sandwich that was not peanut butter and jelly.

He had gotten off the safety cap and swallowed some pretty blue pills once and had to be rushed to the hospital, screaming. There were maddening lights, sounds, and touching. There were white sheets that chafed his skin and cold, shiny things. Worst of all, there were no bathtubs anywhere—no porcelain baths filled with blue water, where he could calm down, where he could get away, out to the three mountaintops that rose from the ocean.

The beings—terrifying tangle of fingers and voices—had put him in the shower instead. He'd acted out his fury and fits with his eyes clamped shut but had to take a shower anyway. More than losing his voice from the screaming, more than the stuff they did when he was finally finished vomiting and had been cleaned with that dreadful soap that smelled like the bottle in the cabinet that read *POLISH REMOVER*, Sephiri was furious that he hadn't had a chance to finish ensuring order in the medicine cabinet. He hadn't had the chance to finish saving the Tylenol boxes from disarray, from their disconnection to their places on the earth.

After the blue pills, and only after his mother fell asleep, he would slip out of bed to open the cabinet, to order and reorder. He promised the boxes and bottles that he would never swallow anything from them again. He had hurt their feelings without realizing it. He had learned his lesson. He would put everything back as it had been, with each item turned at the exact angle of origination, with the pill packs arranged as they were and the lock clicked back in place. And he would get up every night to sanctify what was behind that mirror in the bathroom over the sink, with the distant sound of a freight train's midnight whistle as his cue. Such activity was a deep balm to Sephiri, a way to make everything in the world fit in its precise position on the planet. As all things should. Not the jungle of confusion he was forced to witness, to waddle in, every day of his life.

But there had been nothing like these flying creatures, these wild things that had somehow found him in his head. And for many days and nights, they swarmed the hinterlands of his mind, riding his thoughts, replacing the shadows and the mattress thing, replacing even the medicine cabinet lately. The glowing amber in their bellies was warm and everlasting. That much he knew. They reminded Sephiri of the oily liquid inside his mother's dusty perfume bottles, which he had spent considerable time ordering in the twilight of dawn when the house was still and asleep, when there was less interference from all the other things assaulting his eyes and ears. And every time Sephiri thought of the locusts, he wanted to smile; it was something his mother had often tried to get him to do, something he'd seen demonstrated on the faces of others but had never understood how it worked.

Smiles intrigued him. He spent many days thinking about them, especially at bathtime, when his mother often smiled at him in the quiet. He would scream to let her know that he did not want to be soaped up right away, that he had an important visit to make to the Obsidians, where he might ask the Great Octopus about smiles and other things he did not understand. He flailed and splashed. He knocked the soap from her hands and kicked up enough water to pool on the bathroom floor. Then he would hear the loudness, the oncoming train in her voice. "Stop it stop it stop it stop it stop it." She hissed and held on. He persisted. He hadn't had the time to stop it stop it right then. He had to get into his boat before the water got cold, before the tub stopper was pulled out and the tributaries were drained.

When at last his mother seemed to understand his signals, when she was as soaked and outraged from all the splashing as if she had been dropped into a circus dumping tank, she left him alone to calm down, to absorb the turquoise and warmth, to disembark. It was at frustrating moments such as this that Sephiri wished that they spoke the same language. But he did not speak the language of Air, the land of his mother. He did not understand how things were done there or what occupied the species. There were different sounds and faces that somehow ruled them, and these were attached to meaning that was unintelligible to him. He had no patience for the stops and starts that fell from their mouths. There was no sharing of thought and feeling as there was with his friends of the deep. Sometimes, though, when his mother tired of chasing him, when he tired of screaming, she held him, and he allowed himself to be held. They felt each other. That was as close as Sephiri had ever gotten to reaching his mother and penetrating the Land of Air.

He had discovered as early as two years old that Air and Water were different places with different ways and language. He had been playing with some colored blocks on the floor. He had wanted to line the blocks up and then line them up again. He remembered his mother picking up different blocks, saying something, and pointing. He did not look at her face, but he could see that finger pointing from the corner of his eye and her hand holding the block. She took his hand and placed it on each block, and he felt as if he was being pulled apart. He didn't want to hold the blocks. He didn't want to think about their shape and color and mimic her sounds. He had wanted only to line them up and line them up again. To ensure that they were where they were supposed to be. He tried to explain. But his mother did not comprehend him, and the more he tried to get her to understand, the more it became clear to him that she would never know his language.

Sephiri gripped the crayon and looked down at the paper, thinking instead of the fat-bellied locusts of his dreams again, for he did not want to dwell on things that would make him cry. Why had the locusts come? In his dreams, he saw them growing to bursting, pushing up and out of the earth, taking flight. Above his head, they were waiting, rising, and hovering, as if by their gathering they anticipated something. He began guiding the crayon, his hand moving effortlessly. He first drew the foreground and then sketched a vast plain. In the center, he constructed two towers with a giant iron gate connecting them and an enormous structure behind them. Sephiri didn't know what it was, but it reminded him of the coat closet he locked himself into sometimes at home, but bigger. A giant black box that held things, with a voice that called to him from its farthest corner.

"Come here . . ."

He did not recognize the voice, and he was not sure what the two words meant. Especially together. He'd heard them said before at the Autism Center, and sometimes, he thought, his mother said them too. But he couldn't decide if the two words were the same as other phrases he'd heard: "come home" or "can hear." But all that was too much to figure out now, since the other things were so clear to him at last. His hand moved deftly, sketching enormous mountains in the background, a cloud of locusts flying over their peaks.

Sephiri furiously continued drawing, and at the height of his fever, he snapped his crayon. He threw the drawing down and watched the paper slide under the table. He was angry that his hand had not been able to keep up with his mind, one of many things that frustrated him about being in the Land of Air. He couldn't stand the different regimens and schedules that were not of his own making, how the people were always telling and talking and asking, until it all became a sort of noise that ran together in his head. This place was filled with air, not water, where he felt at home.

He could float out to the realness of his World of Water, where the sea was an endless expanse as turquoise as the liquid in his bathtub. Where he didn't have to try to understand the strange sounds of words dripping from mouths. He could head to his desired destination anytime he wanted, with only his little wooden boat gliding toward the three great black rocks that rose from the ocean. The dolphin waited for his company there, and the Great Octopus sat in majesty in his iridescent lair on the ocean floor. What concerned him in Air did not concern him in Water. He did not need the laws of physics to rein in his terrors, frustrations, and confusions there. He did not need to spin or bang or rock or flap. He could forget about the creatures flying in his dreams, the voice in the giant black box, the meaning of sounds and faces and smiles. He could forget about the words of Air and speak freely in Water, where the language of men was as indecipherable to his friends of the deep as it was to him. An encrypted thing to ponder briefly and release, like the dialogue of wolves and birds in flight.

Burials

"I am dead to you."

These were the last words Brenda remembered hearing her husband, Horus Thompson, say after the verdict was read. Murder. Life. Prison. Seven years later, she was still trying to shovel soil over the sound of this proclamation. On this morbid anniversary, she dropped Sephiri off at the Autism Center and headed to work at the U.S. Department of Agriculture. She was exhausted from cleaning up an accident Sephiri had made on the living-room carpet at four o'clock that morning. He was wide awake after that. She had to lock him in the bedroom with her to keep him from wandering away. He'd spent the rest of the night taking her shoes out of the closet and lining them up along the center of the room. The coffee she drank for breakfast sloshed around her insides, ineffectual against a desperate need for sleep.

The *whoosh* and *clank* of doors opening and closing in other corridors of the building filled the silence as usual. Brenda walked through a cloud of someone's cologne, which mixed with the smell of the building's ancient wooden molding and the pine disinfectant that drifted about. On any other day, she would not have noticed through the regular haze of sleep deprivation. She would have taken on the morning disasters and her overscheduled day as usual. But today marked the anniversary of the last time she saw her husband.

The man she loved, the man she thought she knew enough about, was handed a life sentence that marked a chasm between them forever. Brenda remembered how the earth plates shifted where she stood in the courtroom that day. The ground opened up and fell away when Horus turned around and proclaimed the terrible words to her. She barely heard him in the deafening thunderclap of the verdict announcement. She could still see him shackled. His face was familiar, but a transformation had already begun, a morphing into something right before her eyes. Her bladder emptied where she stood, and she groped in the air for something to awaken her from the nightmare. Manden, Horus's brother, called her name softly in the aftershocks, his strangled voice shattering the glass that held her sanity in those seconds. "Brenda . . ." he said, then faltered. "Brenda," he said again, unable to get past her name, which hung in the air for a moment, then was gone over cliffs.

And there was that other voice of righteousness, of justification and punishment. The defense attorney had long ago faded into the oblivion of her mind, out there where the rings of cowardice and haplessness lay. But the voice of the prosecutor had burned into Brenda like a branding iron as he made his statement. All through the trial, the prosecuting attorney had not been a man. He was an entity. The verbal manifestation of an institution. Crime and punishment. Law and order. His voice felt like a weapon, a malevolent presence that filled her head as she sat there in the wooden pew, as the ground fell away and the roof was ripped from its beams with proclamations, with the electricity of wrath. . . .

"I've told you everything about this case, ladies and gentlemen," he had said. "But most important, I hope I have helped you to understand that Horus Thompson is a lone-wolf terrorist. Now, is that a crime? Ask yourselves. Yes, we've heard the stories. We may even feel some sympathy. We know of his obsessions with the notion that the victim killed his father back when—let us recall the tender age—at the age of seven he claims to have witnessed the shooting death of his father at the alleged hands of the victim. Yes, we have heard of his troubled childhood, his broken family, his alleged psychic break. But his brother, Manden Thompson, was there, too, wasn't he? Why Horus Thompson and not his brother? Why would one take the law into his own hands and not the other?

"Ladies and gentlemen, I'm not going to stand here and deny the statistics. As we have heard repeatedly from the defense, there are numerous reports of the disproportionate number of black men in prison. Record numbers of persons are also being placed under probation or parole supervision. You heard the defense remind us that by 1989, the total inmate population in our nation's prisons and jails is expected to pass the one-million mark. We've all heard about findings claiming that almost one in four—twenty-three percent—of black men in the age group twenty to twenty-nine is either in prison, in jail, on probation, or on parole on any given day. And Horus Thompson is twenty-seven years old.

"In this year 1986 alone, three hundred forty-two out of every one hundred thousand blacks were admitted to state or federal prison. I've read that this is triple what it was in 1926. It's reported so far this year that blacks make up forty-four percent of new prison admissions, though they are less than an eighth of the population. And as the defense has also pointed out, the black presence in the prison population has increased to nearly half this year so far. Citizens, I am not going to stand here and tell you that the Thompson family won't suffer, that they haven't suffered. The Thompson family will most likely struggle under the strain of Horus Thompson being yet another young black male under the control of the criminal justice system at a time when he should be starting a family, mastering critical life skills, and advancing in a career.

"The repercussions of this situation are undeniable. It is yet another assault on community stability that adds to an already debilitated state of affairs. As the defense has said, any potential contributions this man could have made to the community will be stunted. Some will be lost forever. Ladies and gentlemen, this, in a larger sense, impacts us all. But are any of these things crimes?

Perhaps in a larger sense, these things may be crimes. What we've all read and heard about is certainly a shame.

"But is what Horus Thompson did a crime? Is murder a crime? The answer, we know, is absolutely yes. The stakes are high. Because, ladies and gentlemen, what we are dealing with now, who we are dealing with now, is a man who has chosen vengeance for his own misguided recrimination, as his sword. Knowing what we know, we can no longer presume this man here is innocent, no matter his reasons for doing what he did. We must call him what he is: a cold-blooded murderer, who lured the victim from his home and drove him miles away to kill him. Citizens, that is who we are dealing with.

"Let's remember very clearly and without hesitation that a peace officer is any person who by virtue of his office or public employment is vested by law with a duty to maintain public order or to make arrests for offenses. This is who and what the victim was. A soldier of law and order, of justice. This is a fact. And at the very least, we must ask ourselves the most important questions we as citizens, as a nation, face. We must look ourselves in the eye and commit to the dire necessity of ensuring that we live in a society of law and order. I charge you all with committing to the great and important responsibility of guaranteeing that we enforce those statutes consistent with the intention of law and order. We must not labor in doubt, in questioning and quibbling over the determination of rules outside of those great intentions.

"Are we going to invent our own rules and then act accordingly? That's really what we are talking about. We may be tempted to descend into thoughts about Mr. Thompson's reasons for doing what he did. We may even be tempted to think that the alleged murder of Mr. Thompson's father was in some way more significant than the victim's murder. But even with this temptation, we must consider what we know as fact.

"And more important, the so-called slaying of Mr. Thompson's political-activist father, some twenty years ago, is not the concern

of the court today. Jack Thompson is not here today to defend his
son's actions in killing Officer Sam Teak. What is of concern today
is what Mr. Thompson took from the victim. His life. His mortal
connection to his family. His legacy. I don't think you need me to
stand here and give you a history lesson on racism. On bigotry. On
the bitter fruits of this country of which we are all aware.

"I'm not going to lecture you on the litany of racially biased
experiences of black people in America. I am sure that many of you
are already aware of that. I can say that there has been group after
group, legislation after legislation, in my lifetime—even before my
lifetime—established to help black people in their own communi-
ties. To help black people in this country.

"And I won't argue that by and large, history has shown us that
the burden of promoting and protecting the interests of the black
community has fallen to those who may only have an interest in
the black community. Ladies and gentlemen, our quarrel is not
with them. The civil rights movement has taught us much. And if
it has taught us anything, especially now in 1986, it has taught us
that peace for us all is most important. This is America, ladies and
gentlemen. And if any individual can kill even a peace officer—be
he retired or not, he has served his duty to all of us—then we make
the dangerous trip to a troubling place, ladies and gentlemen. We
enter a jungle from which I fear there is no escape . . ."

Brenda remembered how the voice thundered at the end and the
outraged gasps of the jury. They were melted by the prosecuting
attorney's hot fire, forged and hardened into something impenetrable. As Horus was led away, she had to step back, as if from the
edge of something, then step back farther still, as the drop and
descent of things began. The things that she knew to fit into neat
piles, with right and wrong organized in primary colors, easily distinguishable and unadulterated. Foundations collapsed around her,
and the braces she had spent the four-month trial fortifying buck-
led and snapped. She looked on in horror and awe. The free fall of
consciousness and the atrophy of doubt. The tumble of hope and

the fall of dream. In a matter of seconds, Horus looked at her from across a great expanse and said, "I am dead to you." She did not understand what that meant until much later, when the loudness of his absence filled her ears, and she could hear nothing else.

Brenda couldn't wrap her mind around her new title: prison wife. At the behest of friends in those first few weeks after the thunderclap, who quickly retreated to their own lives, Brenda began reading the essays in a newsletter for family members of the incarcerated. *Bound by Love* arrived in her mailbox. She began and ended reading the essays across her cold marital bed in one day, unable to stomach the carnage of words, the cry of phrases. One essay seeped into her soul, so that she could not bear to look upon the newsletter again, for fear she might come across an especially bleak voice that haunted her, which read:

"He did not die. But he is not alive. How can I grieve for him? How can I let him go? What is there to hold of him? His shirts? His razor and deodorant? The shoes still at the bottom of the closet? The belief that he will one day be home when I arrive? No. There is nothing to let go; there is nothing to hold. There are only tears in the dark. There is only the wolf in the wilderness, and I don't know if the wolf is him or me. We call to each other in the blackness, but our lonely howls cannot penetrate the thickness of time. There is only his face in my dreams, his voice in my thoughts. His mannerisms in my children, two boys and a girl who do not know him anymore. They know him only as a word among the many others in the lexicon of their speech, a word that will fade into the Latin of the past. He is only among the shadows of the setting sun. One year anesthetizes the next. One decade lays to rest the one preceding it. He is exhumed only in memory. He did not die. But he is not alive . . ."

Brenda had been unable to read any further. In the beginning, she didn't want to believe that such a thing could be true. How could she have lost Horus to the past without realizing it? She hated herself for believing what he had told her before he left town that day. Before he left town to end their lives without her permission. He was going to work things out with his brother, Manden, he said. Work what out? What was left to work out? Deep inside, she knew that something was wrong. *He'll handle it,* she told herself. It took years to admit that she should have asked more questions, that she knew the morning he left that there was something else.

In all the time Brenda knew him, Horus spoke of his family only a few times and with great difficulty. He talked in that odd way of one carefully reciting a collection of facts, as if saying anything more might conjure the living or the dead. His father was murdered in front of him. There was no justice done for his death. After this, his mother became mentally ill and passed away. He and his brother were raised by an uncle they didn't know and would never come to like.

She listened to Horus each time and allowed herself to be led. She went willingly down a path of simplifications, of illusions. And it still made her face hot when she thought of it: that there had been another man beneath the man she married. But it was this man who took over that night, that weekend, her life, and Sephiri's future. He had his reasons, Horus said when the police came to their front door. There are reasons for everything. This she knew. But where had she been in his reasoning, in his ruminations? What about her life, their life together? The man whose tenor she used to listen to under the sheets at night, the one who held her and called her Baby, so that it meant a million things at once, was now an echo, a resonance left after something larger was gone. Horus Thompson had been reduced to a thought, a concept. A living, breathing man said that he was dead. And it was true.

Brenda struggled to breathe, lumbering through the stale air of the government building. The walk from the elevator to the office suite at the end of the mile-long corridor seemed to take an eternity, and her swollen ankles felt as if they were on the verge of bursting. The 258 pounds she carried made themselves known loudly, tiring her with every step. Midway to the office, she was drenched in sweat, the deodorant under her arms and between her thighs already melting.

She'd had a time getting Sephiri ready for the special van that came to pick him up every day. Dressing him this morning had been like trying to hold on to a slippery fish. He screamed and ran around the house. He urinated on the carpet and threw popcorn all over the floor. She finally cornered and tackled him in the coat closet. She held him in her arms in a straitjacket embrace while he kicked and flailed. After a time, he settled down, and they panted there together in the darkness, listening to their hearts beat through their chests. *A mother should not resent her child,* Brenda thought, rebuking herself. She should not feel apprehension when she puts her hand on her baby's forehead after he has already fallen asleep, when he is quiet and has passed out from jumping and shrieking or filling a house with silence. Shame grew once more in the pit of her stomach as she clutched her son in the dark, and she began the ritual of smothering her disgrace.

Brenda felt her blood pressure worsening as she walked down the hallway to her office. She had forgotten to fill her prescription again. The white slip was still crumpled at the bottom of her purse. She hated those water pills. They seemed to make her gain even more weight. Pounds atop the heap she had constructed to insulate her from the past. She sighed and focused on getting to the office. Her beacon was the water fountain, the last five meters.

She arrived at her desk and collapsed into the chair. The date on the calendar glared at her from the wall. Seven years today, she thought. She looked at the peanut butter candy bars in the open desk drawer. The need to cover it all over and put a gravestone on the memory of things always seemed to make her want to eat. Food was there for her with open arms and offered itself to the great pit at the core of her soul. And every time she bit into peach cobbler, shoveled seasoned pork roast into her mouth, or spooned a gallon of ice cream, she was able to bury just a little more of the memories that kept resurfacing, of Horus rising from the past.

Closing the desk drawer, Brenda thought of how Horus looked when he came home the night that ended their lives. He arrived in their bedroom like an ominous sky just before a storm, his hands shaking but with nothing to say. Quiet. Struck. Waiting. His face was stone. "Jack Thompson" was what he said when he did speak, then sat down on the bed. He said it so calmly, sinking into the mattress, staring at the curtains billowing in the window. Brenda waited for him to say something—anything else—but he did not.

What about his father, Jack Thompson? As Brenda stood staring from the frame of their bathroom door that night, she couldn't understand if he was talking to her or to himself, and it wasn't until the next moment that she realized Horus had said his father's name but meant something more.

Then came the sirens and lights that she expected to be on the way to someone else's house but had stopped in front of theirs.

"Horus?" said Brenda.

The sound of footfalls approached like the headless horseman, louder and louder.

"Horus?"

A knock. Then silence.

"Horus?"

Another knock.

Brenda had blacked out the rest. The things she felt between her husband looking at her and opening the front door to let the police in, between the handcuffs flashing under the living-room lamplight and the pregnancy test in the bathroom trash can. Until that day in their bedroom, with the walls washed in red and blue, she had thought of vengeance only as an abstraction. Years later, she would tell herself that vengeance had somehow become a living being to Horus and that it possessed him in some way. That it was a thing that had been growing inside of him since the beginning. A lethal thing that would claim them both.

Brenda snatched a tissue from the box on her desk and wiped her wet forehead. She had tried to get Horus to talk more about his childhood, but it was like a forbidden room in a house. She later came to respect his silence about his deceased parents and ignored his evasions about his boyhood. She dismissed the oddness of him having a brother in the same city whom she met only once before they married. And she made the ancient mistake with Horus that women make with men: belief that she could renovate him. She believed that her love could make whatever it was Horus chose not to talk about go away. She thought that a new life could be painted over the old one. He was tender and quietly devoted, and he loved her. She would love him and fill in the rest.

Brenda opened the desk drawer, looked at the candy, and closed it again. In the end, she had not been able to compete with the past. Her love for Horus had not been enough to stop him from pulling the trigger. It had not had the reach of justice and retribution. How could she judge him—as society had—for his need to bring his father's killer to justice by his own hand? And she wondered what it all had gotten him and if a ruined life was the reward. She still wasn't sure, and it troubled her that she could not see past the great wall of despair that hid the answer from view. Sundays became anathema to her. Going to church as a means of coping did not soothe her eternal distemper, and in her mind, that place was a graveyard of women banking a river of tears. Each woman's misery sloshed and overflowed and spilled out over the ruined mess of the others, commingling in grief, in wretchedness. She didn't want to see all of that every week.

The telephone on Brenda's desk rang, drilling through her thoughts. Sighing, she picked up the receiver. "Hello?" she said.

"Mrs. Thompson?"

"Speaking."

"Good morning. This is Dr. Susan Watson at the Autism Center."

Brenda tensed when she heard that springtime bounce in the young doctor's voice, so full of things that were nearly weightless, light and airy problems like what color to have her study painted

and whether to plant tulips when a thaw breaks. She remembered
Dr. Watson telling her just a few weeks ago, apologetically, that
she had once put in for a transfer to a different facility in Virginia.
That she thought she could handle the unbreakable silence of these
children at the Autism Center and the stillness that was interrupted
only by their sudden outbursts. After three years, she hadn't understood them any more than on her first day at the center. The
children ignored her still, and she had grown tired of the feeling of
always talking to herself. But she couldn't let these children down,
she'd said.

"Is everything OK with Sephiri today?" Brenda asked. She picked
up a pencil, gripping it so tightly that it snapped in two.

"Yes, Mrs. Thompson. He's fine. I'm not calling about a problem. It's just that . . . your son did something today, something we've
never seen happen before here at the center. I really don't know
how to explain it." There was a long pause. "As you know," she continued, breathless, "we've had Sephiri since he was three years old,
and we have been able to monitor him steadily. We feel we know
him and understand the spectrum of his condition quite well. But
today he has been different in some really rather remarkable ways.
We think at this point, we should all sit down and talk about it. You
and me. And his father."

There was a pause for reasons neither woman spoke of aloud.
Because there was no living father for Sephiri in the sense of the
word. Because Sephiri's father was underground, among the Pa-
leolithic mineral deposits embedded in the earth. There was only
the shadowy figure of Manden Thompson, the boy's uncle and
reluctant stepfather, who appeared occasionally. Manden held the
role only in title. Only in an envelope with a check in it that he volunteered every month. Only in situations like this, when a child's
"father" had to be summoned. Time and again, Brenda penciled in
Manden's name on forms and registrations. She could not bear to
leave that line next to her name blank and be newly reminded of
what was gone forever.

Brenda knew that there was a file somewhere in the young doctor's desk with the details of Horus Thompson's incarceration. She continued to use her married name, even though the title no longer held any meaning. It remained with her like the feeling of a limb still there after amputation. So when the young doctor spoke of Sephiri's father, Brenda felt a twinge as she thought of the scope of what was there and what was not, a half-truth, with the other half capable of devouring both pieces if brought to the fore. She could almost believe when on occasion she spoke of it in the presence of those who did not know that Manden was really Sephiri's uncle. The lie sparkled boldly in the half-light of the pause with the young doctor.

"Is everything OK with Sephiri?" Brenda asked again, louder.

"It's nothing bad. As a matter of fact—"

"In what ways is he different now, Dr. Watson?"

"Well, he's drawing, which is something he's been known to do before. But not like this. Nothing like this. What he did today . . . It's just better discussed in person, Mrs. Thompson. I'd like to set something up with both of you as soon as possible. Today, if you can."

Brenda's throat was dry, and she struggled to control her nerves. She wasn't ready for more issues with Sephiri. She was already overwhelmed by the state he was in now. She could not do any of the things that mothers were normally compelled to do with their children in tow without grave consequences. Simple things like trips to the aquarium or the petting zoo. Even the parks held myriad challenges. She could not take Sephiri grocery shopping with her. All the smells and crowds at supermarkets seemed to trigger his mania. The beeps of the scan machines, the opening and slamming of cash registers, the incessant bell of the sliding automatic doors as customers came in and out seemed to disorient him, so that he became quickly agitated and broke into high-pitched keening, spinning, and knocking things over.

If she attempted to troll the aisles, Sephiri would fixate on a row of something on a shelf, becoming as immobile as a statue, staring and staring, while she tried to pull him away. It took nearly an hour to put ten things into the shopping cart. Other times, he would take the melons, tomatoes, and green apples—always something round, anything round—from the produce bins and arrange them in a long line on the floor down the center of the aisle. If Brenda tried to stop him, he would rage and thrash around on the linoleum, with the old women shaking their heads in disgust and the young mothers looking on with thinly veiled arrogance and pity in their eyes. If one thing changed even slightly in her routine of getting him out of the house and in front of the stop where the van from the center came to pick him up, all efforts were lost to wild tantrums or "accidents" in his pants. What else could it be now? Brenda wondered. Weren't the daily chases, the screams, the silence enough? She was already overwhelmed. There wasn't room for more.

"Mrs. Thompson? When do you think would be a good time?" the doctor asked.

"I'll call you back in a bit to arrange something," Brenda said. Before the doctor could say another word, she hung up the phone.

Brenda heard someone come into the large department space and settle in another cubicle somewhere beyond the view of her own. There was the sound of a photocopying machine sputtering to life. The doctor's request for a meeting churned in her mind. What was to be arranged now?

And his father . . .

She thought of the day she'd received a petition for divorce from Horus's attorney, thirty days after he had been interred at Black Plains Correctional Institute. "No contact from family." That was what the note read that the attorney attached to the divorce papers according to Horus Thompson's request. The attorney urged her to grant it, saying that it had been his "final wish." She had not wanted to believe that the black ink on that line was his signature, the letters slanted and curled in that familiar way. But what was left to believe? Everything they did and planned together was swept aside in one day. The future of the child that was growing inside of her was doused by his father even before birth.

She kept the divorce papers under her mattress for another six months before she was able to open the envelope and read the words, to stare at his signature again. She signed on the line and went to the bathroom to vomit. She signed the papers and screamed and cried in the shower, with Sephiri bawling in his crib in the next room, with the scalding water raining down on her scalp. Since then, her rage had burned down and was molten now. She was too tired, too weighted with unhappiness, to fuel a bonfire of hate anymore. She thought of her signed copy of the divorce papers, buried still in the basement, under the tiles she had ripped up with the end of a hammer, yellowing on the concrete foundation.

Your son did something today . . .

Brenda sank back in her office chair, her face newly coated with sweat. Sephiri. His very name meant "secret place." And that had been true since his conception. She did not have the chance or the heart to tell Horus she was pregnant. After the verdict, after the devastation, Brenda spent days wandering the city and the grounds of the national monuments, haunting the botanical gardens and the corridors of art galleries. She stood in front of a hanging tapestry for hours at a museum, a sprawling emerald world of rolling hills and valleys of flowers, the Indian Ocean crashing on the shores of the South African coast. "They call it Sephiri," a voice said from behind Brenda that day. A museum guide smiled at her when she turned around. "It means the hidden place that exists in your heart," he said.

And Brenda stared at the green tapestry and rubbed her pregnant belly for a long time after the guide had said this. In her mind, she walked into that tapestry, into the downy valley of tender grass and through the meadow of white arum lilies. She knelt at the foothills of Outeniqua and dug a hole with her hands. There she laid the life she was never to have with Horus to rest and covered it over with dark soil. For his body was laid in state someplace else. He was now buried beneath the barren, rocky soil of the Black Plains Correctional Institute, to asphyxiate slowly on what he had done, to starve from what he had left undone.

These were things she once thought happened only to other men and women. And every time she looked at Sephiri's face, the guilt of what she kept from Horus cut into her like bits of glass. Should she have told Horus about his son? As he was led away to face the beginning of the end of his life, should she have told him that a part of him would still linger among the living? Would that have offered him a final psalm to carry through the gates of oblivion? Or would telling him have quickened his death, killed him twice over with the knowledge of something that was evidence of both his power and his powerlessness? She didn't know. She had never been able to understand which would have been better, and now she could only mourn what could never be salvaged.

"Your boy, Horus," Brenda whispered, looking at the calendar tacked to the wall of her cubicle, her tears blurring the date, her body numb. "What about Sephiri?"

Night

Sephiri awoke. He could hear the wail of a cargo train whistle in the night and the rhythm of its movement over the tracks. Hypnotic. Predictable. Soothing. He rolled over without opening his eyes and listened for something breathing, for he wanted to be certain that there was no creature hiding under the bed. Satisfied that he was safe, he opened his eyes and turned over onto his side and was startled by an ice-cold patch on the sheet. He had wet himself again. He tried to think about the steps. But he sometimes got it mixed up. Even after all this time, it was still like a puzzle: release, find toilet, urge. Or was it urge, find toilet, release? These were the kinds of things that didn't order themselves, that did not have a place. They weren't like the blocks or the green apples down the aisle. The steps couldn't be touched. They couldn't be handled. They weren't like the medicine cabinet.

The train horn sounded again, and Sephiri sat up. The train was going to the edges of green mountains, snaking through the plains of tall grass and brush, sliding by mirrored lakes. Sephiri stood up. There was position and sanctity at stake. There were things that needed his help, his facilitation in getting them back to where they needed to be in the world. The sodiums and the phosphates. The melons and the apples. The jars in the pantry. If he couldn't keep them in order, he worried that he wouldn't be able to manage the order of anything else. The things he could grasp and handle, at least. The rest was enigma. He took a step forward and smelled his reek, felt the clamminess of his wet pajamas against his skin. Should he try to change his clothes? He remembered then that there was a different lock on the medicine cabinet. Something shiny. He noticed it yesterday morning as his mother held him still and brushed his teeth in the mirror. There was something with a big ring and a black wheel with numbers on the front, stabbed into something on the side. He remembered watching his mother spin that wheel thing. Was that how it worked? He hadn't been able to concentrate with the fluoride froth in his mouth and the sound of the water running down the sink hole he wanted to explore. He was too distracted by the bottle of mouthwash and its emerald majesty, its greenish gleam against the white porcelain.

He regretted all of that now. He could feel the tension rising in his head, the nausea in his stomach. He spun around until he was dizzy enough to calm down. He would have to pay close attention the next time. He would concentrate on the wheel and what was to be done with it. He would make sure to understand.

Sephiri padded out to the dimly lit hallway. Silence. He liked it when the house was asleep, when all things were motionless with the night. He could enjoy the stillness of things that understood their place when it was not day. At night, there were fewer sights and sounds to take in. But he always found it difficult to sleep, and for as long as he could remember, the Land of Air filled him with so much when he was awake that when he tried to sleep, he could not hold it all. It overflowed and spilled out, and then he had to get up and find a way to clear and reorder his mind. He thought about his mother's perfume bottles, amber everlasting. They were in her room, on the dresser, which was their correct plain of existence, and he headed toward his mother's door. Not so long ago, he held them, caressed them, looked into their incandescent light in the rays of so many dawns. He lined them up along the dresser, atop the white lace, and lined them up again. The last time he was in his mother's room, he thought to check if the amber was the same color as her skin. But in the moonlight coming through the windows, he could not be sure.

So on that other night, Sephiri went over to his mother's bed. He stood over her as she slept and struggled to see her eyebrows, the rounded chin, the twin pillows of her cheeks, the markers he had memorized. He was about to put the perfume bottle on the little soft mound of one of her cheeks, to match the color, as one might match paint to a section of canvas. But his mother woke up wide-eyed, and her face had shifted into something. He thought it looked something like the look she had when he mixed up the steps and urinated on the carpet. Or the times he wanted to feel physics by tossing ceramic plates across the room. But he couldn't be sure.

And he couldn't tell if the look meant something bad or something good. It made him sad that he didn't understand the faces the people made in the Land of Air. He wanted to feel good when he was with his mother, like the feeling he had when he was eating peanut butter and jelly sandwiches. Satisfaction and bliss. He wanted to crawl inside the quiet she always seemed to have at the kitchen table, the humming sound she made when he sat in the tub as she washed him. The humming sound took away the feeling of touch. It gave the soap and water frequency and order. He wanted to find a way to conjure the seconds of that warm sun feeling that sometimes moved through him when she held him on her lap. When he could keep still. When he was able to block everything else out and let the warmth sheath him like a blanket. But he didn't know how. They spoke different languages, he and his mother. And sometimes when he thought of this unfortunate situation, it made him want to cry.

Sephiri took a few more steps in the dim hallway and looked down at the patterns in the Persian rug runner to make sure that they were where he had left them. He thought of that time he had hidden in the crook of a tree trunk in the woods of a park for a few hours. He needed to get away from the playground confusion, from the moving colors and the talking sounds. When his mother came with the men and the dogs to find him, he was counting the grooves in the wood and the termites. Someone pulled him out, and he screamed and kicked and rolled on the ground to tell them he wanted to stay there.

After that, there were special meetings at the Autism Center, more talking. There was that Dr. Watson lady who spoke more to him while he colored. Requests to draw pictures. Requests to listen to sounds. To look at something. To listen to something. To touch swatches of brown fur and palm bunches of white cotton. There were pictures held up to him: butterflies, oranges, balls, chickens, rabbits. He banged his forehead on the table when he tired of the exercises. They tried to stop him but he banged anyway. Then he picked up the chair and threw it to make his point. He screeched and flailed. He jumped up and down. When that wasn't comprehended, he stood immobile, statue-like, to get them to stop the chaos of the Land of Air.

In the hallway, Sephiri paused at his mother's bedroom door and walked on. He would leave the perfume bottles for now. He would not risk changing his sleeping mother's face. His reek grew stronger and wafted up his legs, past his big-boy spot, where it was the most pungent. It filled his nose and the air around him. To distract himself from the smell, he thought of the grandfather clock at the end of the hallway just before the stairs and moved toward it. He loved to watch the pendulum swing and listen to the *tick tock tick tock* in the quiet of the night. The *tick*s and *tock*s knew their order. They understood their place. He pressed his ear to its mechanics, its genius and symmetry. The sound was like his favorite shape: a cube. A shape of perfection, with its height width depth balanced against itself, whole and complete. Like the night in the coat closet. When he was able to enter and close the door, before his mother could catch him, he was encased. He was protected by the sublimity of height width depth. That was how everything should be.

When he had his fill of flawlessness, Sephiri turned from the clock and went to the stairs. One, two, three, four . . . He walked back up to the top to enjoy the start of the count, the repetition, the timing. Five, six, seven . . . It was then that the place he'd drawn on the piece of construction paper reappeared in his mind, the giant box like the coat closet. The flying creatures had been there, too, swarming in the sky above it. And there was the matter of the voice he'd heard that day. If he went back inside the coat closet, would he hear the voice again? Would he have more time to figure out whether the voice was really there and whether the voice knew anything about the place he drew in the picture? Maybe if he got close enough to it, he'd be able to understand. "Come here," the voice had said. What did that mean?

Air had limitations. Like the frozen things in the refrigerator that were too hard and stuck together to take apart. The extra peanut butter he wanted but couldn't have. The milk he wasn't allowed to drink because of the craze that came over him when he did so. The dancing blue flame that lived on top of the kitchen stove he was not permitted to touch, to play with. The static in the television he couldn't pick up and hold (the screen kept getting in the way). Then there was the matter of the holes that he would never be able to explore because they were too small to fit him: the garbage disposal, the sink drain, the washing machine, that tunnel at the bottom of the toilet bowl, the air-duct vent, the little place where the pencils went into the sharpener. And worst of all, the locks on the medicine cabinet that kept trying to stop him from rescuing the boxes. There was always something standing in his way in the Land of Air. And now there was this voice in the clutter of this world to also decipher.

Sephiri finished with the step counting and headed downstairs to the living room. A nightlight extended from an electrical socket. It looked like the flashlight of the anglerfish in the depths of Water, only dimmer. The curtains were drawn like huge blankets over the windows. He avoided the sofa, because to sit on it was to be enveloped, pulled down to the unknown depths of its brownish bulkiness to be caught by some long-fingered monster that lived inside. The man called Manden sat on the sofa a few times, and the sofa never got him. Nor did it ever bother his mother. Why? Sephiri wondered.

He didn't linger on the thought, because now the green carpet looked different without the lights on. He became frightened, and in his excitement, he couldn't remember where the light switch was. It wasn't the dark that worried him. It was the fear that something was different in the dark. In his mind, day things needed to stay day things and not change in the night. They ought not try to become something else. Without the lights, he couldn't see the legions of carpet fibers waving, a comforting reminder of the seaweed that grew where his friends lived.

In the dark, the carpet looked like that enormous bog with the bestial amphibians—just like the ones in his picture books—waiting in the murk to grab him, beings that didn't seem to belong to the Land of Air or the World of Water. In those first minutes when he was climbing into his boat to sail away from his troubles, they would watch him float off with ominous eyes. "Where do you think you're going?" the cricket frogs would say. The mudpuppies and hellbender salamanders crowded around his boat, staring and hissing, so that his departure was slowed for having to shoo them out of the way. The newts and the dart frogs sat around smirking and laughing, and he could hear them for several hundred feet. Amphibians were ambiguous, Sephiri thought, shaking his head. Traitorous. Whose side were they on, anyway? His Water friends? The Air people? He had never been able to figure it out.

But he had to be brave this time in the living room. He had to remember that this was the carpet, even in the night. It was his mother's carpet, where he shouldn't have an "accident." To get to the cube-shaped black, he would have to overcome his fear and keep moving. He scaled the streaks along the wall cast by the nightlight, past the blankets in the windows and the boy-eating sofa, until he reached the coat closet by the front door. It was not locked, to his delight. There was a pile of coats and sweaters on the floor that had been there since the morning he'd lunged inside and pulled them from their hangers. He went in and closed the door behind him.

The darkness was complete, compressed. A safe dark. He sat on the heap of clothes cross-legged, listening to his heart beat. He thought of all the times when his mother would hold him to her cushiony chest, with her big legs hanging out of the open door, him kicking at the tops of her knees and shins with the heels of his feet. She would not let him go. He would get tired of screaming and struggling and grow quiet enough to hear the clouds move across the sky. In that kind of quiet, sometimes his mother would begin to cry. He knew that one thing for sure (what crying was and what it sounded like). He would rise and fall with the heaves of her great chest and listen to her sniffle. He never wanted her to cry, but he didn't know how to get her to stop. "It's OK," he wanted to say.

One of Sephiri's legs was going numb, and he shifted position. He listened to the roof rafters and the floorboards creak. And then he felt the tight space widen around him. The walls, floor, and ceiling seemed to rise higher and away from him. He lost the close-up sense his breathing had before. It was no longer the pressed-together sound he was used to, like when his mother cornered him there and they both panted in exhaustion on the floor. There was the sensation that height width depth had elongated, like a tunnel, pushing farther and farther out.

He held his breath in the thickening silence. Then, far off, he saw a sliver of light drip into the pitch black. It was a faint, fuzzy light, like the television static he had never been able to get in his hand. The blackness was widening and lengthening still, until he could no longer hear even his heartbeat. He had the urge to stand up and start walking, but he was too frightened. But he couldn't stay in the same place forever, could he? That's what the Great Octopus once said to him. He had to do something if he was ever going to find out about the light, about the voice.

There were a lot of things Sephiri wanted to know. For example, he wanted to know if he could will himself to shrink down to the size of ants and follow them down to their kingdom or if he could will himself to be so tall that he could have a look at what was inside the bird nests he saw at the tops of trees. Then there were the practical matters he wanted to know about. Where did music go when a radio was clicked off? Was it possible just to stay awake, to decide that no more sleep was ever needed, and to go about the night as he would the day? How could he save the things he had lined up and organized and delivered from disarray, from being sullied by the meddling hands of the world?

There were many things he did not understand. And it seemed as if the things he was most certain of had no place in Air. Once when he was urinating (this time into the toilet bowl), he had looked through the small window that was set in the wall above the toilet and out into the driveway of one of the neighbors. This way of observance did not disturb him, since peering through a glass window was the same as looking through the windows of the castle in his snow globe, only the objects were bigger, and he could see them better. A blue car pulled up and stopped. A woman got out, talking and talking, and there was that smile on her face.

Sephiri heard the engine turn off and watched the man come around the side of the car. He let out a bellowing laugh before he opened the rear door. He was fiddling in the backseat with something, and then Sephiri watched him lift out a small child. They'd all broken out into something that sounded like what he had learned the Air people called a song, and even the child—who must have been a boy, because he was wearing pants—seemed to follow along. How did that boy know what the words were? The beat and time that went with the words? How did he know the up-and-down sounds of the melody? Sephiri listened to them make the sounds together in the driveway. Then he watched the three of them disappear inside their house. Into a place behind a door that he knew nothing about. What world was it that they were going to? What worlds were there beyond this one and the Obsidians? He didn't know.

So it was the mysterious nature of things that enticed Sephiri to get up and walk deeper into the soundless sightless jungle of black, into the place of darkness with the faraway sliver of light that lived in the coat closet. The dark path seemed to lengthen with every step, but the remote shaft of light beckoned him. He had come too far to give up now. His fear had long since dissipated, and he was curious about what he would find. But as the hours passed, Sephiri's legs grew tired. He began to long for the ease with which he could move under the sea, how he could float effortlessly, how he could glide through the water to get where he wanted. Here, it was as if the farther he walked, the farther away the sliver of light seemed to be.

Fatigue washed over Sephiri, and his eyes drooped. He grew impatient with the endless, unchanging plain of darkness and the slice of light that wasn't getting any nearer. His legs were rubbery with exhaustion, and he felt he couldn't go any farther. "I'll just have a rest here," he said to himself, sitting down on the field of black. His eyes were heavy, but he could still see the thin line of light far beyond the miles of nothingness. His feet were aching, and he was yawning deeply. And just before he drifted off, he thought he heard that same voice from before. But in his drowsiness, he couldn't tell if it was from the blade of light or inside his head. "I'm coming," he mumbled, and fell fast asleep.

Meetings

Brenda stood outside the brick-faced Takoma Park Autism Center, shivering in the morning mist. Sephiri was at her feet, staring at what must have been something embedded in the concrete of the sidewalk. She had been anxious about the meeting with the speech pathology doctors all week, and now her stomach was turning. She took the morning off and cleared her schedule. Longtime coworkers knew of her situation and remained condescendingly silent. They knew her husband killed a retired police officer, that he went to prison, that she was raising a challenged child alone. She now regretted telling Manden that she would meet him at the entrance of the center. She did not like being in front of the brick façade, on display, feeling the eyes of people in cars passing by. Still, she had wanted to avoid the chance that Manden might see her waddling down the platform or struggling up a broken escalator if the elevator was out of service. It was an irrational fear, but she indulged it nonetheless. She also hated standing on empty subway platforms, on crowded elevators, at the entrances of places. She could have easily taken the Metro from the Petworth subway stop just a block away from her house and saved the trouble of time and gas, but she chose to sit in traffic instead. Besides, she was uncomfortable in crowds, in the gumbo of eyes and snickers at her weight.

Or else, she was invisible. No one bothered to open doors for her when she was walking right behind them. No one offered a friendly smile when they met her eyes on the street. They saw, she reasoned, the largeness that framed her. They did not see her. She knew that she was not the only overweight person in the world, but standing alone sometimes made her feel as if she was. Her weight, which had moved in and taken over everything about who she used to be, seemed a thing from which there was no escape. It was a structure she had somehow helped to build in order to house pains she never knew she could have, to press against what was no longer solid ground beneath her feet. Sometimes she felt the weight itself to be a presence, a living barrier to the person she was before, to the person she could have been. Like when she filled the tub and sprinkled talcum powder and bubble bath into the water to hide her body from view, to make sure that the other self she had lost touch with would not rise from the water. Her body had become like a map spread and tacked to a wall. Stretch marks were stenciled in long, meandering lines across her belly, around her ass, along the rolls and folds of her abdomen. Veins swelled to the surface and collapsed back into her tissue. Cellulite and fluid retention made bumps and dunes and mounds around her rotund legs. Her body had become an off-road tract of land, a wilderness where weeds and thorns grew of their own accord, strangling and suffocating it.

Her other self—the self of before—was down there still, beneath the valley of arum lilies, beneath the Outeniqua Mountains and all things still beautiful, a corpse that refused to decompose in spite of the bulwarking weight, her voluntary and involuntary efforts to make it disappear. How had she gotten so far away from herself? She wondered where the person she used to be was. The other Brenda had been eclipsed by her husband's prison sentence, by the enormous block of frosted glass in which her boy was encased.

Not that there hadn't been other things that had draped Brenda's life before. Marriage had been important in her parents' house, for instance. Her mother and father migrated from South Carolina when they were barely out of their teens. For them, the cycle was simple. Marry, start a family, and get old. She was expected to do the same and was told so every Sunday sermon at Our Lady of Perpetual Help in one way or another, sitting alongside her parents. She would watch the ritual of the women serving the men meals at the fish fry in the reception hall afterward and how the men stood up when one of the church "mothers" took her seat at the table, how they looked to their wives before joining in conversations. Like the other women, her mother asked her father how many pieces of whiting or catfish he wanted and whether he would rather have the greens or the potato salad. She'd watched her mother maintain her status of wife for years. Her father did the same as husband. He went to work every day. He was home for dinner. He read the newspaper every morning. He bought his daughter new shoes, his wife new silk stockings. They were married nearly forty years. Whether they were happy together remained a mystery to Brenda long after both of them were gone. What remained was how Brenda found out that she was not her father's daughter.

Her "real father," as it was gleefully explained to Brenda when she was ten years old by her visiting cousin Pam (in Washington, D.C., for the summer from Saluda, South Carolina), was not the genteel man in the living room. The visit was the first time Brenda met any of her cousins. On their very first day of play, Pam (wearing one of the three raggedy dresses she'd brought with her on the bus) pulled the head from Brenda's favorite doll. A fight ensued, ending with Brenda getting the upper hand. That was when she was told about the "railroad man" who was her "true daddy." He had left shortly after her mother "got in trouble," Pam said, sneering. Her father (stepfather), who had been itching to get away from the cotton fields and pine mills, the Klan, and the South, volunteered that he was the father. They married and moved to Washington, D.C. "So don't go actin' like you better than me, just 'cause you got a nice room and a closet full of pretty clothes," cousin Pam said, blotting the blood where Brenda had scratched her arm. "He ain't your daddy no way. I heard my mama say so."

What Brenda felt about that bit of news (which she never confirmed or disproved with her mother or anyone else) floated in the back of her mind that whole summer. At the ice cream truck that often stopped in front of their rowhouse, she heard children taunting others, calling them hurtful names. One of the highest insults was to be ridiculed for having an "Uncle Daddy," a come-around-sometimes man who wasn't your real father, who maybe brought some beer for your mother and candy for you. Silently, Brenda tried to understand how that sort of classification applied to her status. Standing near the window, fanning her face, her mother often made it clear to Brenda, smoothing out her neat hair bun with one hand, that not having an Uncle Daddy meant that she was being raised in a good family. "They livin' different from us. Be thankful you don't have to worry about it, Brenda," she would say.

And Brenda would try to make what her mother said stand next to her cousin's words. She tried to keep the shadowy image of the "railroad man" from bleeding into the clear image of her father cutting her meat into chewable squares for her at the dinner table every night. She tried to understand and appreciate the family she had. Unable to reconcile the truth (rumor?), she began to look only at the surface of everything. Her father was the father she knew, the one who sprayed away the pigeon shit from the front stoop with a hose every Saturday morning and bought her new shoes every three months. Her mother hadn't lied, Brenda reasoned. Rather, she had made for her an alternative truth, filled with the regularity of oatmeal every morning, bleached dress slips and little patent leather purses, school and summer vacation, Thanksgiving and Christmas Eve. Her parents were the people who made up her family, those she loved and who loved her. And this family was a portrait in her mind in juxtaposition to what cousin Pam unearthed. Every day since getting that bit of news (hearsay?), Brenda worked the portrait over, keeping it pristine, dabbing out free radical thoughts, dusting away confusion, keeping it clear of the stains of doubt.

That was when Brenda got into the business, the habit, of fixing things. She kept the house immaculate without her mother ever having to remind her to do her chores. Every stray dog or kitten had to be saved from destruction and carried to the animal shelter. She never tired of tending, of seeing that things were in place. The lie her mother might have bonded to her since the beginning could be shined to the high gloss of a perfect daughter, Brenda reasoned. She'd gone on from Dunbar High School to start a career in nursing, but this had been supplanted by a scholarship to the University of the District of Columbia (UDC). She majored in sociology and landed a job at the Department of Agriculture handling food nutrition warnings and initiatives.

She knew more about bovine health than her own. She knew of hoof-and-mouth disease, of avian influenza, of soybean rust. There were monthly and quarterly reports. There were Government Accounting Office briefings. There were irregularities and loose ends to be addressed in pending legislation. There were mixers at pubs on Pennsylvania Avenue and the modified schedules for motorcades. There was the D.C. when Congress was in session and the D.C. when it was not. Brenda thrived on the back-and-forth of it all, on the illusion of problem solving, the ease of question-and-answer. She fixed and could keep on fixing. Years later, when she sat through her father's eulogy wondering if he had really been her father, she was stricken by the fact that if Pam's lie was true, it would not change anything about the tears in her eyes or the bitterness of looking into his empty chair. And on the day her mother had the stroke that killed her, Brenda felt a sharp and brief regret that she had never asked her mother about the validity of the railroad man.

So it had been the eternal contradiction of things in Brenda's world that allowed the drift to begin. There were boyfriends, men in her life before Horus, who seemed to enjoy watching her conform to their wants and expectations as they would a chameleon. Never their needs. Those were addressed, Brenda assumed, by someone else, someplace else. With the meatpacking-industry lobbyist, she was the perfect secretary with sleeping privileges. The sanitation department supervisor wanted her to be his mother, whom he had never met since she died in his infancy but of whom he had an image and looked to Brenda to shape-shift into the ideal woman he imagined her to be, pleasant and available. There was the freelance architect who was out of work most of the time. He wanted a wonder woman capable of everything imaginable, including sex at two o'clock in the morning on a work night. Marriage, Brenda discovered, was not on any of their minds. All of that had been when she was a size seven.

Then there was Horus. She saw him going into the Martin Luther King Library at the same time every day when she drove by on her way to work. She could set her clock by him entering the building. She often saw him at a local deli during the lunch hour in his security guard uniform. There was a constancy, a kind of steadiness, about him. He was handsome, and his face held a contemplative look that was neither smile nor scowl. He had a quiet about him, a solitude that reminded Brenda of the father she knew, when he was still in his chair reading or thinking late into Sunday afternoon. One day, Brenda sat down on the stool next to Horus at the long diner counter. He asked her if the roast beef sandwiches were any good. That was their casual start.

They spent a lot of time together: free concerts on the Mall, jazz sessions at Blues Alley, performances at the Kennedy Center, food festivals and museums, trips to the ocean. She told him about her unremarkable upbringing (omitting the part about the railroad man), her stint at UDC, her job at the Department of Agriculture. Horus briefly told her about his family, his face holding an expression she had never seen before, an expression she would learn to recognize later. But he had been warm enough and seemed to bask in her company. He did not balk when she spoke of marriage and family. "Beautiful mysteries," he'd said.

In Horus, Brenda saw pliability, a malleable shape from which she could fashion the life they would live together. Or, rather, she took his quiet, his amicability, as an invitation to define and shape him into Horus her husband. Horus the father of her children. Not necessarily Horus the man. In spite of all of Brenda's renovation efforts with him, Horus still seemed to need . . . something. It seemed that the rowhouse they had refurbished, the patio garden, the home-cooked meals, the weekend trips, and all the rest of it only filled the corner of something larger that was missing. She spent the years of their marriage trying to uncover what it was, to repair whatever it was, as she had the family portrait of the past in her mind. All to fashion what she wanted her own family to be.

Years later, from the gray felt panels of her USDA cubicle, Brenda would come to understand that everything she did had been in an effort to repair a kind of cosmic cycle started somewhere in the hot, thick woods of Saluda, South Carolina. After Horus was incarcerated, she developed a gradation system, a sort of clock to delineate periods of her life. Sizes eight and nine were the shell-shocked years, when she was operating on autopilot. The job. Day care. Coffee special of the day. Book club selection of the month. Food to quiet the growing silence of the house, to snuff the fog of uncertain days ahead. When Sephiri was diagnosed with autism, she had been a size ten. Sizes eleven, twelve, and thirteen were the contemplative years, when everything seemed to be in slow motion, and she wondered where she was going, the meaning of where she had been. Size fourteen was a fork in the road, where there were two signs: *What are you going to do?* and *Why are you doing what you're doing?* She grew in size from there, in the haze of everything that already happened and continued to unfold, and she could no longer tell which road she was traveling. She couldn't understand where the beginning of it all had been.

The sound of Sephiri shrieking jarred Brenda from her thoughts. A steady flow of cars rolled by, the last of morning rush hour. She looked down to find him staring at something invisible. What were the things he saw? What was it that captivated him so? She had never known and would never have the benefit of him telling her. She watched him stare more intently, his face descending closer and closer to the concrete, until his nose was almost touching it. An old woman walking her toy poodle across the street stopped to stare, then went on, shaking her head. Brenda reached down and took Sephiri by the hand. He snatched it away. She grabbed at it again. He snatched. This was all part of what was called "Sephiri's autism." Her son's special blend of a mysterious disorder that spanned the galaxy in causes, symptoms, and treatments, with no one being able to put a finger on what the affliction actually was. Autism choked the air she and Sephiri breathed. A substance that loomed always in the sky.

And every time Brenda saw a smiling child, she ached to see a smile on Sephiri's face. Not once had it happened. He had been a fussy baby. And as he grew, his face had held three expressions since infancy: rage, agitation, and indifference. She thought of how she had tickled him so many times, desperate to see some flicker of joy, some sign that there was still good in her life. The little smile that said, *I am the reason for all that you endure.* Because if she could just see that smile, that thing that said he was happy, that he loved her back in spite of everything that happened before he was born, in thanks for everything she was trying to provide for him, she felt she could live with it all.

Brenda read all that she could about autism. There was an array of medications, antipsychotics that worked to some degree or made matters worse: Adderall, Dexedrine, Ritalin, Zoloft, Strattera, Metadate, Focalin, Mellaril, Haldol. There were the treatment therapies: speech and language, cognitive and behavioral, visual schedules, live and stem cells, picture exchange and sign language, applied behavior analysis, sensory integration. Under the direction of Sephiri's pediatrician, one combination or another had been tried, with results ranging from ineffectual to disastrous. There were the nutritional therapies. The quest to be gluten- or casein-free. Sephiri wanted only peanut butter and jelly sandwiches and would eat only a handful of other things, which made food therapy nearly impossible. There was the controversy of medical marijuana. There was the hope of pancreatic enzymes, probiotics, DHA oil, vitamin B-12, flowers of sulfur, intramuscular or intravenous magnesium.

There were the suggestions to remove all stimulants from the living space. But that was nearly impossible when anything around Sephiri could be a stimulant at any time and for any reason. The sound of the blender could set him off. Or he grew upset when the washing machine stopped. A light was too bright, or a bulb had blown out. So much to think about. She could never think of everything, and she could not prepare for anything. He drew on the wall with the permanent marker she thought she had locked away. He pulled out the kitchen trash and arranged it on the table and countertops in little piles. He cracked the window with a mug and again with a hammer he somehow found. He chewed and swallowed pieces of plastic. He relieved himself on blankets and rugs. He screamed and shrieked about things she couldn't see or perceive, and he stared at minutiae for hours on end. How could all the stimulants be removed? How could life be removed?

Brenda was sure of one thing: frustration and fear and the long road ahead. She wanted her little boy, wherever he was inside of the impenetrable thing that held him. She thought of the years of groping through the dark to find him. On the many days she had listened to him scream and bang the wall, she wondered what would become of them. What would become of the lost boy and his mother? Or was she the one who was lost, afraid to behold the tangled forest in which her boy lived?

Now Sephiri stood up and was flailing his arms, gesticulating wildly. Brenda had thought about putting him on the van this morning, instead of bringing him herself and risk driving the whole way with him fussing from the backseat. But she decided against it after the scare she had that morning. She had gone into his room to wake him, only to find an empty bed with a large wet spot. She looked everywhere for him. At first, she thought he had launched into some kind of game filled with mysterious, impossible rules again. Like that time when he climbed up on the kitchen table and held his breath. She went through the list of locks in her mind: gas switch, cabinets, back door, front door, windows, medicine cabinet.

At the height of her panic, she thought he'd gotten outside somehow, and she went out into the yard to look in the bushes. She checked the car and under it and came back through the front door in tears, huffing and puffing. That was when it occurred to her to check the one place she had forgotten about: the coat closet. When she opened the door, there Sephiri was, snoring richly. She was too relieved to be angry with him, as was most often the case. When he discovered that she had picked him up from the floor, she had a time getting him out of the closet. He squirmed against the back wall. In his combustive state, he kicked her in the shin and scratched her arm. He let out a scream that might have shattered glass. Who knew what motivated such fury in Sephiri over the simplest of things? She couldn't ask him, and he could not explain the reasons for his distress. In the end, she carried him upstairs in her arms, with his limbs cutting the air like a helicopter. Somehow she got through the rest of the morning routine, with her shin sore, her back killing her, and a migraine pulverizing her head.

Now, as Brenda struggled in front of the Autism Center to keep Sephiri from wiggling away from her, she regretted her decision to bring him along instead of just putting him on the van. The boy snatched his hand away from her firm grip over and over, and she worried that he would run out into the street. He began spinning in circles up and down the sidewalk. She watched him nervously, calling his name to no avail.

From the corner of her eye, Brenda saw Manden walking toward them from across the street. In those first few seconds, the sight of him startled her; he looked so much like Horus. The piercing eyes with bold eyebrows above them. The prominent jaw and broad nose. The dark lips. Whenever she saw him, she was seized by a panic that was like being plunged into freezing-cold water. Horus and his brother were both quite tall, but Manden walked with a slump that made him appear shorter than he actually was. That crooked walk of his. Even when he was sitting in a straight-backed chair with arm rests, he leaned to one side. The imbalance made his long limbs seem clipped or somehow cropped by childhood polio. It was as if his body was always on guard, bracing for something terrible so it could duck down quickly to avoid impact. His head was completely clean-shaven now, which surprised her. The thick black carpet atop his head, so much like his brother's, was gone. Time had cut only a few fine lines into his face. Except for the hair, Manden still looked the same, with his strange handsome-sad demeanor and the lean-to way he moved. They'd had dinner together once, the three of them, an engagement dinner filled with long stares between him and Horus and silence. It was as if walls rose from the ground between them, and they preferred the shadows. She had tried to bring cheer and conversation but felt as if she was talking to herself.

Brenda watched Manden wait for a break in the moving cars so he could cross the street to join her. When Dr. Watson called to tell her about Sephiri, it had taken Brenda all the next day to gather her strength to phone Manden and arrange the meeting on Sephiri's behalf. She had decided before calling that she would ask him only once; she would not press the issue and ring the bell of truth, which was that he did not have to accompany her on business regarding Sephiri. He was not obligated. Like that time when she needed to tell someone about the baby that terrible week when the verdict changed everything. She needed to proclaim Sephiri's existence, but she did not have the courage, the heart, to tell Horus. She thought about ending the pregnancy but could not get past the feeling that in doing so, she would be helping the court to kill Horus. She could not commit two murders. She held her belly, knowing that the child would never know his father. Horus would be a shapeless specter, as the railroad man had been to her. Unable to control her grief, she had reached out to the only person left in the world who might have known something of who Horus was, the man he might have been. She phoned Manden in a fit of tears. She phoned him to say that she did not know what to say.

And now, with Manden approaching the entrance of the Autism Center, Brenda was again at a loss for words. As she watched him come closer, she saw the face of Horus, the face of Sephiri as he might look when he grew up. It reminded her of why she burned all the photo albums, pictures of her and Horus when they were different people among the living. What little that was left now was crowded with the heaviness of what remained unspoken between brothers, of the helplessness in helping Sephiri, of the silence that banged and clanged them deaf. Now she and Manden could only approach each other with ice picks lodged in their hearts. They pulled them out in moments of necessity, to chip at the cracks in a strange relationship, until they were wide enough for matters to squeeze through. Like at meetings such as this, when an odd alliance stood to save the last trace of Horus Thompson.

Marbles

Manden emerged from the subway stop, three times farther away than necessary for his destination, and began the eight-block walk to the Autism Center. He checked his pocket again to make sure that what he brought for Sephiri was still there. His fingers moved over the smooth glass balls. Real marbles, real toys from a time when his own childhood had been real. He was not sure why he purchased them for the boy, since he could not know what impression they would make on him, if any. But he needed him to have the marbles, for the childhood he might have beneath whatever kept him from interacting with the world, for the childhood he and his brother, Horus, might have had.

As he walked away from the subway, Manden saw a young couple approaching the entrance, clutching a map, looking lost. They were speaking something that sounded Slavic. He half expected them to ask him directions to someplace, which he did not feel like offering. As they approached, the young woman looked at him hopefully, but the young man looked nervous. He took her by the hand, and both moved by quickly. It was then that Manden remembered that he was not wearing his Metro subway employee uniform, the costume, among others, that signaled he was not an assumed threat: policeman, bell hop, chef, fireman.

Manden walked on, trying to clear his mind. He'd had a long

night of tossing and turning and had hardly slept. His sparse effi-
ciency apartment on Connecticut Avenue was furnished with only
a black-comforter-clad bed, a single lamp with no shade, a metal
folding chair, and a refrigerator with nothing but Rock Creek sodas
and stale mambo chicken from the Chinese corner store. It was not
a home. It was merely the place where he showered and kept his
clothes. When his alarm blasted him out of the hazy fog he'd drifted
through for most of the wee hours of this morning, all he had been
able to do was heave a sigh and head into the kitchen to slump over
a cup of bad instant coffee. On so many other mornings, he would
stand over the scratched countertop thinking of his Metro job in
the subways, where he would soon enter the information booth for
another ten to twelve hours, amid the long tubes that emptied into
other tubes in a maze of directed indifference. He had dwelled in
that tunneled underworld of Washington, D.C., for the last twelve
years. And he found an irony in the fact that he had spent more of
his time beneath the city's surface in the dimness of those tunnels
than above ground. More than that, there was a strange and familiar intimacy about the subways, like a place not visited in years but
that called to him even when he was not there. This feeling, which
drifted to him every morning, was precisely the sort of thing that
he did not like to think about, and that first swallow of hot coffee
blotted it out.

Manden turned a corner where a bag lady stood arranging an
old tattered hat on her head. "Smile, honey," she said as he walked
by. He nodded back, making a face mixed with faint amusement,
dread, and pity. He was halfway to the center, where Brenda would
be waiting. He could never get used to these kinds of meetings,
nor did his apprehension ever wane in the moments leading up
to them. They always gave him the feeling of stepping into a
minefield or a forest in the pitch black. Never knowing what was
coming. Never knowing what to expect. Yet he was drenched in a
sense of necessity, of duty to something he had not been able to
name since Brenda called to tell him about her pregnancy. What

was he to do about the child? The question remained still. And yet when Brenda called yesterday about the appointment, as she had called about the others, he was unable to refuse her outright. He could have made up a reason he wasn't able to make it. Something related to his shift at the subway or another responsibility that he could have made materialize as the cause for having to pass. But that would have meant that something else was more important than his nephew. Something else was more important than his own brother's child. Every time, just before he fixed his mouth to tell Brenda that he had other plans that could not be altered, he changed his mind.

He walked a line of rowhouses with quaint little English gardens in the front yards. Now he was going to a meeting with the woman his brother had left a widow in nearly every way. Marriage. It was something he had never been able to bring himself to consider. Sensing how much his mother and father loved each other, for the cause, for their civil rights beliefs, and then watching it all be ripped away in gunshots had cooled his blood to marriage long ago. What had led Horus to it? He could still hear the sound of Brenda's cheery giggles in the background when he phoned him to announce the engagement. The absence of any conversation or event to pick up from where they left off made the phone exchange all the more awkward, for they had left off in the ether of angst and rage. Had Horus called to let him know that it was possible? That it was possible to erase the sight of their murdered father in front of them, their mother's screams, her descent into a realm of despair from which she could not find her way back? That he had forgotten about their father's body on the concrete, their mother in white hospital robes, the way they'd had to live in their uncle's basement? Could loving someone heal what lay agape and infected in him to this day?

It was ever fresh in his mind, when at ten years old he sat down on the curb beside his father's body. He listened to his mother scream above the police sirens. Stood in the door while visitor after visitor came to sit with their mother in the living room. Like that old woman called Ms. Pierce, with the sing-song lilt in her voice, her incessant talking bursting forth as if through a broken levee. They all came to give their condolences, to commiserate, to rage about what could be done about it. Which, after the angry talk, cards and flowers, pot pies and cold chicken, head bowing and tears, was nothing. He and Horus were the spectators of a quiet that settled into the house like poured cement, thickening, hardening. Then, slowly, their mother began to slip away. She sat by the kitchen window and did not move again. Manden remembered watching her fly out of that window on the winds of her mind, day after day, soaring above the city and flying all the way to the kingdom of James in her Bible. One day, her eyes emptied out, and she didn't come back from there, that place. There was only a mannequin left sitting in a white robe in their kitchen, its head tilted toward the sky.

That was when they came to get their mother from the apartment in New York. Someone, perhaps one of the neighbors who brought them food, had finally said something about the fact that Maria Thompson, wife of slain civil rights leader Jack Thompson, had forgotten the names and faces of her children (Manden and Horus), forgotten to eat and to bathe, forgotten that the apartment in which she sat by the window for days on end, urinating and defecating on herself, was still her home. Someone paid the rent for a while, and then someone called about Maria Thompson and her empty eyes and the children alone with her. Manden could still hear Horus cry and shriek (his own horror too vast and unspeakable to utter) when the people from the Utica Asylum came to get her. His little arms were wrapped around their mother's leg as he screamed and begged her not to go, as she dragged him across the floor, oblivious. That was the last time either of them ever saw her again. Years later, Manden would come to think that the Bible she clutched had somehow led her through its pages and showed her a way out, away from her pain, away from them.

Someone came with a car and drove him and Horus down to

live with Uncle Randy, their mother's brother, who lived on the northeast side of Washington, D.C. They hadn't known they had an uncle before. Uncle Randy, as it turned out, hadn't spoken to his own sister in years, hadn't made any efforts to contact Maria when he heard she married that "radical hooligan" they called Jack Thompson. He didn't know he had nephews, he said. He'd keep them out of trouble. Make men of them.

On the day that he and Horus were delivered to the porch of their uncle's rowhouse, Randy opened the front door, his face as grim as an undertaker. Manden felt as if he were standing at the entrance of some funeral parlor. The caseworker who accompanied them in the car introduced them to their uncle, thanking him for stepping up and taking responsibility for their care. "They've been through so much," she said, "what with their father's tragic death. Their poor mother." She told him and Horus to shake Uncle Randy's hand. When Manden looked up at him, there was an echo of familial resemblance to their mother's face, with his yellow skin, high cheekbones, and thick brows. But his eyes were cold and lifeless.

An accountant at a small tax service across the river in Anacostia, Uncle Randy lived alone in a three-story rowhouse painted white, the windows framed with black shutters. His wife had left him years before any children could be born between them, and so he had filled his house with antiques picked up from Eastern Market, garage and estate sales, and junkyards. It smelled of mothballs and Jade East cologne, and everything was layered in dust. At the dining-room table, there was one chair, with others stacked in the corner, which he took out when the mailman or his old friend from the Washington Gas Company wanted to stop by for a "little nip" in the middle of his shift.

Looking into Uncle Randy's hard face, clutching a little bag of marbles in his pocket, Manden could not have known that there was such rancidness between his mother and her brother, much of it from the fact that Uncle Randy had not liked Jack Thompson from the start. In the first place, he was dark, an immediate de-merit. And although Randy Goodwin was certain their family (the Goodwins) had not carried the preservation of status and skin color (or lack thereof) to the heights of vigilant families like the Proctors of Maryland, he had nevertheless been disappointed when he first laid eyes on Jack Thompson. Although Jack's eyes held the amber light of a lantern behind them, he was as dark as a bitter nut. More than that, Randy knew nothing of his family, these Thompsons. What kind of people were they? When he quizzed Jack Thompson at the first visit with his sister, Maria, he'd said that he came from a family of old farmers and dog breeders in Louisiana. That most of them were gone now, and he came up North to start fresh. That was all.

But Randy thought that there was something in the hoods of Jack's eyes, which made him uneasy. Later, he and Jack had words when he pressed the issue about Jack's background again. "There ain't nothin' virtuous about wanting to be the white man's pet," Jack Thompson had said. "See, I look at you, Randy Goodwin, with your high-riding ways and your high-yellow skin. You think it's the most precious thing you have. And I seen millions before you, all of you mimes to who always hated you and always will. I know you think I ain't nothin', but you're wrong. Your sister knows that. Maria's got a good mind and a good heart, you know. But then, it don't look like you ever noticed that." Then, after a silence: "A man's will can't go but one way. Let it be of your own choosin'."

That was the last straw for Randy Goodwin from his sister's beau. But most worrisome of all, even after they quarreled, was what he believed to be the slow, wholesale theft of his sister's mind by Jack Thompson. She had stopped going to the family church and switched to another that was, according to her, more "progressive." She was forever spewing commentary about what was in the papers. The racial mayhem in the South seemed to consume her, and there came about her a graveness that never subsided. All of this, Randy Goodwin felt, betrayed his unspoken belief that he alone was responsible for his sister's safe delivery to a reputable family and life through marriage. He knew that their parents would have seen to her having a different life, if they had not been in the bus accident that had killed them both. The hooligan, Randy Goodwin surmised, had poisoned his sister's mind, already bursting with wild dabbles into the political escapades of the Delta Sigma Theta sorority at Howard University where she was a student, where she'd met Jack Thompson at some rally he'd come down from New York to stir up.

And Randy had been proud of his sister until that point, his ward, whom he alone had been responsible for, even though they were both young adults when they lost their parents. With her fine features and good education, he had hoped—no, expected—that she would marry one of his accountant colleagues and move into a quiet house somewhere as a Goodwin should. They would carry on, he and his sister, as the good family their parents had forged, in their clear diction, culture and manners, and the high-yellow pallor of their skin.

But all of this Maria had thrown away on Jack Thompson, a man from Nowhere, Louisiana. A man with no past and no future, who would lead his sister into the destitution that his sort of social protest guaranteed. It was not that Randy Goodwin was blind to the turmoil of events. Rather, it was that he was incapable of looking beyond the colored glass of his upbringing, where Goodwins were favored by the gods and by the status and connections that years of guarding their lightness and brightness had wrought. He couldn't let his sister throw it all away in a temporary passion of the heart. He forbade her to marry in an explosive argument that would be the last time they saw or spoke to each other again. She had shouted back that she and Jack Thompson were marrying, that she was going back to New York with him. And if she were to strike out on her own, if she were to make a decision that was entirely hers, then what business of her brother's was that? In any case, he was not her father, and she didn't care how dark Jack Thompson was or what kind of family he came from, he was more of a man than her own brother would ever be.

So no one knew that Uncle Randy felt all of this at the doorstep years later, when the caseworker came with Manden and Horus. He first noticed the darkness of his nephews, then looked into their faces and saw Jack Thompson living there still—him, the reason for his sister's demise, the end of his parents' muted hopes, the dilution of the family line that had taken generations to build, now changed forever. And in the two boys, Manden and Horus, he did not see his sister or the Goodwins at all and only saw the dark unknown of their father. And thinking of this in those seconds when he shook his nephews' hands was much easier than thinking of his own empty life, which, save for his tax-accountant job, had been unremarkable, a failure in some ways, even, in its ordinariness. And that was when he had the thought that at last, he would have the chance to stomp out what was left of that black hooligan.

But Manden, standing with his brother and the caseworker, shivering in the cold of their spectacular loss, could not have known about any of this on that first day in front of his uncle's house. After the caseworker shook Uncle Randy's hand, told him how the Lord would bless him, and left, Randy installed Manden and Horus in the basement, where there was no heat in the winter and no air-conditioning in the summer. A thin metal stair rail, which wobbled in its concrete pegs if pushed or pulled too much, lined the narrow steps. Entering the basement had reminded Manden of when his father once took him and Horus to the caverns in Virginia, and from the top of the basement steps he almost expected to see an expanse of luminescent stalagmites and mirrored pools of water at the bottom.

But it had not been so. His eyes, blinking in the dark as his uncle told him to take the first step down, had been unbelieving at first. Then, slowly, he began to understand. In the gloom, on the third step down, with Horus close behind him, Manden heard the creaking noise of the dry, rotting wood, which would be forever imprinted on his mind. The sound of the third step would stay with him always. It marked Uncle Randy's daily approach to bark an order, to remind them not to be like their misguided father and their fragile mother, to say that he was making men of them. The creaking third step was perceptible from every other sound in the world. It was the signal of descent into a long and uncomfortable night. The sound, too, was the trumpet of their daytime escape from their uncle's manhood-training tyranny, for its sound meant two steps to the unlocked door, to the outside, to school, however demoralizing or boring it had sometimes been.

There was a separate entrance in the basement, now bricked over. Two slender windows near the ceiling were frosted and fitted with iron bars. He and Horus spent the rest of their childhood there, sleeping on a worn mattress piled high with blankets or stripped to the bone. Every meal (whether breakfast, lunch, or dinner) was a sandwich: baloney and a thick slab of cheese with a glass of water, or tuna fish and a glass of milk. To pass the time when they were not in school, he and Horus would look through the tiny windows and watch the shadowed feet go by outside and the squirrels that stopped in front of the glass. At night, the door at the top of the steps was locked. In secret, they kept an empty milk bottle to relieve themselves if they couldn't wait until morning. From below, they listened to Uncle Randy's television upstairs, blaring a sports game or the news. Some nights, when they couldn't sleep for the cold or the heat, he and Horus lay on the floor along the wall, listening to the rats living behind the crumbling plaster crawl in and out of the tunnels they had made. They could feel the air moving through the cracks of their tiny halls, hear the freedom they were living.

Manden was fireside to a burning rage back then, when he wished their father would rise from the grave and choke Uncle Randy for his cruelty, when he tried to conjure their mother and have her take wing from Utica to rescue them. "Mama is coming back," he would say over and over, like a chant. Like a prayer. "Soon," he'd say. After a while. One day. Had Horus wished for her too? Had he cried himself to sleep? He did not know, and in his own basement torments in their uncle's house, a world away on the other side of the mattress, he did not cross the icy divide between them to ask. In the slow drip of helplessness, Manden came to view the world as an old house with many rooms, with many happenings behind closed doors. There were events in the common areas for all to see. And there was just as much wonder and spectacle in the time-stilled attic as in the decaying basement. God and the devil dwelled under the same roof, feet apart. Each listening to the other pad the hallways and creep up the steps.

Manden walked on. The Autism Center wasn't very far now. At that hour, store managers were still rolling back awnings, hosing down sidewalks, and putting out signs announcing the lunch special of the day. Walking the last block, Manden could see Brenda clearly on his approach, the center behind her, a box of mystery filled with children like Sephiri, yet all of them different in infinite, unfathomable ways. Without being conscious of it, he slowed his gait as he crossed the street and neared the entrance.

"Hello, Brenda," he said when he got to the curb.

Brenda nodded without speaking, distracted, Manden assumed, by Sephiri spinning nearby. He looked at her in the awkward pause. She was even bigger and heavier than she was when he saw her six months ago. A shiny brown wig sat atop her head like a mop. When she offered a thin smile, he could see her full cheeks push against the deep circles under her eyes. He was newly amazed at how different she was from the vibrant young woman he remembered. She was once a shapely thing, with a glorious smile and an air of vitality. Manden sometimes thought that had he been a different man, he might have reached out to Brenda now. But he was unreachable even to himself, and he felt incapable of helping her in spite of bearing witness to her self-destruction.

Not that any of it mattered now. They had let the past be what it was. He and Brenda did not speak much, although they lived in the same city. They knew very little about each other's adult life, other than the surface of things. Maybe because they knew too much of what lay beneath. Out of a vague sense of familial obligation, perhaps out of some subconscious desire to cobble together some closeness between brothers, Manden once took Horus and Brenda out to dinner at an Ethiopian restaurant as a gesture of goodwill after the sudden news of the engagement, as a gesture to celebrate something he had no plans of ever experiencing. Ethiopian was her favorite, Brenda had said, pulling pieces of injera bread apart and dipping it into heaps of spiced peas and tomatoes.

Manden remembered how she talked incessantly at the awkward engagement dinner like a bird tweeting in the trees—about her new job at the U.S. Department of Agriculture, about all the wonderful things Horus had done for her since they met, about the rowhouse they were buying together and how it had exposed brick with the original molding, about all the money they would be saving for the honeymoon by going to the justice of the peace. It had been a long time since he and Horus had sat together with a woman who was smiling. Her skin glowed in the candlelit room. They were both speechless in its presence, gathered around her like a warm fire.

And Manden had wanted Brenda then, although he would never have touched her. He wanted his brother's woman. But it was not because of her pretty legs or the soft halo that framed her beautiful face. Or how well versed she seemed to be in literature and politics. It was her regal ways. Her sweet charm. It was a loveliness that reminded him of their mother, before her voyage. Before their father's blood had seeped down under Manden's fingernails. The redness that stayed long after he locked himself in the bathroom and washed his hands with bleach, long after he scrubbed them with steel wool, so that he could no longer tell whose blood was running down the sink.

Horus was only seven when their father was murdered. Did he remember Mama the way she was before all of that? Before what came after it, the staring out the window and the house visitors and the white robes and the institution she died in? He wondered if

Horus remembered the big, fluffy pancakes she made for them on Saturday mornings. The steel-drum sound of her voice that filled the house. The way she laughed at his tenth birthday party that January. How she sang when she was cooking dinner and set the dishes on the table as if each one was a crystal chalice.

Manden remembered watching Brenda pick up the restaurant goblet at their little engagement dinner party and how he thought of venetian glass and sterling silver. In the presence of her svelte skin, all butterscotch and creamed caramel, he thought of neat plates of chocolates arranged on a coffee table. Of steaming coffee and gingerbread. Of the comfort and order that used to be. These feelings had always made Manden uncomfortable in Brenda's presence. He couldn't stand the sense that he was trying to hold on to something pure under dirty circumstances. And for years, it was this feeling that kept him distant from Brenda when she could have used his sympathy and understanding the most, even when she called him with a secret too heavy to carry alone.

She called a few weeks after the verdict to say that she was pregnant. In the silence, they listened to each other breathe through the phone. "Remains," she'd said at first. That was how she first described the unborn child. Like a fossil of some fantastic creature known only in mythical lore. Manden had wanted to contest Brenda's choice of silence, but he could not think of any reason telling Horus about his child would be better than keeping it from him. And he was plagued by a new kind of guilt atop the burden of knowing his brother had taken revenge for their father's death and he had not. It lodged itself in his heart like botfly larvae, growing ever larger through the nine months of Brenda's pregnancy, bursting through him when she called to say that it was a boy.

"Hello, Manden," Brenda said now, with a thin smile, a fruitless gesture born from the beast of habit. Then, looking at the boy, she said, "Look who is here, Sephiri."

The child did not respond.

Manden looked at Sephiri. He had stopped spinning and was on his knees, staring intently, as if his life depended on it, at the grooves in the sidewalk. He let out a screech.

"Hello, Sephiri," said Manden, knowing there would be no response. Looking at the deep expression on the boy's face, he was reminded of how Horus looked when they shot marbles together as children.

Sephiri did not respond.

Manden reached into his pocket and pulled out a small velvet sack of glass balls. It was an impulsive buy. He had walked past a little novelty shop on Wisconsin Avenue and saw the marbles shimmering in the window display on a bed of black velvet. He did not think of the possibility that Brenda would object to such a gift, that Sephiri might swallow them, that he could launch them through window panes once he had them in his hands. He had thought only of Sephiri's innocent look of concentration. So much like his brother's face all those years ago when they played the game.

Manden knelt down to Sephiri and sat the marbles on the ground next to him.

"Good to see you again, little man," he said.

The boy did not react.

It seemed to Manden that each of Sephiri's birthdays marked the completion of a deeper, more complicated chamber. The boy sat silently for long stretches of time, pondering a spoon or the buttons on the telephone. Static flickers in the television seemed to mesmerize him. Manden wondered what Horus would have done had he known all of this, had he known of Sephiri's existence. Manden had felt it when his mother died, even before he got word from the psychiatric facility hundreds of miles away. He woke up in a cold sweat, clutching his chest, and saw her waxen doll face. He wondered if Horus felt her go, too, and if he felt Sephiri come into the world.

Later, Manden learned that Sephiri was born with both his eyes and his mind tightly shut, which filled him with a peculiar relief. Sephiri was blocked from it all, as far as he knew. And because the mysterious wall behind which the boy lived was soundproof, the reasons for his father's absence would never have to be explained to him, and he would never pierce the barrier to ask why his father was not there, why he was in a cage beneath the mountains. The ghosts haunting his family would never have to be discussed with him.

Manden watched Sephiri finger the bag of marbles as he sat on the sidewalk. He was fascinated by the velvet sack, not its contents.

Brenda looked at her watch. "I guess we'd better head into the center now," she said. "The appointment is at nine."

"I guess we should," said Manden.

Manden watched Brenda lift Sephiri from the ground like a suitcase. The boy whimpered and kicked, clutching the bag of marbles. The last discussion about Sephiri's state still loomed in Manden's mind. There was always the summary of his condition: behavior mimicking deafness, little or no eye contact, sustained odd play, obsessions with sameness, refusal to accept changes in routine, extreme distress for unexplained reasons, tantrums, bouts of overactivity or lethargy, nonresponsiveness to verbal cues. It was true that all of these things applied to Sephiri. But Manden had only ever wanted to know what was wrong with him—or what was right with him that made him able to sweep a tiring world away.

Apprehension tightened Manden's throat. He would go inside the facility with them as he had done before, and he would remain silent, invisible, during the meeting as he had done before. His support of Sephiri was obtuse, and he was ashamed to admit that he had been reluctant about it from the beginning, never understanding his place, his role. And even in situations such as this, when he was asked to come forward, when he was needed to step in as the man in a certain circumstance, he knew that he would not be able to speak. For what could he say in defense of his brother's absence, in defense of his own paternal impotence? He could not bring himself to cast such shame at Brenda's feet in front of others and heighten the burden she had been carrying alone.

Manden watched Brenda hold Sephiri, cooing to him to come

along, her great arms trembling under the child's weight. Her forehead was thick with perspiration. Manden waited for her to ask him to help carry Sephiri, but she did not. She held him like a heavy basket in her arms and carted him into the Autism Center.

Manden shoved his chilled hands into his pockets and followed behind them.

Observations

The Autism Center was filled with pictures of smiling children that hung along both sides of a long hallway. Skylights above shed a cheerful light on the yellow walls and the gleaming parquet floors. An enormous sculpture of children hugging the earth stood at the end of the hallway near the office entrance. Dr. Robert Peterson, the facility director, was a short, bubbly man with glasses. He was waiting for Sephiri, Brenda, and Manden with a big smile. "Greetings," he said. "I'm glad you could make it today. Shall we go in?"

A redheaded attendant appeared from another door behind the sculpture to lead Sephiri to the playroom. The boy balked, and the attendant produced a bright green ball from her apron pocket. "I brought your favorite, Sephiri," she said. "Remember?"

Sephiri began to flail his arms, ignoring her.

A pleasant chime announced the morning snack somewhere in the facility. Three cheerful-looking assistants came out of another hallway door with trays, chatting among themselves.

The attendant in the apron smiled at Sephiri, put the green ball back into her pocket, and produced a red crayon. "Look, Sephiri," she said, holding it out to him.

Sephiri began to spin around as the attendant drew closer. He let out a high-pitched squeal when she attempted to take his hand in hers.

"Are you upset about something, Sephiri?" the attendant asked. Her soothing voice had not changed. "I'm sorry it is not the color you may have wanted." She put the crayon on the floor in front of him.

Sephiri picked it up and began breaking it into little pieces.

"That's not how we express our feelings, Sephiri," said the attendant.

Sephiri continued on in silence, staring at the crayon intently as he shredded it. While he was engrossed in this activity, the attendant picked him up and carried him away.

Brenda tried to numb herself to all of this, as she had tried on a thousand other such occasions. She always had the unnerving feeling of watching a wind-up figurine when she looked at Sephiri, hypnotized by his strange movements. Each time, her trance was arrested by an overpowering sense of helplessness, a feeling that the hand of God had wound up Sephiri and she could do nothing to control his curious dance, his spine-chilling sounds from the great beyond.

"Thank you for coming today," said Dr. Peterson, gesturing for Brenda and Manden to go into the office and sit down at a large conference table. He had learned to be careful in the way he addressed them as Sephiri's parents, even though Sephiri's file had a letter stating that Manden Thompson was the boy's uncle and had Brenda's permission to attend meetings and discuss all matters related to Sephiri and the center and that on the line next to "Father," his name was typed. A letter from the State of Colorado noting the incarceration of Horus Thompson was at the bottom of the file. Dr. Watson, Sephiri's speech pathologist, had come to him with the delicate matter of Horus Thompson shortly after Sephiri was first enrolled. She told him that Brenda Thompson seemed very uncomfortable discussing anything regarding the boy's father and that she did not make a correction when she was addressed as Mrs. instead of Ms.

Dr. Peterson had seen such things before in his years in social work. Even under the most difficult of circumstances, he always thought it better that children had some semblance of a father as part of the household, or at least their lives. It was a Band-Aid, but it was better than nothing. Because of Sephiri's autism, the doctor was uncertain about the degree to which Sephiri was aware of how Manden Thompson figured into his life or the impact his father's absence had on him. But he thought it best never to bring the subject up for discussion. Sephiri was in good hands at the Takoma Park Autism Center. That was the most important thing.

The table was covered with bottled water, notepads, and folders. A man and a woman were seated at the table.

"You already know Dr. Susan Watson, our lead speech pathologist working with Sephiri," said the facility director. "This is Dr. Edward Smith. He's going to share some interesting things with you today. Please have a seat. Water?"

"No, thank you," said Brenda. Manden sat down without a word. The formality of the meeting made Brenda nervous. It wasn't like the one-on-one conferences she had with the young Dr. Watson periodically, when it was just the two of them in the playroom with a cup of coffee. This looked like a panel discussion.

Dr. Peterson sat down and took a deep breath, a half-smile smeared across his face. "Mr. Thompson, Mrs. Thompson," he began, pushing the rims of his glasses back up the slope of his nose. "Again, thank you for joining us today. I'll come straight to the point. Sephiri has exhibited some remarkable things lately, things I've never seen in my thirty years in this profession."

The others at the table nodded in agreement. Dr. Watson looked at Brenda and smiled.

"Let me first say," Dr. Peterson continued, "that I've discussed Sephiri with some individuals at the National Institutes of Health at great length. They are very excited, and with your permission, we would like to study him."

At the word *study*, Brenda was sickened. She looked at Manden. His face was pained, but he did not speak. A violent cough took hold of her, and she drank some water to calm her throat. "Study?" she asked.

"Excuse me, Mrs. Thompson," said Dr. Peterson. "Perhaps *study* is too strong a word. What I mean is, we would like to take a closer look at Sephiri and the extraordinary shift in what he is exhibiting."

Brenda looked from Dr. Peterson to the other doctors. Sephiri was all she had left of Horus, as painful as it still was, all that remained of him since he had been put away. She didn't want her boy's peculiarities, however profound they were, under a microscope. Although Sephiri had been living bottled in a world of his own making, it was a safe world as far as she knew. His autism had allowed him that, at least. "I'm not sure I understand."

"It's all very special, Mrs. Thompson," said Dr. Watson. Her face was flushed with excitement, and her blond curls bounced as she spoke. "It's an observation of savants, extraordinarily talented autistic individuals. We think Sephiri is phenomenal. There are only a small number of these individuals identified in the world. They're unexpected. They appear like rainbows. I can assure you that Sephiri would not be subjected to anything intrusive, you understand, only close observation. We could arrange for a special room here just for him, with all of his favorite things. Even a bathtub. In fact, this new style of observation allows minimal contact for the levels of sensitivity that we know Sephiri is prone to exhibit. The observation is pure. It is aimed only to enlighten us about the unknown, about the full spectrum of this condition, of the human mind. It could be groundbreaking."

Brenda looked at the animated young doctor. She did not want to say that as far as she could tell, what was amazing about Sephiri was the tremendously thick walls that seemed to shield him from everything and the mysterious mazes he seemed to wander alone. She did not want to say that her boy seemed as trapped as his father, that Sephiri might only be a riddle to them all. "Doctor, what do you mean by an extraordinary shift?" she asked.

The director's eyebrows rose. "Have you seen Sephiri's drawings, Mrs. Thompson?" He reached for a folder and opened it. He took out some papers and spread them around the table. There were enormous illustrations of insects, as if under a microscope. Some were drawn in pencil. Incredibly, others were sketched in multiple shades of brown, amber, or gold crayon. The outlines of things were drawn in the most delicate lines of black. There were fantastical renderings of abdomens, antennae, and wings. The veins across the wings were elaborate webs, with patterns drawn within patterns. From the head of each insect, a bold, piercing eye seemed to rise from the page. "Dr. Smith here can explain it better than I can," said the facility director. He nodded to the other man sitting at the table.

Dr. Smith, a short and stout man with a balding head, pointed to the drawings with his pencil. "These insect renderings are anatomically correct. I've had them checked." He picked up one of the drawings and shook his head. There was a bulbous thorax and abdomen, from which six mechanically drawn legs dangled; joints and musculature were visible, every femur and tibia shown, with finely drawn barbs lining the edges. "We discovered many such drawings stuffed behind the bookcase in the playroom after Dr. Watson retrieved this one from Sephiri." He took another sketch from a different folder and held it up. "But this is the only one that seems to depict something different."

The sketch showed a valley surrounded by enormous mountains. A great wall of dark rock was etched across a pallid-looking sky, and the charcoal-colored jagged heads of the mountains were capped with a smattering of white. Their hulking forms corralled an ominous structure in the foreground. Two towers flanked the extremities of a huge building in the middle. There were shadows of figures standing on the ledges of the tower. Thin rods extending from the frames of their bodies could have been long sticks. Or rifles.

"This really is rather extraordinary, even imposing," said Dr. Smith. "Could it be somewhere Sephiri has been before?" He placed

the drawing in front of Brenda. "Do you recognize it?" He looked
at Manden. "Anything familiar at all, Mr. Thompson?"

Brenda looked at Manden, who remained silent.

Brenda was stunned by the drawings. She looked back again at
the towers and the mountains in amazement, telling herself there
couldn't possibly be a connection to what was creeping into her
mind. It looked like a prison, with the silhouettes of men standing
atop the towers and the ominous-looking walls. It looked like Black
Plains. She had never been able to bring herself to go near there,
and after the verdict, she was only able to look at photographs of it
on occasion in those darkest of times, when she tried to fathom the
place her husband was condemned to. The prosecutor called Horus
a domestic terrorist. The judge said that he would be going where
terrorists go. And she had looked at the images of the perimeter of
the compound, wondering how something so sinister and terrible
could be placed among such spectacular mountain majesty. In those
first months, she had many nightmares of the dreadful place. And
whenever she thought of Horus, it rose in her mind like a mirage
of Hades.

But Sephiri had never been to Black Plains, and he knew nothing
of Horus. His autism had cloaked him, hadn't it? And it was then that
Brenda thought of the tapestry she'd spent so many days in front
of at the museum, for which she had named her son. Sephiri, the
hidden place of the heart. Was this the same boy who threw plates
of food on the floor and banged his head on walls? Who would not
let her touch him sometimes, who screamed when she tried to get
him out of the bathtub? She was never sure if he even recognized
his own name, since he was often indifferent to whether she used
it to try to get his attention or not. How could he know about
insects in this way or Black Plains? Brenda's stomach knotted, and
she swallowed hard, staring at the drawings to glean some meaning
from them, trying to balance an impossible equation.

"Mrs. Thompson?" asked Dr. Smith, louder.

"No," she said. "This is not somewhere Sephiri's been before.

I would never take him to a place like this." She did not look at Manden. They did not discuss such things. What she would never know was that Manden had never gone out to the prison, that he had written a letter to Horus on the anniversary of their father's death every year since he was sent away. Some of the letters were one sentence. Some were pages and pages. Things had a way of coming out on the page, even when he hadn't wanted them to. But he had folded each letter up, sealed it, and thrown it in the trash. He had convinced himself that it was better this way, with the blood dried on the concrete of their lives and certain things left blank.

"Well, it doesn't particularly matter," said the facility director. "The point here is the extraordinary show of mastery. We think Sephiri may be a savant. Such sudden displays of amazing ability have been documented before. There are still so many things we don't know about autism, so much of the brain that has yet to be unlocked. You have to understand that through careful observation, we might be able to learn more of the crucial elements of his condition. It may help you to understand him more."

Brenda looked at the beautiful sketches and was amazed. If there was anything she wanted in the world, it was to understand Sephiri more. He had been unreachable since his toddler years. He had started to speak, first in baby gibberish, then with a few intelligible words. But when he turned three, it was as if language fell away from him altogether, and he descended into a world without words and the feelings associated with them, without facial expression or interaction. He looked at her arm or her hair as if from a distant place, somewhere too far away to hear her calling to him. He had turned to stone before her eyes.

"What kind of insects are these?" Brenda asked.

"Locusts. That's what the entomologist I had examine the drawings tells us," said Dr. Smith. "An extinct variety of locust, distinguishable only by a few specific characteristics. From what I understand, it's a kind of mountain locust that was once native to the western United States. They used to lie dormant for years underground before hatching and emerging. They've been extinct since the eighteen hundreds." The director shook his head. "All the more amazing that Sephiri would draw such a thing and all the more reason to watch him closely. He might teach us something."

The facility director clasped his hands together and smiled. "We will keep you informed every step of the way. As you know, Sephiri will be challenged by a change to a different room, and this is the only initial concern we have. But a room of his own without the possible distraction of other children would be ideal, we think. It is a lovely space, with clear glass walls. We know of Sephiri's fondness for baths, and we have even equipped the room with a tub. Think of it like his own warmed pool, where he can relax. He would really like that, we're sure. Of course, we will have to allow time for him to adjust before we could actually begin noting anything in his behavior. We will have to help him to understand the new environment as being a friendly one, which may be a little difficult for him to realize at first. But we think this arrangement would be for the best. May we have your permission?"

Brenda again looked at Manden. He looked back at her but remained silent. Brenda knew it was her decision. She had been solitary in Sephiri's care. Despite her occasional insistence on this family charade and Manden's monthly check, she had been on her own. She felt her ankles swelling as she fidgeted in the seat. Perhaps this was a way to finally get a glimpse of what was going on in Sephiri's mind, some circuitous route to reach him. This could be a chance to connect with him, to get him what he needed. Maybe then she would have a chance to tell him that he was precious to her in spite of everything, that he had been conceived in love after all. In saving him, perhaps she could find a way to save herself.

Sugar

There are moments that leave a mark. That set in motion a trajectory of events from which there seems to be no escape. There were many such marks for Brenda; pivotal among them was the day her doctor told her that she was heading toward diabetes. His warning came the morning after a long night with Sephiri. He had been agitated by something, and she could not get him to stay in bed and go to sleep. She walked him back to his room over and over, laid him down next to her in her own room, put pillows and blankets on the floor in the hallway, all to no avail. When she gave up well after midnight, she turned on all the lights, locked herself in the bathroom, and broke down crying. She let him roam around the house while she slumped on the sofa. Around three o'clock, he finally settled on the living-room floor in front of the television turned to a channel with nothing but loud static. Exhausted, she tried to cancel her appointment later that morning and was told by the bubbling receptionist that it was important that she not miss it.

"Impaired glucose tolerance," the doctor said. It was a pre-diabetic condition (*pre* meaning one last chance before it all goes to hell). Her cells were swimming in a bath of sugar. Her pancreas was turning on itself. The rest of her would be next. Kidneys. Eyes. Nerve endings. Heart. She needed to make some lifestyle changes.

Eat healthy. Exercise. Reduce stress. Lose weight. She stared blankly into the doctor's eyes, thinking, *When? How?*

The doctor went on about green leafy vegetables and thirty-minute walks, and Brenda drifted into thoughts of how the vortex of Sephiri's autism consumed her. What scraps were left around the edges went to supporting the two of them with her job. The money from Manden helped with unexpected expenses, but she wasn't foolish enough to think that this would go on forever. Eating, as she was loath to admit unless she was in one of those soul-clutching moments late at night, was her only comfort. Often it was the drive-thru, takeout, or frozen meals. Burger King. Checkers. Kung Pao chicken. Sara Lee. Hungry-Man. This freed her to get through meal ordeals with Sephiri, who wanted peanut butter and jelly sandwiches for breakfast, lunch, and dinner. Brenda was determined that he would eat something more substantive. Quinoa and buckwheat. Raw vegetables and fruits. Fresh strawberries and turkey. Fish and eggs. Most of the time, Sephiri was fussing at the table, throwing his plate on the floor, screaming and grabbing the grape jam from the pantry. Or else, he was motionless at his plate, lifeless and staring. There wasn't time for her own meal planning. She couldn't leave him in the house alone to take a walk, nor could she bring him with her. There weren't any yoga classes or gym memberships to fit into her day. Insomnia, which ruled her life by force or default, took what energy stores she had left.

The doctor handed her a Centers for Disease Control brochure on type 2 diabetes and treatment. On the cover was a youngish-looking white woman slicing a tomato in a bright kitchen with a vase of cut flowers on the table. She wore a fashionable yellow sweat suit, and a man smiled adoringly from the doorway of the adjoining room. When Brenda opened the inside flap of the brochure, there was a list of dangerous related conditions: blindness, amputation, gastroparesis (stomach illnesses), atherosclerosis (vessel disease), heart attack, stroke. At the bottom, it read, "It doesn't have to happen to you."

Brenda knew many women with diabetes, including her super-visor, a rotund mahogany-brown ball of congeniality. She was the kindest to Brenda when Horus's trial began and told her to take as much time as she needed when she heard about the verdict. "I'll be praying for you," she'd said. When Brenda started to "show," her boss bought her a gift bouquet with a bottle of prenatal vitamins stuffed inside. "Take those horse pills every day, and take care of yourself, Brenda," she had said. "You don't want to have sugar problems later." In most places she'd frequented, the condition was a casual part of discussions among women. Pricking their fingers with elegant devices pulled from purses, nodding their heads in satisfaction when the light turned green or the white strip came out or when the number appeared on the little digital screen, they acted as if the whole business was a part of life, a part of getting older. Like graying hair or having grandchildren. "Girl, my sugar's up," she'd heard them cluck over salads drenched in dressing and bacon bits. Her mother, too, had been diabetic. It was the contributing factor to her sudden stroke, as Brenda later learned in the meeting with the doctor who performed her autopsy. When Brenda noticed the blood-glucose monitor and the white orthopedic shoes in the bathroom and asked her mother the meaning of it, she waved the question away with her hand as if swatting a fly. "Brenda, when you been through what I been through, a little sugar ain't nothing to cry about," she had said. With that comment, there was the opportu-nity to open a door to the past again, but looking at her frail mother, content only with her daytime soap stories and prune juice, Brenda left it closed. Years later, she would wonder what her mother meant, if it compared to anything she had to face.

"If you want to be around for your son, you will change," the doctor said, looking at Brenda through horn-rimmed glasses. He was a kindly black man, many years her senior. "You have to un-derstand that this can't be taken lightly. Diabetes is no walk in the park. With your weight as it is and from what I've seen with the tests, you're a prime candidate. I've seen it over and over. We all have obligations, but you've got to put yourself first on this one."

Brenda looked at the doctor. He wore an asymmetrical Afro that reminded her of photographs she'd seen of Frederick Douglass. However true it might have been, what he said sounded like a commercial for some pharmaceutical company or health association. The idea of caring for herself had been foreign other than the basics, and those had been choppy. Dental checkups (if she remembered or when a tooth was hurting). Mammogram and Pap smear examinations every year. Well, some years she had missed. The OB/GYN always seemed to be some pearl-necked cosmopolitan from Boston or San Francisco, chatting her up with casual conversation while she dug around her insides with birdlike hands. She didn't want to lie across a slab and pretend to be nonchalant while the cold air raised crops of goose bumps all over her body and the fluorescent lights blinked the way they had when she viewed her mother in the hospital morgue. How many pamphlets did she need to be handed about hypertension, cancer, glaucoma, and heart disease? She knew about the dangers, the risks. At the last examination, two years ago, a young nurse in a pink smock with matching streaked braids in her hair handed Brenda a brochure on obesity and depression. But she hadn't asked her for a brochure. She hadn't asked her for a damned thing. She didn't mind skipping the loud silence of the nurse as she slid the little metal bricks across the bar when she stepped on the scale. Over more. A bit more. More.

Besides, there had been no time. There would be no time. Sephiri's medical appointments and conferences with his caregivers and the hours spent waiting for prescriptions to be filled at the drugstore, at the Walgreens, at the People's pharmacy, ate up her accrued leave as soon as she earned it. In between, there were work deadlines, trips to the store, sitting in traffic, oil changes and repairs for the car, the endless laundry and soiled carpet cleanings. Putting herself first meant letting everything else fall.

If you want to be around for your son . . .

Brenda couldn't stop the words from ringing in her head. The thought of becoming ill and not being able to care for Sephiri, to run the regular and never-ending business of their lives, was too great a thought to fit into her mind. The thought of her boy at twenty years old, or thirty, filled her with angst. If she couldn't care for Sephiri, who would? There was no one else to try to follow Sephiri through the tunnels of his hours, the indivisible spaces of his mind. That she would be the one to do so until her dying breath was something she was absolutely certain of, and yet the road stretched long and bleak. Between his schedules and diet plans and medications and treatments, she didn't have the time to think about her own health, the nature and shape of her own existence apart from it all. She'd lost track of herself a long time ago. She didn't have the slightest idea of how to start climbing the mountain of her own life plan outside of Sephiri. Outside of autism.

"I like to see my patients lead full lives," said the doctor.

But my life is already full, thought Brenda. It was full to the brim with everything. She looked at the poster on the examination-room wall. A woman was smiling with her two children sitting on her lap, a golden cross around her neck. Brenda had not been back to Our Lady of Perpetual Help Church since the last days of the trial. She'd known many of the people there since her childhood, when she sat in the pews as a girl. Horus was not one for church every Sunday, but she was able to get him to go on holidays. She remembered pleasant afternoons on the hill where the church stood, which had one of the best panoramic views of Washington, D.C. From the top, she could see the black Potomac River that snaked the white monuments, the giant obelisk piercing the sky. She had spent countless Fourth of July holidays watching the fireworks from that hill, holding sparklers in her hand as the sky exploded with color. She remembered looking out over the city on that Sunday after the verdict, furious with God. The women had gathered around her in a ring of prayer like moths circling a light, trying to balm her distemper, telling her what they told themselves a thousand times. *God don't give you more than you can bear. It's all part of His plan. The*

Lord is testing you. But Brenda had watched them all try to deal with their own tragedies over the years and was never able to tell if the advice had been applicable to them. The son who was shot. The daughter whose home was visited by Child Protective Services. The mother whose lights were disconnected. The HIV-positive niece. The cousin who lost his job. The uncle whose leg the doctors said they had to take; sugar had gotten the best of him.

Years later, when Brenda was up with Sephiri at four o'clock in the morning (he wanted to spend the night walking up and down the stairs), she sat on the sofa watching a documentary. In it, a Native American talked of his life, of all he'd seen, of what he knew to be true yesterday and tomorrow. "Religion is for those afraid to go to hell," he'd said through watery eyes. "Spirituality is for those who have been there." And indeed, Brenda felt she was living in a hell. One that had swallowed her husband whole. One in which she could see her boy burning but could do nothing to rescue him from the flames. That was when, after holding anger and grief for so long, she made a deal with God, which was this: she would talk to Him about something only if she had the fortitude, and He would listen only if He could do something about it. Brenda had begun to wonder if that private arrangement was coming to an end.

"The truth is," said the doctor, "if you don't start making some major changes now, you're going to get sick." He handed her another prescription for blood pressure and a referral. "Fill this prescription today, and I want you to make an appointment to see a nutritionist. There is only so much the body can take. You owe it to yourself." He patted her gently on the shoulder and gave her a meaningful look.

Sitting on the hard examination bench, Brenda's legs had fallen asleep, and she rose to gather her shoes and purse. Her heart was pounding, her ears thumping with the blood pumping through her. She read somewhere that the heart beats some hundred thousand times a day, thirty-five million times a year, two and a half billion times in a lifetime. Her heart had beaten through so many things.

Thirty-five million beats in each of the years of her life, each beat striking the drum of her heart and then gone forever. How many more beats did it have left? She picked up her purse, clutching the strap. Tired. She felt tired all over, as if she had walked for miles, had swam kilometers in the sea. If she couldn't help herself, how could she help Sephiri? She slipped her feet into her flat loafers, her most worn shoes. They would have to carry her on yet another journey now, one even more ominous. Again, the two signs materialized in her mind: *What are you going to do?* and *Why are you doing what you're doing?* She didn't have the answer to either.

Water World

The little boat materialized. Sephiri blinked to make sure that it was there. He was ready to ride in it, and just as suddenly, he was sitting inside of it, on the little wooden bench, floating atop the beautiful current that was as turquoise as the bathwater he sat in every night before bedtime. He began to float away, the sun's warm rays beaming on his head and shoulders. He blinked again, and there were the giant rocks hailing him from a distance, the Obsidians. He floated toward them. He was enjoying the sounds of the water sloshing against the side of the boat when he heard a voice.

"So you've found us again," said the voice.

This sort of thing always filled Sephiri with a jolt of excitement. In Water, voices were quickly understood. He scanned the blue for the source of the voice. The surface was gilded with sunlight.

"Down here," said the voice.

Sephiri looked into the water. It was his friend, the dolphin, who had been gliding alongside him, his gray skin slick and glistening in the bright rays.

"Hello," said Sephiri.

"Welcome back," the dolphin said. A merry creature, the dolphin always greeted Sephiri when he entered the World of Water.

Sephiri rejoiced. Whenever he was angry or lonely or confused, he knew that he could always travel out to the great ocean. Now he could forget about the things that troubled him in Air. The ocean was the great bath that washed away all tears, the great tranquilizer of fears.

Sephiri had been coming there for a long time. The creatures who inhabited the Obsidians and swam in the currents around them shared knowledge with Sephiri about all the living things that had ever existed and chronicled the alliances, truces, and wars. That was how he learned about the locusts of his dreams. "Well, they only rear up when it is their time," the dolphin said as they floated together on their backs looking at the cloud formations. "They are the message carriers."

"Really?" asked Sephiri, filled with wonder.

"Yes," said the dolphin. "They only appear when something important is going to happen, something that will change everything."

Sephiri wondered what it could be as the wind kissed his face.

The dolphin rose a bit from the surface of the water and looked intently at the boy. "The Great Octopus says that you may visit with your question now." The dolphin knew as well as anyone in the World of Water that an invitation to visit the Great Octopus in his lair was an honor.

Sephiri was giddy with excitement. He plunged into the deep with the dolphin. Down they drifted, deeper and deeper, and when the water changed from turquoise to electric blue to indigo, they stopped. Below them was a void of darker water.

"This is as far as I can go," said the dolphin. "Wait here for the Great One." He swam once around the boy and glided away.

In the next moment, as the ocean held Sephiri suspended, an enormous creature emerged from the abyss beneath his feet. The Great Octopus looked at the boy through two giant orbs and beckoned him to follow. The boy swam alongside its long plum and maroon tentacles, which swirled through the water like massive coils of hair. Together, they descended into the deep, scaling the underwater mountains.

At long last, they reached an enormous den, a jagged mouth

carved into the side of the mountain near the ocean floor. It was a realm inhabited only by the fierce, where there was almost no oxygen, where the viperfish, dragonfish, and other beasts reigned. Sephiri strained to see in the growing darkness, until a school of anglerfish, flashlights dangling from their foreheads, approached them to light the rest of the way. The anglerfish swam ahead, pleased to be a part of such a rare visitation. Sephiri swam behind the Octopus through a maze of jutting rocks. They came to a great cove covered in a blanket of purple and pink coral and stopped. Sephiri seated himself on a huge sea sponge and watched a school of iridescent organisms swim by. The Octopus floated down to a smooth plateau of rock and spread himself out, covering the entire rock shelf in tubes of plum.

"So, Sephiri," bellowed the Great Octopus. "You know I only allow a visit when I can feel that you have a question."

Sephiri hesitated. He indeed had a question, but he was unsure if the Octopus would be able to answer. After all, what he needed to know concerned the Land of Air, not the World of Water.

"Do not delay, boy," said the Octopus. "Remember, your visit must be brief. It is dangerous for you here. You seem to have solved your need for air well enough, and your mind keeps you warm at these depths. But the bottom dwellers will soon sniff you out, and I will be forced to ink even the anglers to provide you with cover."

Sephiri did not want to make the Great One angry. He was upset that things kept changing in the Land of Air, threatening to ruin everything. But he didn't want to waste his chance with the Octopus on that. He needed to know about a different matter. "I heard something," he said.

The Octopus looked at the boy. "We all hear many things, some of which are not worth listening to, some of which are the only things of importance to know. What is it that you heard?"

"A different kind of voice from the Land of Air, I think. But I didn't understand," said Sephiri. "I could barely hear it."

"Did you recognize the voice?"

The boy was silent for a moment. This was the first voice from the Land of Air that had ever drawn his attention, other than his mother's voice. But he was never entirely sure what the words coming out of her mouth meant. He had learned that her voice went with certain things done in repetition, like walking toward that white van that went to the Autism Center or going to the bathroom. This voice was not that voice.

"No," said Sephiri.

The Octopus looked at the tall seaweed wave in the current. In his long years, he had seen this happen before. A voice difficult to hear meant there was a choice to be made between realms of existence. The boy had been a part of their realm for many years, and he knew that this could mean that he would stop visiting forever. But he could not withhold the truth. That would break a universal law. "The voice is asking your permission to be heard," said the Octopus. "It is soft and low because you haven't been ready to hear it. It was waiting for you." He twirled one of his tentacles, sighing. "Sometimes a voice comes to tell us something we do not wish to hear but need to. It can also come and tell us something we always wanted to know but hadn't been able to find out about before."

Sephiri wondered what the voice could be trying to say. "Should I listen to it?"

"If you want to, you'll hear it," said the Octopus. "And once you start to listen, a change begins that cannot be stopped." The mammoth being rose, floating just above the rock shelf. "This is the enduring message of the locusts, Sephiri. When they emerge, what follows is truth. All you can do is bear witness."

Sephiri watched an ancient whale sail over a barren reef.

"You'd better head back," said the Octopus. "As I have said, these visits must be brief. Go back through the coral beds. The iridescent ones will light the way. The anglerfish will take you up."

Sephiri thought about what the Octopus said as he floated to the surface and began his departure, but he was not sure what he should do. He wished he could have stayed longer with the Great One and asked the million other questions he had. How does one smile? Why do children play together? As he drifted back over the ocean to the shores of apprehension, Sephiri closed his eyes, thinking of the Obsidians and all he learned and discussed with the inhabitants. And he wondered what the voice would tell him if he listened.

There and Not There

When Sephiri felt brave and adventurous, when he did not long for the blackness and the ordered space of the coat closet by the front door, he ventured to his mother's closet. It was like a small room with a door that he could close. He enjoyed the two sides. One side had the swish and swirl and scratch and fluff of his mother's clothes, with the smells of coconut oil and cinnamon. The other side was completely bare, with a single wooden pole running across its width. He loved the dichotomy of the space. One side was filled to the brim with fabrics and belts and stockings and hats. The other side was filled with emptiness.

One day, he was exploring the shoe boxes on the floor while his mother was in the bathroom, and he saw something glossy stuck under the iron grate covering the air duct on the nothing side of the floor, ruining the emptiness. He lifted the grate, with some difficulty because it was old and rusted around the edges, and pulled out a photograph.

There was a man in the picture, wearing a big white shirt and black pants. His brown skin glowed in the sunny day and the green trees behind him. He held his arm around a woman standing next to him. She wore a patterned sundress the color of lemons and melons and candy. She was slender, and big peacock feathers dangled from each earlobe. Sephiri had a picture book with something in it that looked like the feathers and thought that this woman might have been someone in the book. But he looked again at the woman in the picture, and something called to him about her face, and then he realized that the woman looked like his mother. Her body was much smaller, though. At first, he thought the photograph must be a magic trick and wondered how she could be so differently shaped. But when he stared carefully into the woman's face, one of the few things in the Land of Air that he was sure of for as a long as he could remember, he knew that the woman was his mother.

But who was the man standing next to her? Like many things Sephiri could remember with great precision after looking just once, faces were like maps when they didn't move. An expressionless face was easier to see. He could remember the geography of eyes and eyebrows and nose and frame of mouth. The man in the picture looked something like that person his mother called Manden. He was the one who came to sit on their dangerous sofa, the same man who came to the Autism Center with his mother sometimes. His was the deep voice that stooped down to him, that talked at him. A bass sound that quivered the fine hairs in his ears.

But the man in the photograph was not the bass-voiced man, the man with the funny walk. And when Sephiri stared longer, he thought that his face looked something like his own. Still, the hair above his upper lip and on his chin got in the way, so that Sephiri had to turn the photograph over and back again to see if the magic would give him a clearer view. Sephiri looked at the man's face staring back at him through the surface of the picture and felt something: absence. The opposite of his mother. He knew her by the alarm in her room, which sounded at six o'clock every morning; the cake she baked every thirty days (that was how he knew it was a new month); the scrambled eggs for breakfast (he did not like eggs but liked to stare at the yellowness of them while he ate cereal). She soaped him in the bathtub through his rigidity or tantrums; she held him when he screamed; she smelled of coconut oil and cinnamon.

Always. That was her regularity. That was the order and symmetry of her being.

But he liked the photograph. The left and right and known and unknown of it. The big man in black and white clothes on one side and the little color-laden woman on the other. And he looked at the kaleidoscope of the closet on one side and the white-walled emptiness on the other and thought that perhaps the empty side was this man's side. That the filled side, the side of lemons and melons and candy and peacock feathers, was there. That the empty-poled, barren side, the picture man's side, was not there. Something on the blank side had once been filled with something and then was not. Sephiri figured that this man had been on this side of the closet, and then he was not. He (the absence) was now the regularity of not being there. Sephiri was satisfied with the duality of this. He lifted the grate and dropped the photograph into the air duct. It slid down into the worm of black and disappeared. The empty side was not like the other constants and timetables that went with the order he knew of his mother—the nightly ritual of baths and pajamas, the steady emerald green of the mouthwash, the sanctity of the medicine cabinet, the peanut butter and jelly sandwiches, the *tick tock tick tock* of the clock in the hallway, the repetition of the steps.

Sephiri looked again at the hole beneath the iron grate where he had dropped the picture. It was gone now, where it was supposed to be. He hid the picture where it wouldn't ruin the emptiness, in the order and safety of the black. Sephiri wondered if Air people knew about the dark and if they hid in it too.

PART II

Black Plains

The Rocky Mountains walled clear up to the sky, grim and mean, daring anything but the wind to cross them. Without mercy, they looked down from crinkled, frosty faces at the vast, desolate plain that lay at their feet, naked and helpless. And in the lonesome valley, the Black Plains Correctional Institute stared back at the Rockies with equal malice, cold to the core and just as heartless. The men who peopled Black Plains, those entombed behind its walls, those trapped at its core, those who guarded the concrete, the men who walked its watchtower ledges, perimeters, and corridors, all were covered over with the frost and had long been frozen in the deep of all things lost. The prison, endless in its intricacy of halls that led to other halls, rooms and spaces within other rooms and spaces, turns that led to other turns, shifted and reshaped itself according to the mind of the dweller, whether prisoner or guard.

Warden Andrew Stotsky walked the halls of Black Plains like a seasoned soldier, the angry wind howling outside in the dying twilight. He was no longer a young man, his grayish face etched in deep wrinkles, but he still moved with a steady gait. From above, fluorescent light showered down in chalky beams, and tiny flecks of paint coated the walls like chips of ice. He turned the corner of the corridor, the sound of his polished black loafers echoing through the interior. In all that solitude, the hush only increased the volume of memories. Often, against his will, each pace dislodged the past; he walked one hallway to another, one turn after another, and each step in the thick quiet only awakened Stotsky's thoughts as ceaseless rattling loosens the hinge screws of a lock.

At such times, he would sometimes think of his dead mother's face, when he was nineteen years old and had stood over her in that pitiful funeral parlor. It was filled only with the neatness of dark, empty chairs, the smell of carpet cleaner, and the perfume of dying hyacinths and lilies. His father had long been in the ground. His mother had no connection with her own family, and they had lived in a town of others too engrossed in the squalor of their own lives to notice that one of them had departed. He stood before the stillness of her body, nestled in the stiff white satin of the coffin. Staring down at her pale skin, Stotsky had been appalled by rouge too red hastily applied to her thin lips and the perfect circles of pink powder brushed onto each sunken cheek. It had all come together like a thick, clownish smattering of oil paint on a canvas. Viewing her face in this way—not so dissimilar to what it was when she was living, except that then the colors were made by his father's fist—lit a match to something within Stotsky.

He did not believe in second chances, as his mother did with his father. He remembered watching her cry at the kitchen table. She would sob into her hands, nursing her face. His father loomed somewhere else in that quiet house, a silence so much deeper than any silence in the halls of Black Plains. Somewhere in the darkness of the rooms his eyes flashed cobalt with anger. Stotsky remembered peeling the limp fingers from his mother's swollen eye, cupping the blood dripping from her nose with his hand. As she always did when he touched her, she would wince and wave him away. "Stop," she would say. "Don't ax me nothin' about it." She would later declare, as she did a thousand times, that his father hadn't meant it, that she was giving him a second chance. At this, Stotsky would look at his mother slumped in the chair and run outside. On and on he would run, until he came to the outskirts of an abandoned factory. He would press his face against the cold fence that rimmed miles of barbed wire, taste the acrid air and the dusty remnants blowing in the wind, and vow never to go back.

Stotsky's legs shook when he stood before the coffin. He stared at his mother's face, a portrait of ruin, a face that became the face of all women. And he could only stand, helpless, in the murderous outrage of that moment, with the cheap wall clock ticking. Then, from inside the wax-encrusted ear of the body crawled a bug. Stotsky recognized it as a potato bug, those gray ball-like creatures always in the stacks of yellowed newspapers his mother kept by the kitchen door and the damp food sacks in the pantry. As a boy, he toyed with them on the floor. He would watch them scurry, as he had scurried through the rooms of the house, as his mother had scurried from the kitchen to the bedroom and back again. And he would pick one up and marvel at how it could curl into itself, how it hardened into its own suit of armor. He admired the exoskeleton, a thing so small yet capable of repelling so much. At the coffin, Stotksy watched the potato bug crawl across the side of his mother's face, over the bridge of her nose, and settle on the pink of her other powdered cheek. There the thing held court; there it held dominion over his mother's wasted body.

And as Stotsky looked at the insect, oblivious to his mother's death as it stood atop the zenith of her cheek in triumph, he felt that smallness again, the raw vulnerability that haunted him during his father's rages, when he was an enormous mound of moving flesh and shadow over his mother, over the house, over all of them. In those moments cringing under his bed or in the closet, when he could scarcely stand to be in his own skin, he hated his father and loved him too. And he hated his mother and loved her too. And he could not bring himself to allow the last testament to this small woman and her small life ever having existed to be defaced by something that crawled from the wax of her ear. And he lifted the potato bug from his mother's cheek and held it tightly between his thumb and index finger. And when he could no longer feel it moving, when he was sure it had given up its last, he put it in his pocket. Years later, he would realize that had been the moment, not when he felt his father's fist or when he listened to the ominous sounds of flesh on flesh in the rooms of his boyhood house. It had been that squeezing moment, when he held that ball of smallness, when he stifled that defiance in the vise of his fingers, that the hunger had been born.

Warden Stotsky walked down one wing and turned the corner to another. Thick columns of stone flanked the Black Plains corridors. *The Roman Empire*, he thought, passing through a tall iron gate. There had always been other empires, other dominions. He thought of his old Japanese comrade, Hanamitsu, who had been an orderly in a death camp in Manchuria. They'd been exchanging letters ever since the Japanese corporal's days of serving time in a Russian prison. Hanamitsu had plea-bargained at the Khabarovsk War Crime Trials and was granted leniency because of his low rank in the Japanese Imperial Forces and his detailed disclosure of the nature of the camp experiments. They had a strange admiration for each other, Stotsky and Hanamitsu, which continued long after the old Japanese soldier settled into an obscure thatched hut in the blue mountains of Hakuba. In their long letters over the years, they discussed life and death and the various ways both needed to be controlled. In spite of all the things they agreed on, Stotsky always felt that Hanamitsu was slightly off the mark when it came to certain matters. For instance, Hanamitsu did not believe that human will could ever be turned into something else.

Coming to the end of the dim prison corridor, Stotsky supposed that the hunger to know the secret of what his father certainly must have known (what it took to break the will of another) only grew after he buried his mother, locked up the house, and enlisted in the Army. He turned a corner that led to another corner, thinking of his old days in Vietnam, the lush treachery of the jungle, and the place he and his men called the Kennel. He thought of the seven women he and his squad had captured and locked into empty pig stalls. "She wouldn't bark," he said out loud to the dark, thinking of the seventh woman. But why? He could still feel the oppressive humidity and smell the stench. After all these years, his curiosity about why had never waned. They had the women there, nooses around their necks, cowering on all fours, knee-deep in manure, as they sodomized them for nineteen days. "Bark," they had said to them, yanking their heads by their ponytails.

By the tenth day, the women barked and howled on command. By the twelfth day, the women barked on their own. Except for one, the seventh. No matter what they did to her, no matter how far they went with her, she would not bark. Stotsky brought her extra food and water and asked her questions in broken Vietnamese to test her faculties. She answered him, as clear as rainwater.

If she had been insane, Stotsky felt that he would have been satisfied. He would have gone on raping her with the understanding that she was silent not because she did not want to bark but because she couldn't. On the fifteenth day, he loosened the seventh woman's noose and smeared iodine on the oozing infection ringing her neck. "Bark, bitch, and I'll let you go," he said as he looked into her red, furious eyes. He loosened the rope a bit more and kicked her stall door open. But she did not, would not, bark.

On the nineteenth day, the section of the jungle where Stotsky and the others had been camped was attacked. The women howled through the gunfire until someone freed them like horses in a barn, and they ran about amid the burning foliage, crying and barking. The seventh woman was running, too, until she saw a knife lying next to a dead Vietnamese soldier and picked it up. She ran up behind one of the American soldiers and put its tip to his jugular, just as Stotsky was approaching. And he could see by the look on her face that she was impenetrable even at that moment. She was unreachable, even as she slashed the soldier's throat and Stotsky shot her.

Stotsky arrived at the end of that corridor and turned a corner that led to another corner. The question concerned him still. Would she ever have barked, had it been the twenty-third day or the fortieth? He had no way to be sure. Looking at her face in those seconds, he still wanted to know before putting her down. Later, he wondered why he felt no remorse for needing to know this, although he had no intention of sparing her life. But it all ran together in his head long before he left the jungle. He dreamed about that woman still, and she glared back at him through the foliage of time with the same resoluteness, with the same citadel in her eyes.

What he felt about all of that was something like the disgust at having been the victim of a practical joke. Could a man's will ever truly be broken by another, snapped like a twig and reattached in a different manner? Reactions could be had through various measures, through persuasions. This much he knew. But after the blood dried, after injuries healed and compliance was obtained, he wondered if soul and will could then be repositioned, morphed into something of another's making.

"Warden." A sullen voice plowed through the stillness of the hallway.

Stotsky turned around to find Secured Housing guard Jimmy Eckert, always severe in demeanor, with his crooked mouth and his stringy blond hair plastered to his forehead. He was Stotsky's most dedicated guard. It seemed as if he was on duty no matter the day, no matter the hour. The way he crept around had always annoyed Stotsky, and he would have long ago dismissed him except that he valued his special skills in the Secured Housing wing, also known as solitary confinement. He was useful, and Stotsky had always been mildly amused by the zeal with which he seemed to perform his duties. Besides, Eckert rarely spoke. Stotsky immediately assumed that he was approaching him with a matter of importance.

"There was some trouble," said Eckert, looking gravely at the warden. It was at times like this, when he was standing in front of Warden Andrew Stotsky, that his disdain for Stotsky's smugness and arrogance was acute. Eckert was never troubled in this way when he was down below, where he ruled the rodents, where time itself was of his own making. It gave him much pleasure, however, to bring news of a certain rodent under his watch, since he had caught a glimpse of the warden's discomfort in his presence all those years ago. "There was a problem with one particular rodent," he said.

"What is it? Which one?" Stotsky snapped.

"There was refusal to comply," said Eckert, enjoying the slow disclosure. "He wouldn't eat. He's on lockdown now."

"Well?" Stotsky asked. "Is it all under control?"

Eckert nodded. "Yes, sir," he said.

"And? Which one was it?" asked Stotsky.

"Zero-two-seven-six-three," said Eckert. He looked at the warden evenly, showing neither respect nor scorn.

Warden Stotsky was momentarily silent. Besides that look that had been in the eyes of 02763 on his first day at Black Plains, there had been other things Jimmy Eckert had said about him since. How he was not like the others in the solitary confinement wing. How he seemed to survive on something other than food and water. "A feeling I have," the guard would say. Eckert claimed to have learned to sense the flavor of an inmate, what he would and wouldn't do, what it would take to crack him, turn him into something else. He claimed that there was a wildness within this prisoner, not like an animal in the woods but like a bird that might take flight. It was all ridiculous to Stotsky. How would Eckert know? How would a man whose entire past and present had become the prison know anything about what made someone different? It was impossible that this strange troll he depended on to stomach the fatal intimacy of the solitary confinement wing knew about anything other than being buried alive.

"Are you sure it's under control?" Stotsky asked.

Eckert spread his hands out as if affirming an important truth. "Yes, sir," he said.

Stotsky looked from Eckert to the shadows in the corridor. Horus Thompson. Inmate number 02763. Twenty-five years to life for the stalking and cold-blooded murder of a police officer. He thought of Horus Thompson's induction day, how he glared at him even after the beating he had taken. "Welcome, rodent," he had said to him. Normally, Stotsky anticipated the arrival of a new one like the opening to the first chapter of a book. Stotsky looked forward to what he liked to call the "interview." It was the gateway experience of a new inmate, when he was made to feel the fullness of Black Plains for the very first time. This event still brought him satisfaction. It filled him with the sense that it was not important what a rodent expressed at the beginning. What was important was what he came to realize at the end. What he himself and all that came to Black Plains, willingly or involuntarily, came to realize: there was no escape.

But there had been this look that remained in Horus Thompson's eyes, even after the code violations and thresholds they broke with him. It reminded him of the look of the seventh woman in the jungle. A kind of certainty. Breaking Horus Thompson was important, because it was atop the minced souls of men that Black Plains had been built. Stotsky did not have a name for the fracture point, but he knew what it looked like, and he had seen it on the faces of countless other inmates, something that crept into the eye when it looked back from a narrow, desiccated place. Something that crawled in and stayed. In spite of Stotsky's efforts to achieve that frequency to which he could key this prisoner's—every prisoner's—vulnerability, that coolness in 02763's eyes remained. Horus Thompson looked up at him from a tub of water, from a pool of urine, through the brownish-red rivers of muck running from his eyes, with such gameness. A bewildering sweat formed under Stotsky's collar when he saw it. He had wanted to drown the prisoner then but decided instead to bury him alive, to suffocate him in the confines of the earth.

And the warden couldn't put his finger on the threat this inmate posed, even now. What was it about him? If he could have gotten away with blocking Horus Thompson's allowance of sixty minutes in the confinement gym for more than three months at a time, he would have done it. But he knew that this hastened dementia, and although he was not yet ready to pull the cord that led to madness, he was nevertheless reluctant to face the possibility that such measures might have no effect on this rodent. For these reasons, Warden Stotsky limited his thoughts of 02763 to the steady knowledge that he was encased in rock, three levels below him.

Sometimes, though, in the quiet of the shifting hallways, the warden thought about what he feared the most: the chance of escape. Not physical escape, since every precaution known to man had been taken to block all manner of leaving Black Plains except in a body bag. Rather, he worried about the possibility that an inmate's sins and the sorrows and years of misery could somehow be pushed back like the pane of a window in the mind and allow him passage to someplace else. And if that were true, it meant that what they said about the Mummy, the longest incarcerated inmate, was true. And it pained Stotsky to think, even for a second in the deepest of privacy, that there might very well be a way to jump the fence of the world without dying first.

Above, fluorescent lights flickered and the shadows in the corridor shifted their positions and he thought of his wife. Stotsky had taken a wife, reluctantly, after washing the blood spatter of Vietnam, the pig stalls, and all the rest of it from his face. It had been the advice of his commanding officer the day he returned stateside. "Get a wife," the man had said, after reading Stotsky's psych evaluation, after a long silence. "It'll help you remember what life was like before all of this." After his debriefing and out-processing, the young Stotsky tried to digest the superior officer's advice. The memories of the foreign place he had left were like blood smears turned to dark ink now, with the unknown fingerprints etched in by unspeakable stories, immortalized in silence. *Get a wife* rang in his head as he went to a bar that night. He smiled at the friendly waitress who served him and took her back with him to the room he was renting. He married her, and he loved her, he thought, even as he beat her. Eight months later, when he got to the police station and was handed the report, he found that he had again been outwitted by will. His eyes raked over the words: "single-car accident."

He mulled over a long description of the tree they said she must have willingly crashed into. How there had been nothing mechanically wrong with her vehicle. How she had missed the last three appointments with a social worker. That given the initial autopsy, which indicated that she had been pregnant, her file read, "presumed suicide." Stotsky had never decided on his final feelings about the pregnancy. At first, he felt a surge of anger, as if some important property of his had been confiscated without his knowledge. But he was more bothered by the fact that his wife had chosen the tree over the life she was living with him. That even though she yielded to him in every way, he still had not had the final say in the end.

In spite of himself, the thought of children would cross Stotsky's mind on his birthday. More and more, as time went by, he was struck by the finality of leaving no one behind. For all he accomplished with Black Plains, there would be nothing but ashes. In spite of the facility, over which he held God's mercy and wrath, his life was as finite as the years scheduled out for the condemned men he ruled, and he could not see his way to push what troubled him aside and climb through the windows of his own castle.

But when Stotsky was putting on his tie in the morning, when he was pouring his coffee in preparation to face the unyielding stance of the Rockies and the glory of the fortress in his charge, he had to put away such thoughts, for he could not bear to make space in his mind for the fears of small men, peering out at a world that had thrown them away.

Jimmy Eckert was waiting for the warden to respond.

At length, Stotsky nodded to the guard and sighed. "You did right by informing me, Eckert. You can go," he said, waving him off.

"Yes, sir," said Eckert.

Stotsky watched the guard back away into the shadows from which he had emerged.

Alone again in the corridor, Warden Stotsky walked on, pushing thoughts away and welcoming others. The silence in the vast facility was profound. It was something the administrators always complimented Stotsky about when they visited. "How can there be seven hundred twenty-nine people locked up in all this quiet?" they had asked. It was an astonishing feat, they marveled, indicative of the atmosphere of absolute control that Stotsky maintained, a control that was in danger at any given moment without vigilance. At this, Stotsky was heartened. If one understands the nature of a thing, Stotsky reasoned, one can know its capabilities, its look, feel, and movement beneath fur and flesh. Black Plains was a man-made wonder, a technological success complete with automated cameras, self-contained lights, water systems, and pressurized doors. The Great Room was a masterpiece of machinery and orchestrated labor. When Stotsky took the reins of Black Plains years ago, when it first opened its gaping mouth, he even had the banner "WORK SETS YOU FREE" set on the Great Room wall himself.

But the crowning achievements were the three sublevels omitted from tours and annual facility reports: level one was a security floor that divided the sea level from all the other sublevels; level two was a storage and supply floor for the entire facility; level three was Secured Housing. Supermax. Secured Housing was completely self-contained, with its own ventilation and water system separate from the rest of the facility. Tubing ran through it and beneath it, and life and death were connected to a shutoff valve that controlled air, water, and lighting. The administrators weren't given tours of this hidden jewel, although they read Stotsky's modified report about it. They shook the warden's hand, enthralled but eager to return to sound and sky. Black Plains was a petrified Noah's Ark, immobilized for all eternity in the hardened soil of Colorado, beneath the glare of the Rockies. The facility had been manned optimally, Stotsky reminded himself. He had been able to keep the population busy, more or less, ensuring that their focus remained inward and strained, guaranteeing total immersion in the Black Plains world. His world.

He reached his office, a great wooden door with his name embossed in gold, and walked in. As always, a feeling of ease and leisure washed over him. He sat down in his chair, ignoring the stack of papers waiting for him. Instead, he looked at his collection of Greek marble figurines lining the top shelves of his many bookcases. His books, which filled the shelves of his office, were elegantly bound with emerald-green and blood-red leather. There were rows and rows of scholarly works on psychology and the history of penal traditions over the centuries.

He even had a special edition of the 1842 travel journal written by Charles Dickens, *American Notes for General Circulation*, about his touring visits to a series of prisons. Stotsky went over and pulled it down from the shelf, as he did often, to reread what he liked to call the "opposing view" to his job, to the institution he upheld. He did not read it because he agreed with any of it, nor was it because he was trying to understand something he might have missed in all his decades of experience. Rather, he read it as a reminder that others looked upon his world in the extremities of right and wrong. But he knew that this was only because as outsiders looking in, as mere aliens visiting, they could never know the natural laws within the walls that formed the nature of the beast, the living, breathing structure built by man but which, by man's oppression and depravity, submission and rebellion, had taken on a life of its own. The blue satin bookmark was right where he left it, and he opened the book to read once again:

"Looking down these dreary passages, the dull repose and quiet that prevails, is awful. Occasionally, there is a drowsy sound from some lone weaver's shuttle, or shoemaker's last, but it is stifled by the thick walls and heavy dungeon-door, and only serves to make the general stillness more profound. Over the head and face of every prisoner who comes into this melancholy house, a black hood is drawn; and in this dark shroud, an emblem of the curtain dropped between him and the living world, he is led to the cell from which he never again comes forth, until his whole term of imprisonment has expired. . . . He is a man buried alive; to be dug out in the slow round of years."

Stotsky read on and stopped at one of his favorite parts.

"And though he lives to be in the same cell ten weary years, he has no means of knowing, down to the very last hour, in what part of the building it is situated; what kind of men there are about him; whether in the long winter night there are living people near, or he is in some lonely corner of the great jail, with walls, and passages, and iron doors between him and the nearest sharer in its solitary horrors. . . .

"I believe that very few men are capable of estimating the immense amount of torture and agony which this dreadful punishment, prolonged for years, inflicts upon the sufferers; and in guessing at it myself, and in reasoning from what I have seen written upon their faces, and what to my certain knowledge they feel within, I am only the more convinced that there is a depth of terrible endurance in which none but the sufferers themselves can fathom, and which no man has a right to inflict upon his fellow creature. I hold this slow and daily tampering with the mysteries of the brain to be immeasurably worse than any torture of the body; and because its ghastly signs and tokens are not so palpable to the eye and sense of touch as scars upon the flesh; because its wounds are not upon the surface, and it extorts few cries that human ears can hear; therefore the more I denounce it, as a secret punishment which slumbering humanity is not roused up to stay."

But the whole business had gone on, Stotsky thought, closing the book and returning to his chair. It was preserved by the millions who committed every act imaginable, by the countless who were guilty but not sorry. And it was for those whose acts could not be imagined that places like Black Plains Correctional Institute existed: the child rapists and murderers who laughed and jeered about the long list of children the authorities would never know about; the men who had chopped their families into pieces small enough to fit into a deep freezer; the drug kings and human traffickers who had lost count of how many they killed or made disappear. Worst in Stotsky's mind were the enemies of the state, those who had no respect for the centuries-built power and authority that come with the military or police and had taken law and order (or chaos) into their own hands. It was not so much what these types had done that bothered Stotsky; rather, it was that they felt they had the power and authority to do it.

He spun his chair around to Biderman's Chart of Coercion pinned to the wall. When Stotsky had first made warden, he'd gotten it retyped according to his own liking, and had the word "victim" changed to "prisoner" (there had been no distinguishable difference in his mind) and "effects" changed to "results," and had the text enlarged into a poster and framed. It hung behind his massive desk like a piece of art. And just as he liked to read from his books of the opinions of those who would never understand the world in which he breathed, he liked just as much to recite Biderman's chart, which had been written in the language of rules that made places like the Black Plains Correctional Institute work.

A social scientist at the Maxwell Air Force Base in Alabama, Dr. Albert D. Biderman had written and later published what was to become known as Biderman's Chart of Coercion, a delineation of tactics the Communists had used on U.S. Air Force prisoners of war in North Korea. In letters over the years, Stotsky and Hanamitsu had discussed the document at great length, and they had agreed that the techniques noted were no different from what they themselves had seen and done in their own war careers, and were consistent with the behavior of overseers and enforcers throughout the centuries of time. Stotsky had liked the chart at first glance. There it all was, in written form, the process and tutelage— the science—of breaking the will of another. And when he thought of his time in the jungle, of the question of will, he felt that the Biderman chart articulated the beginning of an odyssey that he would, time and again, bring the Black Plains inmates through, the nature of which he was sure his father knew. And so Stotsky faced the beautifully framed chart and read it over as he had done a thousand times before:

Method 1. Isolation

Result: Deprives prisoner of all social support of his ability to resist. Develops an intense concern with self. Makes prisoner dependent on captor.

Method II. Monopolization of Perception

Result: Fixes attention upon immediate predicament; fosters introspection. Eliminates stimuli competing with those controlled by captor. Frustrates all actions not consistent with compliance.

Method III. Induced Debilitation and Exhaustion

Result: Weakens mental and physical ability to resist.

Method IV. Threats

Result: Cultivates anxiety and despair.

Method V. Occasional Indulgences

Result: Provides positive motivation for compliance. Hinders adjustment to deprivation.

Method VI. Demonstrating Omnipotence and Omniscience

Result: Suggests futility of resistance.

Method VII. Degradation

Result: Makes the cost of resistance appear more damaging to self-esteem than capitulation. Reduces prisoner to animal-level concerns.

Method VIII. Enforcing Trivial Demands

Result: Develops habit of compliance.

Stotsky spun around again in his chair. Yes, that was the order of things, the necessary mythology that made Black Plains a masterpiece. The code was the pith and tithe of one day to the next. And like the real hell, this was a torment from which there was no escape.

Amenta

Horus Thompson, inmate number 02763, sat on the floor in the corner of his cell. It was the time of the lunar eclipse in the solitary confinement wing, the cusp of a perpetual dim, gunmetal light. It was the time between shifts from blinding beams to deep-space darkness and back again. Such things were on some sort of timer, but Horus was not able to recognize the pattern. He sat in the gray stillness, the nerve endings needling his backside like pins in a cushion. His eyes twitched in the gloom, trying to catch some stray ray of light that might stimulate his corneas. The cement on which he sat sloped toward the center of the floor, where it met a small corrugated drain, which held Horus and the meager contents of the cell like a sink. He couldn't always see the drain clearly, but he knew always that it was there, the threads of copper and green around the drain drawing his eyes as he wondered when he would liquefy and run down its open mouth.

Horus could still remember the pull of gravity when he first arrived at Black Plains, how the elevator scaled down each sublevel, the click and scrape of metal that grew muted as it neared the lowest level. He had ridden it down with the guards slowly, and it landed at Secured Housing elegantly, as if touching down on the surface of the moon. The elevator doors hissed open with the release of pressure, and he was led to a cell door on the day that would begin his life in a crypt. The day he would enter Amenta, that ancient Egyptian underworld where the sun had set and rose no more, where the dead and all last things were buried, where the lingering spirits roamed. He stumbled over his chained ankles as he was brought down the corridor by two guards, their demonic faces shifting in ghoulish delight like holographic jack-o'-lanterns. A consecrated silence descended when they arrived at his designated vault.

The steel door slammed open, and Horus beheld Amenta: four walls, a thin mattress atop a bed of concrete, a sink, and a toilet. The ceiling was embedded with some contraption behind bulletproof glass that dimness obscured. He could feel a weak stream of air from somewhere, a maddening riddle against the impervious look of the cell. The rest of it was a thick dreariness that filled the cavity like a dingy foam, and Horus was overwhelmed by the sensation of being plunged into something. He felt he was about to enter the dense atmosphere of a chamber, filled with an unnamed substance meant to dissolve him. He would later freeze this moment in his mind and understand that this substance was time itself.

Horus was pushed inside.

In the first seconds, he was struck by the sense that he was again, somehow, in a basement. But this place was secreted beneath a sprawling miscreation, a living institution of which he was the blood host, and there were no steps leading up and out to the world. He looked into the space of his demise and tried not to see his uncle Randy's face.

"Take a look, rodent," one of the guards said. That was when doom welcomed Horus at the end of the eight-foot box, as his senses washed in like a tide and crashed against the walls. He looked about and witnessed the enormity of his end, drawn and atrocious. "The Cask of Amontillado," a story he read so many times in his school years, one that began to speak to him, materialized in his head with every inhalation of the foamy air. He was Poe's Fortunato now. He could smell and feel the mold and damp. Horus was ordered to move forward. The two guards put him facedown on the stiff bed, unshackled him, and left him there.

And from the beginning of his time in the mausoleum, when Horus Thompson was not made to submit to hoods, strip searches, cell raids, penis measurements, or water torture, he was plagued by two great tormentors: Light and Dark. In the darkness, he tried to keep track of the passage of months by counting the occasions he was allowed to see the sky. One-hour sessions in a special roofless cubicle, which seemed to be about every sixty days. Or was it every ninety? And when darkness completed its course, the inverse (Light) circled around to take its place with the scowl of twenty-four-hour fluorescent lights. The bright white drilled through his crusted eyelids, unremitting beams of judgment that pierced his pores and shrank his pupils to specks of dust. The light rained down, drenching Horus in thousands of watts, until he was convinced that the Dark had been a thing that dwelled only in his imagination. At the height of his confused senses, he awoke in the pan of a polar desert, shivering under a white winter sun. His head banged on as his ears rang, as he swooned. He felt as if he were falling from some great height, falling through the earth.

Then all the pivotal moments before the instant of arrival in the sepulchre broke away and fell into the substance that was enveloping him. The moments flashed like the disintegrating frames of a silent black-and-white movie: his mother's smile, his father's bloody chest, Manden's blank stare, the police lights running along the walls of his house. There was the image of the contents of the bathroom trash: crumpled tissue, a spent razor, and the inky dot of a pregnancy test.

Worst of all were the flashing images of Brenda the Beautiful lying naked on the bed. The sight of the worried, ruined landscape her face had become. Horus felt he needed to begin erasing those images as soon as he sat on the bed that night and waited for the police, as soon as the sirens approached, as soon as the gavel fell. He needed to forget the long licorice locks that framed her magnificent watery eyes and the coconut oil that dressed her supple legs. He needed to forget her dark berry lips, round and firm, her slender frame and inviting hips.

Brenda the Beautiful. The erection that once overtook Horus when he thought of her vanished in the undertow of grief. Form-aldehyde filled the blood vessels of his member now. The miracle once manufactured in his loins by the millions ceased, the turbines and pistons shut down, rusted and inert like an abandoned steel mill. Brenda the Beautiful. He wished to God that he never met her, that he never saw the test in the trash can, the mark of a new life that caught aflame and would grow without him. By doing what he had done, he killed his own past and future and buried his chance at a family. Thinking this, he turned to Brenda slowly as the cops approached that night, as if moving through primordial water. He discovered in those seconds that not speaking was easier than what remained in ether.

He was unable to manage more than a glance at her tearful face that day in the courtroom, those same pained eyes that would look back at him through Plexiglas for the next twenty-five years, for the rest of his life, asking him silently, *Why?* It was a question he would never be able to answer in a way that Brenda could understand, and the look of her eyes through the glass would have meant a different kind of death that he could not stand. "I am dead to you," he'd said. And he said it out of love, a mercy killing of everything he knew she would cling to, of all he would never find the words to say. The divorce he would later ask of her would erase the rest.

Horus did not want to think of such things, and yet they rose before him in his mind every day like the sun. And his first vow to himself after the prison doors slammed shut, when everything went black and cold, was that he would will it all not to be there. And after the dementia and the mania and the death wishes that the vow would bring, there would only be the sounds that lingered in his mind, echoes left as if in an empty house: the wheels of the car on the highway that night he drove to Upstate New York, the rhythm of the windshield wipers, the driving rain, the gunshot. There would only be the echo of policemen knocking, the verdict, and the gavel. The structure of why it all happened had yet to come into full being. When it was ready to form, he would know and understand it himself.

He paced circles in the cell and tallied the pulses of his heart. He once tried to stop it by sheer will, but the thing marched stubbornly on. In the torturous silence, when his bug-eyed stares at the walls of the cell stretched taut, he was plunged into obsessions of the natural world, the realm that seemed to function without the sun. He marveled over the female menstruation cycle and the magic of bears hibernating. Under the weight of time, Horus pondered such things, until he could no longer remember his own face. Shadows, those illusionists that subsisted on panic and fear, dislodged themselves from the edges of spaces, accosting him. He curled in a fetal position on the stiff bed that first night, watching them float down to him and recede, loom and ebb.

Horus wondered if it would have been better to be on death row. In the execution line, there was a semblance, at least, of some appointed time to end it all. There were others he imagined, like himself, housed somewhere in the hallways within hallways, rooms within rooms. And these condemned souls knew a specific date was set when they would surely die. He wondered if the lethal injection that awaited them was a nervine, a relief, even, against the hours that led to more hours, days that led to other days.

Somewhere in the cavernous corridors, Horus could hear the cackle of the beast he called the Bean Hole Man, the prison guard Jimmy Eckert. Sometimes Horus thought that he and the Secured Housing guard were the only inhabitants left in the world, that since the earth plates shifted and all of the dinosaurs died, it had been just the two of them. When Eckert wanted to taunt Horus, to remind him that torment would prevail for all his living days, he spoke of old man Edward and his decades in the penal system. "The Mummy," he called him. "Old Edward tried to escape another federal facility years ago," Jimmy Eckert said, sneering through the envelope-sized slot of the steel door. That was how old Edward was transferred to Black Plains to die.

The guard enjoyed telling Horus that he was bound for Edward's fate, that the old man who had already been inside Black Plains for decades had been institutionalized in other places totaling forty-seven years, the longest of anyone. The walls claimed his mind. "The Mummy's only joy is the Great Room," the Bean Hole Man said, chuckling. He spoke of the horrors of the Great Room, a crucible of machines and hisses, where men lost fingers and limbs in the faulty equipment, where buzzers announced the shifting from one rote activity to another, the movement of every inmate timed. "Only the lucky ones are allowed to slave there," the Bean Hole Man whispered to Horus through the slot of the cell door, peering in with his dilated, Ouija-board eyes, "to be flogged by the minutes and the hours."

Horus wanted to ask the Mummy what it was that he had done, if the Act was ever committed by anyone at Black Plains. Written in the invisible scripture of the prison, the Act was the cardinal sin of speaking aloud about that which had been responsible for one's imprisonment, the highest offense. For nothing that happened outside of Black Plains mattered. It was no longer real. To speak of the Act that led to imprisonment meant that something of meaning outside of Black Plains had actually happened and therefore existed.

One day, as Horus stared at the wall from his bed, he saw from the corner of his eye a cockroach making its way. The fat roach crawled across the ashen wall near his face, brazen and without fear. It stopped as if to look at him. Horus stared back. He couldn't remember when he had started eating roaches in the times when Light reigned, when his brain turned that corner where such an idea was not repugnant. He had learned in the thick solution of time that the mind was free to bend itself into new shapes of being. He couldn't remember how he developed the quick-twitch skill of catching a roach, looping his forearm up and around as it ran frantically across the back of his veined hand, so that it leaped from the cliffs of his fingers and dropped into his mouth.

The roach had been busy on its way, crossing what for it must have been like kilometers over the span of the wall. Horus assumed it was headed for a meal at the toilet, where there was always a generous lining of microbial slime and water. It seemed to stop and look at him with curiosity, and Horus could see its antennae rotating in their sockets. Perhaps the insect thought that the threat that existed with other humans did not exist with this one, and it stopped to take a look. Horus thought of swiping at the bug to startle it away or snatching it up and chewing its insides between his teeth, but the roach scurried on and disappeared into a crack.

And it was during these cycles of rule by his two great tormentors (Light and Dark), in the seventh year of condemnation to the solitary confinement wing of Black Plains Correctional Institute, that Horus came to understand the great drain into which he was being emptied day by day. Like an equation, he was being reduced.

That was when Horus found the Catacombs.

Catacombs

*U*nbeknownst to the Rockies and long before Black Plains had been built, generations of locusts had been growing underground . . .

The Catacombs, that place of the damned and the blessed, of chilled limestone and granite and gypsum, of ancient growth crawling out of ancient things, lay in wait for Horus. It was the place where memories of the past rose like corpses and the extinct lived. Where the hieroglyphs of meaning and consequence were scrolled on the walls, invisible until the soul was awakened, until the world vanished into the dream it had been. The endless tunnels were hundreds of feet below, deep beneath the layers of Horus's mind, long, dark mazes that went on forever. The entrance to the Catacombs appeared to him one day of its own volition, an archway framing something blacker than his cell in the time of Dark rule, the death grip of the time of the eclipse. The entrance held a silken calm, and Horus felt as if he were looking into deep space. Its open mouth was an invitation to its wonder.

Horus entered the dank chill that led to the tunnels of a million paces, infinite strata and gradations. The dark rolled out before him like an open road in the night, and he could no longer feel even the presence of the shadows of his cell that stood panting near him always like fiendish familiars. At the archway, the scope of the place lay mysterious.

He took the first step forward. His bare feet were unsure on the dusty path beneath them. Was it dust? Or ash? He looked down and saw nothing. His eyes were of no use to him, and he came to understand that he would not need them where he was going. He would not need them to see. He reached out and touched the sides of the narrow passageway and felt the slime that coated the stone walls. What realm had he entered? In other floor-pacing nights of foamed mouth and crossed eyes in his cell, he was convinced that he had fallen to the lowest depth, a dimension burrowed in the deepest pit. And yet here was another doorway to another place. He thought of turning back to the familiarity of that hell behind him, the known Amenta that had held him these past seven years. But the stagnant, primal air of the Catacombs cloaked him, beckoning him further.

He took more steps forward, stumbling over what felt like jagged bones and cracked skulls scattered on the ground. Were they bones? Or his own twig legs and scaled feet? It smelled of myrrh and roses and death, of the dust of lives once lived, of final breaths. And somewhere he thought he heard the roll and crest and break of the ocean.

More than the substance that filled his cell, the walls and spaces of the Catacombs amplified the smallest decibel in his ears. Sighs and whispers leached through the pores of the granite. Spaces and walls, upper and lower realms, made their presence known by the green velveteen quiet that caked them. There were things awaiting the breath of life that remembrance would give. They waited for Horus to resuscitate them. And Horus could feel their infinite patience, ground as sharp and aged as flint, a waiting presence that needed the permission of a living being to live again.

Horus looked into the darkness. The sound of the ocean rolling and cresting and breaking came up from somewhere in the cauldron of time. The smell of seaweed and foam rose from the black. Dare he think of the Caribbean Sea crashing against the shores of Jamaica,

where he took Brenda the Beautiful? It was she who revealed to him
the enchantment of getting away from the grind of life, the tedium
of doors and keys. It was she who reminded him that there could still
be splendor out of the thorny past he did not discuss and the forested
way ahead. Brenda the Beautiful. Her dark skin shimmered in the
sapphire light. Her intricate coils of braided hair were coiffed into
sculpture, her dark shapeliness was exquisite crystal. Her sweet smell
blended with the salt breath of the ocean. They had made love under
a midnight sky, diamond-encrusted with stars. They moved with the
tide. He flowed into her like a hungry delta. They receded together
and turned their backs onto the wet sand. They glimpsed the icy blue
point of light that was Venus, close enough to touch. Horus could
have pulled it down from the heavens and set it in Brenda's earring.
Was that when she conceived the child?

He walked on.

There were other memories waiting, serene and petulant. They
were smaller and required less breath, less flesh. They called to
Horus from the corners and crevices of stone, from the particles
floating around him. Like the smell of coconut oil and cinnamon.
Like the deep blue of blueberries and the royal purple of plums.
Like fireworks over water. But there were beasts that needed more,
those memories that needed lungs filled with what air there was
to breathe. They glowered through the stone, waiting for Horus,
waiting for him to think of one beautiful day, of white picket fences
and coffee, of the straight white lines of the interstate, and of storm
clouds.

Horus felt faint and struggled to right himself in the passageway.
The silence was steeped in itself and waited for him to continue,
but he could not. He looked into the endless maze. The labyrinth
looked back at him from oblivion. "If I think of it . . ." Horus said
to the darkness, his voice echoing through the chambers. He knew
that thinking about things, remembering, was dangerous. It was
pain beyond pain. In the clutches of torment in his cell, he had
learned that the beginnings and endings were the least of worry.

There was always a beginning to something, and there was always an ending. But he had learned that the most troublesome was the middle of things, that which happened after a beginning, that which forced the end of something else. The middle was unsafe. It was what blotted out who he was before the middle, what he became after it. He was at risk of that box of teeth-chattering cold, of mind-numbing heat, of slowly dying as he inhaled something designed to poison him. It would put him in danger of not surviving another hour, another minute, another second in that place back at Black Plains. But he had found this place, this secret wonder, hadn't he? To think of any of it might mean something else this time. A way out, perhaps.

Horus looked into the darkness and felt something inside him quicken, and the thought surfaced before he had a chance to push it away: the child would be seven years old by now. The only remaining proof that there may have been something that was not ruined by what came before the middle, evidence that there may yet be something left of the man he meant to be. And the child had been there all the time, growing through the years without him. The bricked-up child was there, behind the limestone and granite and gypsum of his thoughts. Hidden since Horus looked at the pregnancy test and listened to the sirens and the *knock knock knock*. But he would not try to imagine the child's face (was it a boy or a girl?), for fear that he would not have the strength to go on. He would be forced to retreat, to walk the miles back through the Catacombs to Amenta.

The thought of going back to that place of endings, that realm away from this realm he'd found, drove him forward. He felt his way down a sloping path of the Catacombs, until the passageway turned and dipped into a deeper labyrinth. He looked into the dark. And slowly, a thin gleam appeared as if from miles and miles away, a tear in the sheet of black where a prehistoric torch of light stabbed through. He moved toward it, tracing his way along the gypsum walls. What had spilled inside coursed through him, and he could feel the memories that lay waiting behind the great boulders of stone, how they lived still, even after he tried to put them to death, how they ached to live out loud again.

Horus looked ahead to the cavernous depths. The light was still there, a seduction, a warning. Before his mind could stop his heart from resurrecting it, out of the black, he saw the sunny sky again. He saw his mother's smile again. He heard his father's voice again and remembered July 21, 1966.

Empire and Sky

The basketball court in New York on July 21, 1966, was alive with color and pride, blanketed by hands waving flags of red, black, and green. The crowd was a vivid, glorious patchwork quilt of colorful dashikis, head wraps, and sunbursts of African cloth, and it moved like the sands of a kaleidoscope. The air was thick with anticipation, and everywhere was a heat like the fiery blast of an explosion. It was electrified by voter drives and the Vietnam War, by riots and slums and sit-ins, by white crosses and the Klan, by Night Riders and the police, by rent strikes and cotton-picking minds. Malcolm X was already dead. He had been murdered the winter before, with his wife and four children looking on, with twin fetuses swimming in their mother's fluid, listening to the gunshots. Some traveled to Southern churches to hear Martin Luther King speak of having been to the highest peaks. The truth was revealed to him, he said. Had he really been to the highest peaks? The people weren't sure. They needed proof in 1966.

From the makeshift stage, Jack Thompson wiped his brow and looked across the field of faces in the crowd. He was no longer concerned about the death threats he received the week before. The assaulted protesters in the streets and the accosted women who stood in front of municipal buildings. The midnight shootings. The dawn beatings. He did not think of the lynchings of his boyhood in Bed, Louisiana, and those he read about in the paper. How his grandfather dropped from the tree he'd swung from and walked away. How his grandfather cooled his broken neck in the Pearl River and sat by his wife's bed at night to watch her sleep. Jack Thompson did not think about the rape of his young sweetheart Delia by Judd Baker in the high grasses of Boudreaux Field back in Louisiana or the things that grew wild inside of him when he grabbed the shotgun. Nor did he think about the cold New York alleys he slept in when he crossed the scratch line at last. He set it all aside and thought only of the promise he had made to himself at the Hudson River. He thought only of the promise of starting anew.

Jack Thompson looked over the faces of the people. It did not matter that he didn't recognize them individually. He didn't need to, because he knew them all anyway. They were the men at the barbershop. They were the women of the church and the market and the children of the parks. He looked at the bright eyes of his boys, Manden and Horus, and his wife, Maria, holding each by the hand proudly. And when all of it had filled him to fullness, Jack Thompson began.

"Brothers and sisters. Friends and enemies. Another of our slain black knights has left us with some important questions."

The crowd hummed.

"Who are you? What was your name before you were brought here, and why ain't it that today you don't know what your name was? How come? If your name is Smith or Jefferson now, what was it before it was Smith or Jefferson? Can you tell me? No, you can't. Because we don't know. But that's not the point anymore, brothers and sisters. I am not here today to speak of our suffering. We know the stories. We all got a trunk full of our grandmothers' memories and what our grandfathers told us in the fields. We all got a river of tears we've cried, people we've buried, women and children we couldn't save. These things are burned into our souls without us speakin' of them. But today I am here to speak of rising. I speak of rising to who and what we are. What we were. What we are meant to be. And to know who and what you are is only half the journey. To be who and what you are is the prize."

Jack Thompson paused and looked at the sky. The men nodded, and the women hugged their breasts. They were all transfixed in the throng of testifying to what was being said, together fed by hope and outrage, a moving, living mass of energy. On the edges stood an assortment of onlookers. A few whites bothered with the spectacle, among them a man with crystal-blue eyes who no one knew was a police officer because he was not wearing a uniform. On the edges, too, stood the junkies, whores, pimps, thugs, and others who had long ago sat down on the curb of life.

"Those of you with children, hear my words," said Jack Thompson. "A man gotta know who and what he is before he can name himself, before he can understand anything, before he can show his children the way through. Because this place—this country—has made the black child, the black man and the black woman, invisible, brothers and sisters. And so a man has got to name himself anew. He gotta rebirth himself again before he can live. Before he can stop himself from dying." And here he thought of his grandfather, Nathan Thompson, and how he died, and the thought fed the fires of his passion.

"I got children, brothers and sisters. And I considered them before they was born. I considered what they would face. A world that hates them and would do anything to erase any trace that they ever existed. Even the ghost. You know, my grandma Lucy, God bless her soul, used to say that the ghost comes back and stays around sometimes to give the reasons. It stays to give the living some understanding of the reasons of a man's life, of what he did and why. What are our reasons for what we did and what we tryin' to do?"

Jack Thompson looked down at his sons standing next to his wife. "I love my boys too. I want my boys to hear what kind of man I am now and understand what I was when I'm gone. And after I'm gone, I want to be nearby in case they got questions, in case they lose their way. I want my boys to live and thrive and streak the sky with all they can do, just like you, brothers and sisters. And I named my first boy Manden, for the great Mandinka empire that once was. Right now, that empire is far away from the South we know. It is far away from New York and the United States we know. But I put it in his heart. An empire in his heart. Not like in a book I read, not just in words, not in faded pictures, but in his heart. To remind him that empires lost can be built once again. That he is the keeper of greatness. And then I named my second boy Horus, ruler of the sky. Any of you heard of it? Read about it? About the son of a king who could fly? The sky is there for him to touch, brothers and sisters. It's there for him and others like him to soar to. Always. That's what I want my boy Horus to know. To remind him that he can be free anytime he wants. That he must—"

Pop pop pop

There was a loud sound that cracked over everything. Horus felt his mother drop his hand. He saw her open her mouth and scream—an otherworldly Jurassic scream, a sound made in the time of calcite seas, supercontinents, gastropods, and mammoth flora. His mother screamed, and the sound of it broke through the crowd like a shock wave, knocking Horus back. People dropped and ducked like a flock of startled birds. Legs and arms flailed everywhere. Bodies rocked and shook. Heads were thrown back. Hearts dropped and shattered into a million pieces. And there was much screeching and squawking and shouting, and there were murmurs and cries from women framed in apartment windows above. People ran in straight lines and circles. There was the loud, tense pulse of throbbing hearts thumping the ground. There were curses of men, unintelligible individually but audible in unison, that said, "They have taken another one from us."

Horus blinked in the unreality, wondering what his father was about to say. What was Jack Thompson going to say before the bullet stopped him? What else was he going to tell his boy? Then time thickened to a sludge, and in the long seconds, Horus watched his father falling, falling forever, like a razed skyscraper losing to gravity, imploding from interior detonations. Layer by layer. Story by story. A vertical descent of stone and concrete, of steel and iron, cascading down like a waterfall in great thundering shoals, like the apocalypse, like the End of Days. Horus could still feel the warmth of his mother's hand in his palm, and in the sludge of time he looked down at it, thinking that the comfort of moments before would return time and dimension to where they once were. Horus looked for his brother, Manden, but could not find him. It seemed his own eyes had turned to rubies, for everything was bathed in red, crimson like his mother's wet hands outstretched over his father's body.

Three days later, at the funeral, it seemed to Horus that all the world was chalked and shaded in charcoal. His father was pieced together in his coffin in a gray heap of ruin. Horus stared and stared, unable to understand how such a metamorphosis could have taken place. He sat in the pew as the cold overtook him, as the winter solstice rose above the altar, as his heart floated away on glaciers. He looked to Manden, who sat next to their mother like a ventriloquist's doll. Then, from the satin-rimmed coffin, Horus thought he heard his father's voice.

"Promise me . . ."

Horus looked around, then back at the coffin. Did he hear his father say something? Was his father really dead? Horus peered into the coffin, but his father's eyes were closed. Horus looked at the women fanning their faces with the eulogy program and the men wiping their foreheads with monogrammed handkerchiefs. He looked at his big brother again to see if he heard the voice too. But Manden was leaned into a permanent crook, holding on to their mother's limp hand. And then the animated choir behind the coffin rose like an electrical storm, the wrath of organs, the fury of tambourines, the whipcrack of claps. A woman moved to the center to sing. An old Negro spiritual rose from her throat like an obelisk, the mezzo-soprano of Isis in the flesh. Horus clutched a marble in his pocket, hoping it would steady his grip on the world.

Later, as Jack Thompson grayed in his grave and the eternal snow of ashes fell on his face, Horus, together with his brother, watched their mother leave. It was a long leaving, first begun when she dropped his hand and screamed, then when she sat by the window of their apartment. Horus and Manden would never know the nature of their mother's journey when she departed from that window. Barefoot, she walked the hot coals of the *Psalms of Solomon*. She ice-climbed *Corinthians*. She rode bareback up the rocky inclines of Shomeron. She snaked black lakes and crossed the slate rock valleys of the Shadow of Death. She swam the rivers of Abana and Pharpar until her skin grew raw and iridescent. She blistered and scabbed atop a raft in *Genesis*, adrift on the ocean on the day it had been born. And when, at last, she stood before the burning bush, naked and bleeding, she asked why all that happened in her life had happened and got no response.

That was when she turned to leave for the desert. There, amid a sea of sand, the question blazed in the sky above her and made beads of glass beneath her swollen, blistered feet. The sky burned above her head, and the question remained in heaps of ash that rode the acrid winds of her thoughts: Why was her husband murdered? And the question swirled around her, until dust clotted the last tear she would ever cry.

But these were things that Horus and Manden knew nothing about. What they knew was the last time their mother cooked and they had dinner at the table, the last clean stack of folded shirts and socks in their drawer, the last night she kissed them and tucked them into bed. The two boys listened to her slip-down sounds by the window, the sing-song sound of her mind letting go and something else taking hold. She spoke only once and then no more:

Butterfly, Butterfly
Fluttering your wings of
Emerald and amethyst
Butterfly on the quick wind
Fierce you are

Ready you are
Riding the quick wind across
The seas and
The lakes and
The rivers and
The creeks
Up to the tall oaks
Past the hawk nests and squirrel holes
Down to the ivy and snapdragons
Shining your wings in the sun
Afraid of no one

Years later, Horus would picture his mother in that sing-song way, with her shimmering butterfly wings, with the sun warming her back. Horus and Manden were never to hear their mother's voice again. Whether she heard what she last said from somewhere and repeated it or she dredged it up from her soul, they would never know. Near the end of their mother's leaving, her sorrows hung in the air like notes, and despair dripped about the apartment like a ceaseless rain, and she looked at them without seeing that they were there. And that was when Horus and Manden understood that they were alone: one boy with an empire frozen in his heart and the other who could no longer see the sky.

Heart and Mind

Beginning with the coldness of his uncle's basement when he was seven years old, Horus had the eerie sense that the heart could make a decision long before the mind had realized it. This feeling, which dwelled somewhere in the ether of his subconscious, grew stronger as he grew older. He had the sense that the heart, with its own barometer of scope and impact, could experience something and make a choice that the mind would be helpless in resisting. The mind, in its arrogance of understanding and control of matters it has neither understanding of nor control over, could preach long and hard to the heart about what was and what wasn't—never once realizing (until it was too late) that the heart has already decided.

Secreted in Horus's subconscious was the truth that no two hearts process anything in the same way. The tree limb from which two birds take their first flight does not wonder what is to become of them. It does not ask the questions: Where will one of them go? Which path will the other one take? No. It bears witness only to their departure and the wind left in their wake. And even if Horus and his brother had been through what they went through as twins, there was always the reality that each of their hearts would have had its own voice, its own calling. As it was, he and Manden, although they were from the same nest, felt what was to be felt differently. Two hearts made different decisions.

For Horus, this dynamic seemed at first to be sparked by happenstance. Later, it seemed to him that it had all been mystic, almost destiny. He was at work, making his usual security guard rounds inside the Martin Luther King Library on Ninth Street. With his usual precision, he was checking that the employee-access areas were locked and securing the conference rooms. He headed to the library archives, which were always immaculate and empty. On a great wooden table were huge leather-bound books that had been left out, big black serious timeless books that held the recorded history of the world.

Horus went over to the table and began thumbing through them. One of them held the entire *New York Times* newspaper printings starting with the year 1940. His eyes roved the pages, looking for nothing in particular. There were stories about the war. There were stories about the presidential election of Franklin D. Roosevelt. There was an article about the wave of black tenants in the New York rent districts that the Jews had abandoned. Then he came across an article about the first Negro Day Parade on August 16, 1940. There was a list of some of the participants. And there it was: "Nola M. Pierce."

At first, Horus wondered what the M stood for without realizing why. He stared and stared at the name, as if circling the rim of something. "There could be a million women with the same middle initial," his mind said. But only one awakened his heart: Nola Mae Pierce. She was the old woman who had spoken boldly to the police, who said that Jack Thompson's killer was a member of their fraternal order. They brushed her aside as if she was raving mad. Her name was one of the few his mother had murmured before the time of her leaving. Horus wondered how it could have been possible, how it was that he went to work on that day of the year, at that library, and picked up that big black serious timeless book and turned to the name of Nola Mae Pierce. And then the question floated up through the blackness of stealth, and Horus did not feel it bursting through the surface of his mind until it was too late: *Who killed my father?*

It was twenty years after the fact. He was a grown man now, with responsibilities. But over the weeks and months since the name of Nola Mae Pierce reappeared in Horus's mind, he tried unsuccessfully to brace the gate against the memories the name would trigger, the thoughts he had put away in a box in the cellar of an abandoned place, far away from his mind so he wouldn't have to think about it while the rest of it happened. Because to remember her name meant remembering what she said. Had he imagined it all? He was only a child at the time. He was no longer sure. Memory had become a clever chameleon, changing colors and hiding in plain view, in the light of what he did not want to see.

Whether or not it was the same woman became irrelevant as his agitation, restlessness, and insomnia grew. In the daytime, he was stricken with fits of mania and could not calm himself unless he was constantly in motion. He walked flights of steps. He took circuitous routes everywhere. When he looked at the simplest of things, even something as ordinary as the kitchen stove, his mind ran long lists of strange details: the six seconds that the electronic wick clicked before the blue flame jumped, the lone elbow macaroni trapped just under the range cover, the pottery-kiln look of the inside of the oven, the mixture of sauce and cheese and gravy drippings fire-glazed onto the aluminum, the engaging smell of the gas.

Anxiety coated him like a film. He began to worry over the smallest things: whether or not it would rain or if he had locked the upstairs windows, whether there would be Saturday mail, how many times the electric company sent someone to read the meter (did the man who came really work for the electric company?). In the nighttime, Horus would wake up after only a few hours to stare up from his pillow. In those endless trances, the ceiling became a fifth wall that held a giant screen. There he saw flashes: his mother's smile, his father's shoulders, his brother's eyes, his uncle's basement. Horus lay there next to Brenda as he struggled to blink away the wisps of light and memory, the moving figures, the undulating mouths. He often got up to roam the house. Things in the night seemed to take on different shapes and significance: the paintings with faces that looked back at him in the dimness, the little sculptures on the bookcase that seemed fixed in macabre contortions, the condensation on the windows that ran down the panes like black tears.

Horus told Brenda that lower back strains were keeping him awake (he was walking and standing on the job too much), promising that he would have it checked out by a doctor. After she fell back asleep, he would stare into her velvet skin and wonder how long he would be able to deflect the few questions she was starting to ask. Was he sick? Did he need her to get him something? She was asking questions and she might ask more. Until now, Brenda's lack of questions about his past, about what he might be thinking when he was suddenly very quiet, was one of the reasons he had married her.

He had also figured out when he first met Brenda that she was of a rare breed, one who could look at something that was damaged and still hope for the best. She could look at him when he wore an unexplained scowl, when silence settled over him like a thick blanket, and still smile. She could rearrange a bouquet of dying flowers, picking off the crinkled brown leaves and the wilted petals, and reposition them in a vase of fresh water. She could look at a rowhouse, its windows hollowed out by crackheads, its walls defaced by squatters, and see a home that could be yellow with hope, green with prosperity. He had watched her sleep in those insomniatic nights, thinking of the time when he used to believe that perhaps one day, she could repair him too. That she could wash the melancholy, the memories, the history away. But that was something he no longer believed. In those weeks and months, Horus learned (or, rather, he remembered from watching his mother) that self-destruction, that slow, lumbering roll toward death, was an all-consuming process. It was a thing that happened in stages, a series of essentials falling away. Nola Mae Pierce's name became lodged in Horus's mind like an aneurysm, a gnashing parasite in the silence of his head. Years later, Horus would come to understand that a memory exists always behind the doors of the mind, to be pulled like a file by some seemingly small thing.

Horus remembered when the old woman came to their apartment the day of his father's funeral. "My name is Nola Mae Pierce. Sorry for your loss," she said when she arrived at their door. His mother invited her in, saying, "Thank you," in that robotic, unfeeling way that shock brings to the voice. Horus and Manden hovered in doorways and corners, in the shadows that their father's death had cast. Horus came out to look at the visitor, before returning to his solitude on the floor of the next room. Like the others who came to pay their respects to Jack Thompson, the old woman sat down on the little sofa next to his crumpled mother. The elderly lady was small and shriveled, her gnarled hands betraying the decades of hard labor that had been the whole of her world. All of the years and experiences of her life seemed to gather in the deep lines that creased her walnut-colored face. She wore a blue cotton scarf about her head and a long, sweeping housedress with the faint markings of a flower print. She smelled of the black cake and blood sausage that she had been up most of the night preparing, which she brought to Maria Thompson as gifts for her grief.

Talking incessantly as soon as she was seated in the living room, Nola Mae Pierce began a litany of condolences and confessionals about knowing Maria Thompson's unique pain, looking meaningfully about the room at the lit candles and flowers and trays of food. She continued on with proclamations about the hurt she had known all of her life. "Ah, New York. This country. This world. Look like there ain't no end to despair, Ms. Maria," said Nola Mae Pierce. Her voice leaned like a coconut tree, and remnants of her Trinidadian roots were like flashes that appeared and disappeared as she spoke in her quick-tempo manner. "I know it seem like the Lord God Almighty decided to strike you down. I mean, it seem like a curse been put 'pon you, and He grinding you down into the good, dark earth with His great foot. But I seen a lot in my day, and I'm tellin' you to hold fast. Hold strong, chile. There gonna be many a day and night when you feel like your heart won't never be healed, and maybe I think that there ain't no healin' to some things—take the loss of my boy, for instance—but if you can hold on a day, and then that night, and then hold on till the morning, and so on, you gonna carry on, chile. You got them two chil'run to look after—two boys, at that—and Lord, I know it is awful hard to think about how you gonna raise 'em up now, but you got to. You got to. This ain't no promised land, like they say, like they tellin' and givin' over to everybody else. We know the look and ways of the hard, hard, road, don't we?"

Maria Thompson nodded, her eyes blank.

"We got to carry on with babies, anyway. And even then . . ." And here the old woman's face closed up like a door, and her soft, watery eyes hardened to a high sheen. "They slaughter our boys, and snuff 'em out like candles. Yes, indeed, they do. They ran my boy in the ground. Had him cornered in the ally, they tell me—Ms. Robinson's little niece Sunnie run to my house and told me—and I run as fast as these legs could carry me, like I was a schoolgirl, chile. I run and run, and when I got there, they was like a pack of wolves on him. Little Sunnie screamin' behind me and the sight of my boy on the ground, beaten, mashed down like a breadfruit, took my breath. I mean, the savagery struck me dumb. Now, you tell me. What did he do to deserve that? What kind of sin can lead to that from a hand that ain't God's? And then them cops—God, strike me down if I'm lying, they was cops with badges shining—they scattered like a pack that got finished with a meal, drippin' blood and spit, and they got to scampering away. I wanted to die that instant. And I got sight of one of 'em. Yes, he looked me dead in my eyes. And all I could do was look at them eyes and then look at my boy. Ain't no words. Ain't no words for certain things, certain sights and feelings and such. Just like you ain't got no words now, chile, I couldn't think a single sound in the queen's English what could be spoken. And the police didn't want to hear nothin' about it later. But how could they? It was them that did it."

A fresh tear dropped from Maria Thompson's yellowish face, which had lost its buttery tone and had given over to the look of brittle leaves in autumn. Her trembling hand held a cup of coffee teetering between her fingers.

"And I took sick many days long after that. Just keeping to myself and waiting on the Lord to call me home . . ." The old woman let out a sigh that seemed to expel all of the air inside of her that had been keeping her alive. "Well, I know who done it," she said at last, straightening her dress and clutching the handkerchief in her lap. "Just as sure as I know my own birth name is Nola Mae Pierce."

And here the old woman set her cup down and took Maria Thompson's lifeless hand. "Can't forget eyes like that, chile. Cold and blue. Wolf eyes, they were. The same eyes that ruined my boy in that alley. And they was the same eyes I seen at that basketball court. Near that big tree. Yes, he was there, standin' in his clothes, plain as day. The devil walking 'pon the earth. He didn't have no uniform, but it was him. I learned his name and where he worked and what else he done in the ten years of digging to the bottom of my boy's terrible end. I tried to report it, for the sake of you, a young mother with two baby boys. But who will listen to an old, angry woman? But I know, as God is my witness, if Sam Teak was there when your good man Jack Thompson was speaking the truth, wasn't no good come of it."

Sam Teak's name fell from Nola Mae Pierce's lips and filled the air and Maria Thompson's mind like a poisonous gas. What no one knew in the subsequent seconds, including Nola Mae Pierce as she talked on and on in outrage, and as Manden stood dazed in the doorway frame, and as Horus slumped in a nearby room, was that a split occurred within Maria Thompson at the exact moment the totality of her husband's death came into being in her mind. She thought, *How will I . . . ?* (for she was no longer listening to anyone and was talking to her two selves now as if in private conversation, split versions of herself seated across from each other in a parlor). The two Marias (the wife Maria Thompson and the maiden Maria

Goodwin) talked quietly in her head like two old enemies forced together to discuss a common threat, each questioning the other. *Who
will protect me and the boys now?* Was there ever any real protection
in this world? *How can such evil exist?* Wasn't it always so? *Can I bear
this?* Shouldn't you know what you can stand? *What will I do?* Don't
you know? *I am alone now.* Weren't you always?

The two voices—the two Marias—grew louder and louder in
her head, and the sensation faintly reminded her of the day her
mother confessed (in a moment of weakness, undiagnosed ovarian
cancer can soften the edges of the mind) that in truth, the Goodwins had not a drop of prominent white Goodwin blood in them.
There had been no freedman's contracts or latter-day marriage, as
each generation had been telling the next. Rather, the highly prized
blood of the Goodwins (according to the oral stories of the eldest
women in the family) was merely, and unremarkably, the result of
plantation rapes. Maria (as Maria Goodwin) remembered the sensation of that split feeling then and pondered the question of whether
she should plant her sense of self in the bit of news her mother
disclosed to her or the more familiar, comfortable lie.

And there again, as Maria Thompson sat on the couch while
old Nola Mae Pierce talked, was the feeling between the two minds
that one self would have to be chosen over the other. And in those
moments when the two Marias yammered on about what was and
what was not to be, she thought that she was again at a split, that
she would have to choose, yet again, the Maria Goodwin she had
never really known or the Maria Thompson she had not had the
chance to fully be.

In the mocking voices of both sides of her was another lingering
question. Now that she and her brother had disowned each other
and now that she'd made her own way and had begun a life that had
already been ended, what was she going to do? Now that she had
dropped out of college and was a revolutionary homemaker, a role
she'd fashioned out of thin air, out of what she thought might be
needed without being certain of what was necessary, what role was

she to play in her own life—Maria Goodwin or Maria Thompson—now? And sitting in her apartment with a dead husband and two children, she wondered (both Marias wondered) how it was that at the age of twenty-nine, she still did not know.

The old woman was finishing now. "He's a cop, you know. In this here precinct. The devil's name is Sam Teak, chile. I know 'cause I seen him come up from the fires of hell myself. Run our men into the ground. That's what they do. 'Specially those that got something to say, that stand up for something. Well, well and so, Ms. Maria," and here at last the old woman rose slowly in preparation to depart. "God hears the child who cry out and is prepared to receive and keep us all in the by-and-by."

And it was at that moment, when the front door was closed and Nola Mae Pierce was gone and Maria Thompson was again seated on the couch in the quiet, that there was the spigot sound of coffee spilling from the cup that she let drop onto her lap and run down to the floor. She let go of more than just the coffee cup, something bigger.

But sitting on the floor by the bed, crying intermittently and listening in the nearby room, Horus could not have known about the two Marias or what had finally slipped away. In the weeks and months to follow, he pondered how the gunshot, the man named Sam Teak, and his dead father connected. And in his seven-year-old mind, he tried to summon the logic of the combination. But before he had the chance to understand the horror in its entirety, the worst part of the family's descent began. Someone had called about the "changed" condition of Maria Thompson, how her mind had seemed to shift from clear, distinguishable colors to gray. Years later, what Horus would remember the most was the scent of the spilled coffee, which seemed to last forever in the carpet and hung in the air of the apartment long after his mother drifted away.

Nightmares served as caretakers of the seen and unforgotten. He sometimes dreamed of the drive down from New York to Washington, he and Manden in the car with the caseworker taking them to another place, where they were put in the miserable care of Uncle Randy. Horus watched Manden shrink down into someone else in those days. His brother, too, Horus had always supposed, watched him drown in his own rancor. It was this feeling of watching, of being in a constant state of powerlessness, that made Horus despise Manden somewhere inside.

Once, in the early-morning stillness of the basement, with the periwinkle of dawn spilling though the tiny windows, Horus got the courage to ask Manden if he had heard their father's voice the day of the funeral. Did he hear what their father said from the coffin too? "Our father . . ." Horus began, unsure of how to ask such a question. It sounded almost like a prayer, the beginnings of a catechism. "Our father . . . Manny, did you hear what Papa said?" he asked. Manden did not respond. "Tell me," Horus demanded. In fear of what he thought he heard at the funeral, wondrous and so impossible, Horus wanted a yes or a no from his brother. Manden stirred, betraying that he was awake and listening, but he did not answer the question.

Perhaps that was why, years later, Horus worked with doors and locks. Security. An artificial realm in which at least he had the key. His mind compartmentalized and warehoused his life. And somehow, without his mind knowing it, his heart decided that the annihilation of Sam Teak could wash away his father's blood and resurrect his dignity, and he could reclaim his mother's wandering soul and bury his uncle in a great black pit. With the removal of the source of the sorrow, he could preserve the children he and Manden were before it all happened, untarnished in time.

And wandering about the sullen library shelves at his place of work, Horus reasoned simply (his mind fast at work) that he just wanted to see where this man Sam Teak lived and how he had gone on living after his father was dead. And he was not hard to find. A retired police officer listed in the directory. Horus wrote the address down neatly on a little white piece of paper. His heart played along while he did his research, waiting for the opportunity to reveal the truth, feigning agreement with justifications for satisfying curiosities. Such tricks! Such mastery of line of sight! And Horus might have been able to go on like that for many more weeks and months and years, with his heart and mind looking at different parts of the whole, if it wasn't for the marbles.

Coming home from a long day of locks and doors at the library, his polyester uniform stuck to his overheated body in all of the most uncomfortable places, Horus parked his car on the crowded street and walked to his house. There was a group of children playing on the sidewalk in front of his rowhouse when he arrived. They were huddled like a mound of Neapolitan ice cream, laughing, colorful in their play clothes. The soft chatter of childish concerns flittered through the air.

Horus stopped to look at them. To his surprise, there were two little boys in the center with a cluster of marbles. They glittered in the honey sun of late afternoon like semiprecious gems. An older boy heckled about the marbles not being as great as street tag or Hot Wheels cars or basketball. "Sell 'em for snack money," said one boy. "Who cares about some stupid old marbles, anyway?" said another boy. These boys reminded Horus of how the children in his second-grade class teased him about his "African-booty-scratching father and his African ways." They did not understand Jack Thompson's talk of a history that extended thousands of years before the four hundred years of slavery drilled into their heads. They did not understand his "outfits" and the slow, deliberate way he talked of the lynchings and atrocities of the South, of taking a stand, of power and destiny. They called him and his brother "Sons of the African Booty Scratcher," until Manden punched the biggest boy in the face.

"Sell 'em for treats," the boy said again. But all of the children looked on still, the little solar system of glass holding their gazes in varying degrees of wonder and delight. Horus had not seen such a sight since the summer day of his father's murder. It was the last day his universe had held intact, the last time he had a brother and a mother and a father and a family. Sam Teak exploded all of them apart and spread them to different parts of space to disintegrate, where they were unable to find their origins or evolve into anything else.

On the sidewalk, Horus looked at the twinkle in the boys' eyes, the concentration, the purity, and saw himself and Manden as children, bickering and smiling, oblivious to the horrors that awaited them later that day. He saw his favorite marble, the cat's eye, which he later gripped in his pocket at the funeral. In the light and magic of the choir and the shadow of the coffin, he dropped it. He never found that cat's eye and supposed it dropped into the hole where sorrows went. And twenty years later, on a sidewalk in front of his house, he was watching the dazzle of the glass balls again. And somewhere, between the glittering glass and the dripping honey sunlight, his heart decided that he would kill Sam Teak for what he took, for what he destroyed, for the people his people had not been able to become.

Horus took Sam Teak's address out of the bottom of his dresser drawer, where he had stuffed it weeks before, and put it in his pocket. He told Brenda his story (his mind still culpable in the half-lie) about going up to New York with Manden to revisit the past. He would leave early that Saturday morning. He would go up there to see, as a scientist able to travel back in time to witness a catastrophic event would wish to see it and prove how it happened, to prove that it actually occurred. Oh, the mysteries that could be solved, the destruction that could be explained, just by going to see how a man who murdered lived.

Later, when Horus was able to think of it, he would take that moment on the sidewalk from a sealed Mason jar on the highest shelf of his mind. He would take out that moment of watching the children play as he would a preserved peach. And he would hear a clicking sound in his mind, but he could not tell if it was something locking or unlocking. The little slip of paper on which he wrote the name and address of his father's murderer called loudly to his heart. "Come and see for yourself," it said. And the swell of all that had been destroyed and could never be regained welled up inside of him, until his heart trembled and could not hold it any longer.

And then there were the locusts. Loud they were, like a million little sirens, trumpeting a day filled with something he would not be able to fathom until later, when the fathoming of the thing itself spread before him on the highway with Sam Teak in the car. With the gun in the glove compartment. He rose at four o'clock in the morning that Saturday. Brenda slept soundly. The air seemed heavy with a dew that dripped from everything. In the subway-tiled vestibule of the rowhouse, his hands slipped on the knob when he opened the front door.

Later he would think of that early dawn, when he stepped out of the house and smelled the exhaust-filled air, stood looking at the mulched tree boxes and dead grass in the shadowy light, and heard the locusts. It was a wonder, an omen, that such a sound of Southern, swamp-hot night air should be heard in the early morning of the city, a place of car horns and buses and traffic-jammed streets. Even at that hour, the pigeons were already about, picking up stale McDonald's french fries and bits of candy on the sidewalk. The locusts droned on, brazen in the bluish light, preening from wherever they were. Countless and unseen in the dimness, the darkeners of the sun.

But on the early morning that Horus headed for New York and heard the locusts, sudden and unannounced but for the sirens with which they greeted him, his heart knew that one door had been locked and another opened. And his mind looked on helplessly. For it could only marvel at the means and speed of his falling, and ponder what "Promise me" meant.

Mama

On the morning Horus left for New York, Brenda pretended to be asleep. Earlier that week, he told her he was going to meet his brother, Manden. And as Brenda lay in the bed listening to Horus go out the front door, she tried to convince herself that he told her the truth, even though deep inside, she knew that there was something else. Something was wrong. She had noticed changes in him that she kept sweeping to the back of her mind—his irregular sleeping, his obsessions with things being locked, his tendency to eat large plates of food or nothing at all. In bed, he reached for her with a desperation she hadn't felt from him before. Days before that morning he left for New York, their conversations had become exchanges of minutiae: what they might have for dinner, whether or not there were any more clean undershirts, when the Blockbuster movies needed to be returned. Sometimes she would wake in the night and discover that he was downstairs in the kitchen. When she asked him what he was doing, he gave the strangest responses.

"Brenda?"

"Yes?"

"Have you ever gotten something back that you thought was gone forever?"

"Like what?"

"Just gone."

"Like a lost ring?"

"No, a person."

"What do you mean, Horus?"

"Nothing, baby."

He became more and more quiet, and there were days when they hardly talked at all. "See a doctor," she wanted to say. But she had learned from her father that men handle things, and she had learned from her mother that to say too much to a man was to interfere with what he had to handle. She wanted to believe that the silence was Horus working things through, that her love for him and plans for their life would keep him grounded. Suggesting that he see a doctor meant that she had missed something.

Now the only evidence that Horus had ever lived in the house was his large black umbrella. It was still in the vestibule corner, bent and dusty. Brenda sometimes thought she heard the doorbell ring and imagined that it was Horus wanting to come home. He was sorry about all the pain he caused her. What the courts said he had done never happened. He had stayed away to work things through, and now he was back. But she knew that no one would be standing there if she opened the door. His car would still be absent from the street, his side of the closet still empty. In those early months after the verdict—pregnant and miserable—she could not sleep in the bed they had shared, and she would get up and move to the bedroom chaise and then finally the couch downstairs. After Sephiri was born, she returned to the bed, and they cuddled there together on a fragile island of comfort. When he got older and she started struggling with him through the night, she was back on the living-room sofa. Staring into the shadows, her strained eyes had learned the shades of things, how light and gloom made war, how the living-room carpet moved in the dimness, ebbing and flowing in tides of indigo. Restlessness and exhaustion stalked her through a fog of fits and distractions that did not lift in the day. She tried everything to calm her nerves: chamomile tea, deep breathing, relaxation tapes, warm milk. Nothing helped.

Brenda struggled up from the couch and adjusted the wig she'd fallen asleep in. Sephiri had been awake most of the night, and she'd drifted off there. Horus had liked the soft, free-flowing natural she once wore. Her hair had long since thinned, and small patches had fallen out in some areas. The sides had already begun to gray. She looked on the floor and found that Sephiri was asleep where she'd spread his pillow and blanket. The television crackled with the static that had been playing on a channel all night. She stood up stiffly, her back aching, and opened the window curtain. She could see the perennial flowers she had planted in the small fenced front yard when she and Horus first bought the house. She hadn't gardened in years, and the bright patches of black-eyed Susan and butterfly weed came up on their own now. In the months after the verdict, she thought about selling the house and moving. She felt it no longer housed the life it was meant for. But the rowhouse had been an abandoned crack den they bought for a song and renovated beautifully, and now she could not afford to live anywhere else so nice for the cost.

Brenda lumbered to the kitchen and brewed a pot of coffee. It would take three cups to get through the morning and have Sephiri ready to go to the center on the van. There would be the long process of getting him upstairs and into the bathroom to help him use the toilet (if he had not already relieved himself on the bed or the floor), brush his teeth, and wash his face. She expected him to fuss through that. Then dressing him and fixing his hair. There would be some game he would start in between that involved him running through the house or hiding or climbing up and down the steps. Then there would be the ritual of making scrambled eggs and putting a plate of them in front of him so he would eat his breakfast cereal. She would eat them later, when they were stale and cold. Then there would be the rush to get herself together in the bathroom, all the while wondering what Sephiri was doing, listening for any sound that he might be in trouble or some other disaster he had caused. She would have to make sure his shoes were by the front door, so he would step into them when she opened it.

The thought of having to stop and speak to neighbors who were also starting their day when she came out of the house sickened her. The nosiness and insincerity was obvious in their veiled greetings. "Good morning, and how have you been, Ms. Brenda?" they would ask. Most of them knew all about Horus, having heard about the murder in the local news reports and discussed it with one another. Then they'd ask how Sephiri was coming along, all of them having watched his meltdowns in front of the house or heard him screaming through the windows. They knew that their children laughed and pointed and made jokes about Sephiri. Brenda would respond with bullshit, how she was well and couldn't complain, how her boy was growing faster than wildfire, how she'd been working and getting on with everything. "Well, I've just been busy, you know, what with Sephiri and work and running the house," she would say. It was all a beautiful lie, as iridescent as the Coral Paradise polish she brushed over her chipped nails at two o'clock in the morning.

The coffeemaker beeped, and Brenda poured a cup. She didn't worry about what the neighbors said or thought anymore. But sometimes, in the brief pauses of the craze and haze of her life, she could feel the isolation. She could feel the loneliness. The marital bed remained in the room she once shared with Horus like an altar. She wondered if she ever would or could be with a man again, if she could feel desire and be desirable again. Sometimes she tired of that empty feeling and padded into the dark kitchen in search of mercy and grace from Häagen-Dazs. She stood in the light and frosty freeze of the opened refrigerator door, contemplating Rocky Road or Fudge Truffle.

Brenda took out a bottle of ibuprofen she kept in the locked kitchen-sink cabinet and swallowed three. A boom shook the ceiling, and she heard Sephiri shriek somewhere upstairs. She listened closer. There was silence for a moment, and then she heard him walking up and down the steps. She had learned to tell the difference between the sounds he made when he was upset, hurt, or occupied. When something did upset him, she would not know why, and he would not be able to tell her. Sometimes, when she looked into the bright little faces of other children, eyes so full of the wonder of bubbles and cartoons and laughter, she wished such joys for her boy. She had begun to fixate on the small things she felt she could offer him, although she had no way of knowing if what she did could ever make him happy: peanut butter and jelly sandwiches, daily baths, cake once a month, television at four o'clock in the morning. She went over to the kitchen pantry and opened the door, studying the cereal boxes on the shelves.

Brenda heard another shriek, this one distressed, and she left the kitchen to find him. He was not on the stairs. She climbed the steps to see what was going on.

"Sephiri," she called, now just a maternal reflex that held no purpose other than to announce that she was approaching.

She heard banging and then another shriek. She hurried up the last of the steps.

"Sephiri," Brenda called again. She went to his room and scanned the floor: a few scattered toy cars turned upside down, bits of paper, broken crayons, a row of blocks down the center of the room, picture books stacked according to size. On the windowsill was a neat line of marbles. She pushed the bed aside to see if Sephiri was under it. Nothing. She was about to check the hallway bathroom when she heard him scream. It was coming from her room, and she rushed down the hallway.

He was in her bedroom closet, jumping up and down and flailing his arms. When Brenda tried to come near him, he only screamed louder. "What is it?" she asked, more of herself. Many of her things were disheveled. A blouse sleeve was ripped. Scarves were pulled from a basket. She saw that the blanket she had taken out of the storage bag in the closet the day before was on the floor. She'd been meaning to wash it later and hung it along the empty pole on the other side of the closet until she could get to it.

"Come out of there, Sephiri. It's time to get ready to go to the center."

The boy shrilled, violently beating his fists about his face.

Brenda was afraid he would injure himself and reached for his hands.

Sephiri picked up a shoe box and threw it. When she tried to take it from him, he grabbed one of the shoes and threw it at her, hitting her on the forehead.

"Dammit!" Brenda cried. "Stop, Sephiri." She held his hands down to restrain him.

Sephiri screamed louder and louder, and Brenda felt a stabbing pain go through her head like a bolt of lightning. She thought of the day she knew something was different about Sephiri. When he was two years old, she took him to the National Zoo. She thought he would be thrilled to see the giraffes and the tigers. All through the outing, she tried to get his attention as he sat in his little stroller. "Look, Sephiri," she said. But he kept staring down at a string he was fingering. She took him very close to the elephant habitat, and he did not look up once. Children holding ice cream cones and balloons walked by unnoticed. A little boy of about five years old proudly held his stuffed gorilla toy out to Sephiri, but he did not even glance at it. "Look, Sephiri," she said. Her boy did not respond.

Now Sephiri struggled to break free of Brenda's grasp, kicking at her legs as she tried to hold him still. When he kicked her in the stomach, she lost her grip on him.

It was at times like this that she thought it was all her fault. Somehow she caused the autism. She made it happen by hiding Sephiri's existence from his father. God said that Horus had a right to know, and she ignored a law of nature. And this was her punishment: a child who was hidden from all reason, from his family, from the world.

Brenda went numb while Sephiri's meltdown raged. By the time he was finished, he had pulled down all her clothes from the hangers, taken out every last shoe, and torn many of the shoe boxes to pieces. Then he shrank down on the blanket he had pulled to the floor and stared up at the empty pole, panting heavily.

"It's OK, Sephiri," Brenda said in a cracked whisper. "Mama's here." She touched his hand, unsure of what her words meant.

The boy did not move.

After Brenda got Sephiri on to the van to the Autism Center, she went back into the house. She called her job to let them know that she was going to be late. She went to the kitchen to get more coffee, sat down at the table, and held her head in her hands. Her temples throbbed with pain, and her backache had become more severe. A welt had formed on her forehead where Sephiri hit her with the shoe. She felt she couldn't manage anything more this morning.

Brenda finished her coffee and headed upstairs to take a bath. She turned on the gushing water and looked at the wall behind the tub. There once was a panel of mirrors there. She and Horus used to stand together naked in front of it, his arms around her waist. She had talked of having children someday, and he had nodded. She used to consider herself lucky to have married Horus, a man far away from the Uncle Daddy her mother warned her about as a girl and the railroad man they never discussed.

Brenda had the mirror panels taken down and the wall painted white. They were in the basement now, a graveyard of things. The divorce papers were down there, too, decomposing with everything else. Her mother once told her that a good woman is a married woman. "In my day, vows wasn't nothin' to play with," her mother said. Divorce was the way of the coward. "Husband and wife should hang in there," she said. But when the verdict was proclaimed and the divorce papers from her husband came and she saw his signature on the line, she did not know what hanging in there meant. "He doesn't want you to see him like that," her husband's attorney said over the phone. "Believe me, it is better this way." She held on to the papers for months, anyway—wondering what was better—all through the morning sickness and the prenatal visits, the nights of turning on her side, and the baby's delivery. But as time ground on, she couldn't understand what she was holding on to. So she signed them and felt angry for years about it, until she was too exhausted to carry the outrage. She needed her strength for Sephiri.

Brenda turned off the tub faucet and undressed. It was a beautiful and deep claw-foot antique tub. It no longer held her comfortably, but she could at least sit down in it.

In those first days after the verdict, she submerged herself in it, trying to drown her sadness. She pressed her back against the rubber mat at the bottom of the tub, melting into the heat, plunging her head deeper under the water. And she thought, just for a second, about staying down in the water. Staying and never coming up. But the life inside her beat with her heart, and she could hear her mother's voice. "A woman's got to carry on," she would say when times were tough. "What are we gonna do, Mama?" Brenda would ask. "I ain't startin' to quit now," her mother would answer. But Brenda wondered if she had ever wanted to.

Squeezed into the tub now, Brenda looked over at the scale in the corner along the wall behind the toilet. She hadn't been in to see her doctor again since he referred her to a nutritionist. The slip of paper was still at the bottom of her purse. In the long nights with Sephiri, she snacked on bags of potato chips and watched infomercials, awash in a sea of wealth-enrichment seminars, self-improvement retreats, and dietary programs. She consumed the ads like opiates, addicted to the solitude and fantasy of instant prosperity and losing ten dress sizes in thirty days. And she tried to imagine Sephiri's smiling face.

The phone rang in her bedroom, and Brenda wondered if it was someone at the center or her job but made no effort to answer it. The machine picked up the call, and she heard one of the physician assistants from her doctor's office leaving a message. "Please give us a call," she said. Brenda soaped up, climbed out of the tub, and toweled herself off. She grabbed the little mop she kept in the corner, scooted the scale out into the middle of the bathroom, and stepped onto it. The scale read 273 pounds, fifteen more than the last time she checked. "You need to take care of yourself," the old woman cashier said to her when she was loading the conveyer belt at the grocery store the other day. "If Mama goes down, everybody goes down."

Brenda kicked the scale back behind the toilet and looked at herself in the mirror above the sink. She hardly recognized the woman looking back at her. "When I'm gone to glory, you keep on keepin' on," she could hear her mother say. "Try," Brenda said to her reflection, her eyes welling up with tears. There were nights when she looked up at the stars and wondered if one of them was her mother twinkling.

Beautiful Day

That spring morning was unusually balmy and bright, the sky a swirl of blue watercolor. Horus parked across the street from a handsome brick house with a white fence and pink and red begonias in the yard. Seated in the car, he could see that there was a swing bench on the porch, and hanging fern plants suspended from a beam cascaded down in long tendrils. There was a tan Lincoln Town Car in the driveway. A blue water hose was neatly rolled on a spindle next to a flowering azalea bush. In the air was the sweet smell of new grass and firewood.

On the side of the white mailbox, which stood proudly on the strip of grass near the curb of the lovely tree-lined street, were the words "The Teak Family" in press-on letters. Horus saw it the day before when he arrived in Scarsdale, New York, when he had driven by the house and back to the motel. He drove by three times. At the motel, he slept a sleep of bottomless soundless tumbling. He thought he dreamed about the press-on letters in the endless fall, except that in his dream, they read "The Thompson Family." He thought he dreamed that he pulled the gun from his bedroom closet shelf and put it in the glove compartment of the car before leaving the house. He was not sure if he'd actually done that and did not want to spoil the meditative calm by leaning over and checking. It was still early, and he listened to the birds tweet in the trees and the squirrels start their day on the bark. The Sunday paper, wet with dew, was lying on the green carpet of the lawn. He wondered how long he could wait there before someone noticed a black man sitting in a car on a pretty street in Scarsdale and called the police.

He learned that Sam Teak had retired from the Brooklyn precinct. He wrote the address on a white slip of paper and carried it in his security uniform pocket, in his pajama shirt pocket, in his sweating palm. As he contemplated unlocked windows and ovens, as he sat up staring at the wilting flowers on the dining-room table at three o'clock in the morning, he thought about what it would be like to drive up and look at the house. To see one of the pillars of a community, a retired police officer, who was expecting to always be needed and kept his name listed in the phone directory so that someone who needed him could find him someday. People would vouch for him, protect him, turn the past into what his police reports said they were. He sent his kids to college and tithed at Christmas mass. He paid his mortgage and taxes.

Maybe it *never happened.*

Horus stared at the house across the street. The shots had been real. The blood had been real. The picture, too, of a man twenty years older, with wolf eyes that stared back at Horus from the microfiche he dug up, had been real. Horus learned that not sleeping could augment perspective. It could allow one to see things that couldn't be seen before, enable one to think of things never thought of before. Like what he told Brenda about coming up to New York to put closure on things. "I need to do it," he said. That wasn't a lie, not entirely. It was a piece of some larger truth, snapped between two slides of shaded glass and placed under a different kind of light.

He hardly remembered the drive from Washington, D.C. He hardly remembered who he had been, the made-up figure he sculpted to get through the years on his security job. Then the nervous breakdown he had two years before he'd met Brenda—that's what the therapist he went to a few times called it. "Take some time off," the therapist said. The job could wait. There were things to be discussed, uncovered, and faced. "We'll get you some help," the professionals said. There were appointments made that he did not show up for. There were remedies he did not believe would work; they were not designed to address the unnamed maladies he faced. What did work, for a while, anyway, were the doors and locks at the library, the satisfaction of putting *it* away, which before all of this had been everything after that day on the basketball court. Then came Brenda, a balm and gauze, a comfort among other comforts. Her healing properties were undeniable, although she was ineffectual against the deepest wounds. But she tried; that was the point, the comfort. She tried without asking certain questions. But Horus would not think of her soothing powers now. He would not try to find the man he was trying to be in the thought of her now.

From across the street, there was the sound of the front door cracking open. A man with silver hair and rotund build came out onto the porch. He was dressed in casual pants and a light flannel shirt. He strolled down the whitewashed front walk of his yard, then stepped onto the grass to pick up the newspaper. After shaking off the droplets of water a bit, he tossed it onto the porch. He turned back and walked the rest of the front path and out onto the sidewalk. He stopped to check the mailbox and, finding nothing, closed it and looked at the man in the car looking back at him.

Horus watched him walk across the street to the car. The sound of the birds and the squirrels on the bark fell away, and he could hear only his heart beating, his breath, the flatline tone that rang in his ear. The time drip was unhurried, lavish, one step for each year, twenty steps across the twenty years, and the man was there at the car.

"Can I help you?" said the silver-haired man.

And Horus thought that he had something big to say, something deep and wide and old, but in the unexpected feeling of the expected, he could only manage his name. "My name is Horus Thompson."

The quiet remained in the man's eyes, pool water, undisturbed.

"My father was Jack Thompson," said Horus.

There were ripples in the pools then, which started in the center of Sam Teak's pupils and expanded outward. His eyes grew sad and celestial, primeval with inevitability. And in the dimension in which the two men were, after one earth orbit around the sun, he said at last, "God told me this would one day come. My wife did too. She's dead now." The eyes rippled again, and he looked as if he wanted to say something else but folded it up and put it away. "Would you like to go get some coffee?" he asked instead.

Coffee. In the time drip, it seemed to Horus like such a simple easy understanding thing to do, because coffee is a thing that can easily be offered and easily accepted. The word "Yes" fell out of his mouth. And after Sam Teak got into the car and they were driving along the lovely tree-lined street, Horus tried to think only of the cup of coffee and what that kind of gesture could mean or not mean, not the look of his father on the ground, not his mother at the window, not the gun in the glove compartment. And as he stopped at each stop sign, looked both ways, and pressed the accelerator, he listened to the man talk of the nice, quiet café that opened early on Sunday mornings, how it was at the edge of the neighborhood that he had lived in for the last forty years, where he raised his children. They could go there and talk things over.

But what could there be to say? Horus tried to keep his mind blank as he listened to Sam Teak give directions to the place: three more streets and turn left; the next right at the light; go down a little ways past the fountain and the cemetery. It was quiet then, and Horus could hear the sounds of the turn signal clicking, the car pistons firing, the transmission shifting gears. His heartbeat synchronized with the uniformity of the asphalt breaks in the road. *Da-dum da-dum.* And that was when the smell of his mother's spilled coffee, Maria Thompson's coffee (cream with a sprinkle of real vanilla bean floating on the top), filled the car. The smell from the cup she dropped on the rug in the wake of what Nola Mae Pierce said.

Maybe he didn't do it.

Horus had the thought that perhaps this man in the car had only Nola Mae Pierce's curse crowning his name and that he did not have, nor had he ever had, anything to do with the death of his father or the atrocities she claimed. Memory could fool the mind, couldn't it? Maybe the old woman was mistaken (grief and rage could cloud the mind) and fixated on this man, as he himself had come to do, for the lack of a clear target on which to lay the blame. He might have heard the whole thing wrong as a boy. The repressed memory that crashed through the apertures of his mind, that took on skin and eyes of its own and breathed in the car with them now, might have somehow, through the brine of time, been changed into something else. But how could such a thing be forgotten? How could a thing that stains the soul ever be rinsed away? A constellation of happenings had gathered to bring him to this point, to this place.

Horus drove past the triple-tiered fountain, which sat in a median filled with bright red tulips. Nearing the cemetery, he could see rows of headstones in the bed of green. Behind them was a stand of white birches haunting the meadow. The silence in the car seemed to harden as they drove by.

After a time, the silver-haired man said, "It didn't happen like you might think."

All the air seemed to drain from the car at that moment and was replaced by a substance that filled and flowed through the lungs like water through fish gills. What Horus felt as he breathed the substance during those first few seconds could not be later remembered, for his heart took hold of the wheel, saying, *For the promise. Do it for the promise.* There was justice against the debt owed to his father and his ruined family to be collected, it said. But his mind, in the habit of rationalizing a battle it knew was one to be lost, said Horus owed it to himself and to his father's memory to soldier on, in spite of what Sam Teak had just confessed. *Leave it be and carry on*, his mind said; that was the promise. Not to exact retribution and make this day the day of reckoning but to go on in spite of everything. Which of the two was right Horus did not know. That was when the middle of things took hold, and he could no longer remember the beginning. He could not stop the progression to the end.

Passing the cemetery, there was no room in the silence of the car for anything more. There was only the full tank of gas and his foot on the accelerator; the bottomless soundless tumbling and the dreamed gun in the glove compartment. Nearing the café parking lot, Horus saw the adjacent ramp that led to the highway. At its entrance was the red, white, and blue interstate sign, the colors of the flag, the gauntlet. And he heard the tornadoes and sandstorms that roared from his mother's mouth when she kneeled over the little burgundy lakes that filled his father's chest. Horus remembered his mother's firm leg as he tried to stop her from going with the people from the Utica Asylum when she dragged him across the floor, deaf to his pleas. His heart asked his mind how he could drink with the man who spilled his mother's coffee and was the reason for the emptiness of life and the fullness of death. And instead of turning into the café parking lot, Horus turned onto the ramp going north.

"What the devil are you doing?" asked Sam Teak.

Lessons

orus heard a scraping sound cutting through his mind. From the slot on the cell door, there was the familiar fumble with the metal. He could hear the needlelike scratches traveling across the eons from Black Plains to the Catacombs, and it was then he realized that he was back in his cell. Had he been here all the time? He remembered all that he remembered: the dew on the front doorknob and the locusts, the mailbox, the hypnotic highway. He tensed and clamped his eyes shut, fighting the urge to scream. He did not want to do it, because if he heard himself scream, he would know that he was back where he did not want to be. Horus thought he might die from the thought alone, with scraps of his sanity strewn about the sticky floor, with Amenta rising again before him. He opened his eyes to bright lights raining down. The light stabbed into him like swords. Then he heard the Bean Hole Man laugh through the slot on the cell door. The familiar cackle of Jimmy Eckert, half-human, half-jackal.

Horus wanted to believe that he had been someplace else, that the Catacombs were real. But if that were true, how had he gotten back to his cell so quickly? So easily? An empty metal tray was pushed through the door slot. Horus imagined the Bean Hole Man's smirking orifice hovering in the blackness of the narrow opening. His crusty mouth. The grayish teeth fanned into a smile

149

in the symmetry of the metal. And out of that, the ghoulish whispers, the chants meant to harpoon his spirit, the litanies of madness. For years, the guard spewed desolation into his ear, dispensing his wicked wizardry. Jimmy Eckert's whispers were like crushed glass blown into the air, dropped into every meal, every tin of water.

I know a boy
With nowhere to go
And for his deeds
I own his soul . . .

What dragged Horus back from the Catacombs was the scraping sound and the chant. Enraging moments of realization such as this, when the savage facts of existence jeered in his face, made Horus long for the patch, the hidden country in the back of his head toward the center of his scalp. The Bean Hole Man's voice seemed to be one and the same with the wish and will of Black Plains. It filled Horus with chaos and abhorrence when he heard it, so that his fingers slunk to the private spot on his scalp instinctively. He moved his thumb and index finger deftly to that small, barren lot at the back of his head where anything at all could be plucked clean. Where he could weed and remove his feelings of rage and abomination a single hair shaft at a time. There he could pickaxe the unyielding terrain of helplessness. He could grub-hoe and root out the feelings that had no words and the words that had no sound and the thoughts that had no resolution. He could seize them from their places of refuge and watch their roots scream and die in the glare of his revulsion.

The ritual with the Bean Hole Man began, one of many.

"You're going to die here, rodent," said Jimmy Eckert.

Horus thought of the boundless depths of the Catacomb, and a quiet entered his mind. "There are other places," he said.

"You'll live like you'll die," snarled the guard, "wretched and alone."

Horus was silent.

"Tell me you're hungry."

Horus was silent.

The guard tapped playfully on the cell door with his baton. "Tell me you're hungry, and I'll go."

"I'm not hungry," said Horus.

"Do you know why you're here, zero-two-seven-six-three?"

"Yes."

"Kidnap and murder is what got you here."

Horus felt his legs going numb, his throat going dry. He would say the same thing today that he'd said yesterday, that he would say tomorrow. "I didn't mean to kill him. Not at first."

Jimmy Eckert laughed from the other side of the cell door. "But you did."

Horus stared at the drain near his feet. As he drove in the car on the interstate, the beautiful day faded and the sky darkened. A cloud front approached, a moving city coming toward the car. And Horus felt he was putting something on as if it were a suit, with a hat and a mask, covering that which fueled what he was being led to do.

Horus listened to Sam Teak say over and over that there was a list; that the Brotherhood, of which he had been a part, enforced the list; that it had all been a matter of pressure (him having been a new initiate at that time); that the names on the list were chosen by the others (who were all dead now); that Jack Thompson had been designated for him (not a choice of his own). And even before he joined the Brotherhood, even during the other times before when he might have been present, he had only watched, not participated. But after all the others became members, he had to join too. Expectations were made clear to him. There was his family. His career. His pension. He didn't want to get involved but he didn't have a choice. "It was a different time back then," he'd said.

A river ran free inside of Horus as he listened, as he drove the car. There was only his question. There was only Sam Teak's answer, the marble and the shooter. The roads rolled by. The Catskills slipped into thickening mist and clouds of ire. The sky opened up and cried, and Horus snatched the gun from the glove compartment and put it on his lap (it had been real after all). He felt his blood go hot, the gun resting on his thigh like a lapdog—loyal and waiting.

Now Horus stared at the prison-cell toilet, stained and atrocious in the bright light. "I pulled the trigger, but that's not how it was."

"Oh? Tell me, rodent, how was it?" Jimmy Eckert's raspy voice was laced with mockery. "Warden Stotsky talked about you. Son of a black separatist. Jack Thompson was his name, right? Your father. One of those militant revolutionaries. Anti-American. Then there's you, cop killer. Murder one. You stalked him, then kidnapped him. Took him upstate and shot him, didn't you? You don't snatch and snuff a police officer on a whim. You don't do a white-knuckle ride through Upstate New York with a gun on the spur of the moment, do you?"

Horus was silent.

"But it don't matter, rodent. Nothing matters now."

Horus thought of the fork in the road, barely visible in the driving rain, and how he drove the car into the woods, a stand of black pines. He looked away from the cell-door slot and put his hands around his aching head, now talking only to himself. "The weather closed in."

Jimmy Eckert snorted. "Well, you know we have our own weather down here, rodent. Special weather made just for you. Ask the Mummy. He'll tell you. A two-hour glass ceiling above your head, rodent. You might not be able to see it, but it's there. Forever. Made to take the assault of a sledgehammer for two hours. Did you know that? Bang on it, if you can reach it. There's a tiny little hole for you to breathe. That's it. You won't find nothing but lights and cameras behind it. We're always watching, rodent. Always. Permanent emergency. Containment. Control. There will be other days, zero-two-seven-six-three, a trillion days like this one."

Satiated for now, Jimmy Eckert stepped back from the slot. He stared into the dusky corridor of the Secured Housing wing, as he had done a thousand times. "Black Plains is made to kill you, that's for sure. But first, it'll teach you how to die."

Bean Hole Man

Jimmy Eckert walked swiftly through the massive front gate of the Black Plains Correctional Institute to his car in the cold night air. Chafing wind cut into the folds of his jacket, chilling him. Wispy blond hairs whipped about his balding head as the cold rouged his pale nose and cheeks. The walk ended a double shift he'd started the day before, when the sun was already recoiling behind the Rocky Mountains, when an ashen shadow spread over the plains behind him like an evening tide, swallowing light as it washed over the Supermax facility.

Now, in the dark, he hurried to his car. The parking-lot lights were out, and there was a quarter-moon visible in the starry sky. He had memorized the way and knew the paces, the spaces, the distance by heart. As on so many black nights, the stars looked down at him through the veil of eternity in that cold, familiar way. And like other such nights, when he looked up at the distant constellation of stars, detached observers of all he had endured, he thought of the fire. The blaze that had burned the barn, his family's livelihood, his inheritance, to the ground.

The sound of horses screaming shook him awake in that long-ago time. He ran out into the black night, a wedding quilt of dark velvet over the land. Clouds snuffed out what lay beyond the sky. In the full dark, in the split-second slide of reality and unreality, he could see only the nebula of fire in the distance. The barn burned brilliant, like a dying star. In those moments, he could not explain what froze him there, mute and shirtless. The clouds cleared then, like a great curtain moving across a stage, all the better for the stars to see the spectacle below. He had looked up at them in the seconds his mind was able to pluck from the flypaper of awareness and beheld a cold, unfeeling audience.

The seconds smeared into time and dripped like wax. He arrived at the inferno first and stood before it as he would before an altar of death, awestruck by its grandeur and terror. Waves of crimson and gold climbed to the sky in spectacular peaks and crashed down onto the falling beams, the screaming horses, the billowing white bushes of burning hay. He stood hypnotized in the heat and glow and wax melt of dream and purpose. From the edges of the barn, he could just make out the figure of one of the great black beasts. The money and years his father spent breeding perfection made no difference in the blaze. Its coat melted into black oil and ran freely in the flood of liquid fire. What might have been left of the other horses dissolved into the sound of his father shouting, "You left the lantern in the barn!" The one he had been using earlier that evening because he liked to polish rifles in the deep calm of firelight? He did not want to believe what his father was saying. No, of course he hadn't left the lantern there. It had been someone else, that other part of himself that would not have thought such a slipshod act could lead to such devastation.

As the fire swept aside their lives, the stars looked down at them all, unchanged, unmoved by the singular event that was to shift the course of their destiny. The fire burned everything to the ground, and those same stars watched as his family tried in vain to right what could not be altered. Guilt and bitterness coated Jimmy Eckert like the mess from a slop jar. Years later, when he learned about the inevitability of all things within Black Plains, he came to understand that it was fate that held him transfixed before the fire. It held him now in the vise of daily shifts.

The wind swooped down from the Rockies, and Jimmy Eckert shivered, pulling his coat tighter over his body. All those years ago, when he had tried on his black polyester uniform for the first time in the mirror, he did not know that his shift would be the start of his own prison sentence. He didn't realize that he was beginning a life on the inside that would change him into someone who could not function outside the walls of Black Plains. He would not have thought that the facility would author his destiny when he first reveled in his uniform and weapon, the license given to him to inflict his will.

He could no longer see beyond the Rocky Mountains. He no longer felt himself to be a free man. He could not hear man's flurry of murder and procreation, debauchery and virtue, living and dying. He stopped watching television, since he could no longer relate to simplistic scenarios solved in hourly frames. He had long ago stopped wearing a watch and threw all his clocks away. Women, enigmatic creatures that they were, held little interest for him, and he had no patience to decode the endless combinations of their words and feelings. He could take himself in his hand or take an unfortunate to bed. The pithy feeling was the same, an unremarkable sensation that gathered and dispersed. He had become one with Black Plains. He breathed its stale air and tasted its tinlike water even when he was alone in his dead parents' house. His pillow and bed were framed in concrete. At night, when he closed his eyes, he saw only steel doors and stone floors. He dreamed of scalps rippling with ringworm and rotting flesh. He awoke to the sound of a loud buzzer in his head. There was no escape far enough away from the facility. There were no books, no fiction or autobiography, that could capture what he came to inhabit, for the world outside had nothing to do with the world in which he lived.

It was as if Black Plains, the Secured Housing Unit, Warden Stotsky, the horses, the liquid fire, and the stars—everything—had always been. It had always been as it was in the swirl of time. He began to ask himself difficult questions with difficult answers. The

kind of time Jimmy Eckert had come to know was born of something else. He didn't know if it was evil or justice. It did not have a
beginning, a middle, or an end. He was certain of one thing: he was
bottled in it, along with the prisoners he guarded.

Jimmy Eckert fumbled with the frozen lock on his car and got
in. In the world of the facility, the inmates held infinite combinations, infinite possibilities of wretchedness. He observed them for
the specimens they were, for the natural enemies they were. In the
showers, each held his own genitalia, the last of what he was, the
last of what the prison would take. Each of them with his reasons
for crimes committed. And when Jimmy Eckert looked at them,
he saw only that they were once males, not men. And inside Black
Plains, they were no longer males, they were rodents. There were
exceptions, of course. Anomalies. But not enough to change the
numbers. Not enough to change the form of the prison state, this
hidden nation. None of any of it mattered in Black Plains, a realm
unto itself, a world away from the world.

Sometimes, when he stepped into the vomit-green walls of the
receiving room for ID check-in, he pushed his baton into its holster
and was struck by the fact that he was not permitted to carry a gun,
nor had he ever fired one. But in such a place as Black Plains, his
real weapon was more powerful than batons or bullets. His weapon
was control and the deathlike stillness that came with it. The only
currency to be had by any of the rodents was worthlessness. He
had earned a wealth of it himself; he would dole it out to those who
earned the right to receive it. He reminded himself of these facts
daily, as he nodded to the guard at the elevator, as he prepared for
his descent. Each day, the elevator awaited Jimmy Eckert to escort
him to the underworld, where the souls in the Secured Housing
wing writhed in cages seared with fury. Where fluorescent light
embedded in the concrete beamed like an Alaskan midnight sun,
and he, the falcon, roamed a fiery, encased sky.

He spent every day ambling down the wing, the line of sol-
itary-confinement cells standing eternally at attention, the seal

of each steel door interrupted only by the slot through which he would shove a tray. He would pick up the stack of food rations to be distributed to the fated men and begin walking the row slowly, pushing rations through each slot. He could hear the rodents in the wee hours of his shift, the conversations they had with themselves or other personalities inside of them, how their voices changed to mimic other people. Sometimes he wondered if what they talked about had come from reality, or if it grew from what Black Plains ladled into their minds.

From behind the door marked 02763, there was usually silence. Staring at that door always filled Jimmy Eckert with excitement. He would stare at the numbers stamped onto the steel, listening. He had grown tired of knowing the ending of each prisoner at the beginning. But when he stood by Horus Thompson's door, he imagined that something was growing inside of the cell, something coveted that he had a hand in creating, a thing he came to own. And it was in certain moments, like when he opened the bean hole and pushed the tray through, that Jimmy Eckert felt as if he was feeding something besides a prisoner.

And sometimes it seemed, even in small acts of rebellion, that Horus Thompson was trying to move to a place where he could not reach him, where Black Plains could not reach him. It reminded Jimmy Eckert of the Mummy. The old man was a sort of mascot of Black Plains, with his weeks of eating three beans a day and cupping his own urine and swallowing it. The Mummy refused food numerous times before escaping into the opaque realms beyond insanity, to which there was not even a window for spectators. He assumed the old man's mind was too feeble even for nightmares or babbling, and he lived in his own sarcophagus. He worried that 02763 might follow.

He turned the ignition over and listened to the engine struggle with the cold. These were concerns that he could only admit in the backwaters of his mind. Because he needed Horus Thompson there to punish, to talk to, to listen to, to act as an accelerant of his misery—the only feeling he had left. They talked, if you could call it that: him peering through the bean hole to whisper and 02763 writhing in silence, in delusion, in rage. Jimmy Eckert hated and needed all of this. He had given up understanding why.

He put the car into drive. And as it moved forward, he was overcome with the creeping feeling that his relationship with the prison was the relationship he would have had with a whore. Even in brief moments of pleasure, he wanted to strangle the life from her. The years had become one repetitive motion, one rising and falling of the moon. What was left at the start and finish of each day was the call, the obligation, to step through the ruthless jowls of Black Plains yet again. He sat in his car and listened. The wind whipped in short bursts. Coyotes bayed from distant lairs. It was cold and getting colder. Dark and getting darker. He ground his teeth and pulled out of the parking lot. The Rocky Mountains pressed against the starry sky. Through the frosted glass of his car, he could not see the white flickers of the stars piercing the black, but he felt their mockery as he drove away.

*V*isitation

*T*he construction of the facility had not disturbed the beginnings of the locusts at all, since they were many meters beneath the lowest point excavated. And below that, there was streaming water that no one knew was there, moistening and nourishing an earthen bed for ages. . . .

Horus lay in his cell bed, shivering, his head throbbing. It was the reign of Light. Beams shot like daggers down from the ceiling, and his eyes were tightly closed against them. He tossed and turned for endless hours, taking cover under his blanket, under his pillow, as if avoiding artillery shells. Horus felt around to the back of his scalp, the territory that he was clearing bit by bit. His fingers came to a spot that was wet, and he wondered if it was sweat or blood or the slime that had coated the walls of the labyrinth. He couldn't be sure.

Time descended on him once more, and he felt that an incantation, a mind pickling, was accelerating. There was a briny taste in his mouth. It bloomed first on his tongue and then sat at the back of his throat. It was so long ago that he was a part of that alien world of tastes, in that foreign time when such things other than the occasional peanut butter taste of roaches might have existed. The briny taste sat at the back of his throat nonetheless, and Horus was sure that it was some new cruel trick of his senses, an imaginary flavoring to accompany the metallic taste that was always in his mouth. But now there was this brine, too, this pickle that he could not explain. And the years were evaporating in the sunless moonless substance in his cell, so that he no longer recognized the functions and features of his own body. He was now a part of Black Plains, and the prison was now a part of him, and each day embalmed the day before.

Under the explosion of light, Horus prepared to open his eyes. It was a stronger dread than the sound of the air vent being shut off or when the Bean Hole Man crept near his slot. He opened his eyes and felt the sharp pains of his corneas, and he cradled his head in both hands as if to stop the drilling inside of it. He then looked around. The toilet was where it had been, stagnant and reeking. The drain at the center of the cell remained the endless, ominous hole into which he would one day slink. The walls remained a floodlit white, stoic and bleak.

Horus pulled the Catacombs back to the center of his thoughts. Had it all been a dream? But he was sure that he had been some-place else. He could still smell the dank mold, the roses and myrrh. He tried to sit up on the bed, but the room began to spin, and he collapsed back onto the stained mattress. He turned to his side, ineffectual against the light beams. He felt as if he was closed into a Mason jar and left under a lamp. In the cell, he was bobbing in a suspension, sinking to the bottom and floating to the top like a trapped jellyfish. His eyes grew teary, and he looked through the watery light and thought of the sea. And there was the audible memory of the ocean's roll and crest he thought he heard, and he wanted only to float away with it. Sleep and float away.

But then Horus thought of that light in the Catacombs, the warm, clean light that was nothing like the torturous glare of his cell, and wondered where it came from. It was so far away, and he was so tired from the endless walking. He remembered collapsing in the passageway but nothing else. "I was outside of Black Plains," he said desperately to the ruthless Light. "I *was* outside."

Something was dripping inside the mechanisms of the toilet, and Horus listened to the steady beat. The drops grew slower and slower, like the gentle rock and sway of a buoy. The heavier his body became, the lighter his mind became. Balloon-light. Rising. Drifting in curls of smoke. He rose higher and higher still, until he felt himself floating down the prison corridor. And without his heart telling his mind, he knew he was in search of the Mummy. Somewhere in the fog of his mind, he thought the old man would know about the blade of light in the Catacombs. By now, time would have splayed him open like a piece of fruit. He would be pliable. Open. Horus knew that there were many debilitated minds in Black Plains, but none like this one. A mind like this would know something of existence and nonexistence in such a place as a cell, and all the different kinds of cells a man could spend his life in. Or at least, that's what Jimmy Eckert said about him. Surely the Mummy would know what might be beyond the cages of buildings, the barracks of the mind. He would know the sort of alchemy needed to look into the great expanse. Horus needed to understand more before he traveled any further down the Catacombs, before he tried to reach the light again.

Horus had never been beyond the Secured Housing wing, beyond the shaftlike lift that led to the walled, roofless cubicle where on rare occasions he was permitted to glimpse the sky. And he had never seen the old man's face, but he was certain that he would find him. He would feel his presence like an energy and move toward it. Black Plains unfolded in his mind like the smooth paper of a blueprint. He was three levels below the surface. The small boxed earth of his subterranean chamber was all he knew for the past seven years. He would see more. Stepping over the Catacombs entrance was a choice. He would choose this too.

Horus lifted, upward through the three levels the elevator traveled. At length, he drifted to a great atrium at sea level that was the heart of the facility. He drifted further still, through the eerie light of hallway after hallway, corridor after corridor, until he came to what he had always envisioned as Lucifer's chamber, Warden Stotsky's office. The walls emitted heat. The closed office entrance, with its heavy wooden doors, was less opulent than he thought it would be. Even at this late hour, he could hear someone talking inside. Perhaps on a telephone? He could barely remember what one looked like. He looked at the warden's name emblazoned in gold lettering as he drifted by. He moved down a long corridor, weaving in and out of the uneven fluorescent light and the tall shadows that hung along the walls. There was a small window at the end, through which he could see the black night. The moon was bright, and the baked ground looked as if it was drizzled with mercury. How long had it been since he saw such a sight?

Horus turned a bend and floated down another long corridor and was filled with wonder. There were a handful of men wandering it. They walked listlessly, a few steps in one direction, only to turn around and walk back to where they were standing just a moment before. Horus watched them go back and forth. One stopped to stroke a huge gash in his head. Another was skipping as if in a game of hopscotch, slicing his fingers off one by one with a makeshift knife. Another had a rope around his neck made of sheets. There were two other men huddled together, as if in a lover's embrace, in front of a door in the middle of the corridor with a sign that read "Special Room."

One said to the other, "You wouldn't quit on us, would you? Me, Billy, and the others?"

"Would I ever do such a thing?" answered the other.

The fingerless man noticed Horus. "Waiting, too, are you?" He gestured at the door, his hands bloody mittens. "We can't leave until our request is granted."

Horus looked at the fingerless man. In the strange light, he could see the twin black holes of his eyes. "What request?" asked Horus.

"That we live again," said the fingerless man.

Horus watched him walk a few steps and turn back again, and that was when he understood that they were lingering spirits, restless and unable to leave. "Is that possible? To live again?" he asked.

"Yes," said the one with the rope of sheets around his neck. "But if you were one of us, you would know that."

Horus did not know what to say. Would he wander the corridors of Black Plains forever like these spirits, on and on, from one millennium to the next? The thought filled him with trepidation.

"You should know that," said the fingerless man as he disappeared. "It's a sin to offend the dead." Then he was gone and the others vanished in his wake.

Perhaps the specter was right, thought Horus, alone in the corridor. Perhaps that was what he had been thinking on the day he found Sam Teak. A day of pink flowers and sweetness in the air, when the brazen pistols of tulips shot unexpectedly from the ground. But Horus would not think of such things now.

He floated on.

He could feel the Mummy's energy drawing him, closer and closer. He went through two sets of double doors leading to a long hallway. At the end was another set of double doors. He drifted through them, and they emptied into a large arenalike room. He looked up and saw three stories of cells where the rest of the prison population was kept. It was like a small city housed inside a building. There were overhead lights along the rows, but the cells were not lit. Here the prisoners did not sleep under fluorescent sunlight or grope in the dark. There was a lonely skylight high above the fifty-foot ceiling, blacked out by the night.

Horus ascended. There were rows and rows of cell doors. He moved through the muted light. From the dark cubicles and hanging in the air were the smells: rotten feet, urine, armpits, unwashed genitalia, shit, curdled blood, the decay of souls.

At last, Horus drifted to a single cell. He was sure this was the one. He could feel the pulse of reason and unreason from within. He moved through it and hovered in the corner, blending with the shadows. The Mummy was lying in his bed along the opposite wall. Horus did not want to move his ragged slipper or disturb his blanket, lest he give the Mummy a heart attack. He would whisper into the rooms of his thoughts.

Hey, Mummy. Listen . . .

Vine of the Earth

Edward, also known as the Mummy, thought he heard a voice in the early hours. Overcome with expectancy, he had been wide awake, awaiting the morning prison buzzer. And unlike most nights, he had not rested in the pleasant arms of a deathlike sleep. Dreams were a thing of long-gone decades, when his subconscious had been able to cut through the brush of disbelief with a machete, when he had the strength to clear a space and glimpse alternative realities, to see the infinite variations of what could have been his life, not this devastating reality.

With increasing impatience, Edward waited on the filthy padding of his cell bed, anxious for the buzzer. For that daily scream, always prompt, always clear, announced the beginning of his day and reunited him with his dearest. He was no longer a young man, and it had taken thirty years for the raging fires of his heart to die down to the sleepy hues of sunset. And even as his bones creaked under the hanging folds of his chestnut skin, his body warmed under rays of anticipation as the morning hours clicked on, like the blood of an old scorpion heating on the sands of the desert.

But he thought he heard someone speaking to him in the early hours, as he clutched his pillow and reflected on his dearest in that drifting state between lucidness and slumber. It sounded as if someone was talking to him from the end of a long tunnel. It got closer and closer, until it seemed as if the voice was right next to him, in his cell. He hadn't heard the other voices since before he found his dearest. Those others spoke of things he hadn't concerned himself with in years. He had long since lost interest in the sky, in terrain, in the elements, in other human beings. Consorting with men was now a preposterous thing to him, as foolish as jesting with death. Was this voice just an echo of all the other voices he heard inside his head all these long years? Was it like the voices that spoke of things he no longer wished to think about, those unimportant things like freedom and family and money and plans that faded from the universe he created each dawn? He couldn't concern himself with such things now. *Soon, my dearest,* he thought, curling tighter under his thin blanket, imagining the delicate, lovely limbs leaning toward him, bending under the water spray of his love.

The precious thing was all that mattered now.

He spotted it alone in the cracked floor of concrete along the eastern wall of the prison's Great Room, where men became one with machines. At first, he thought it a mirage, a trick of his cataract-plagued eyes. After twenty years in other prisons and more than ten in the one that now caged him, his eyes had convinced him that black, white, and gray were the only colors left in the world. "They are all gone," his eyes had said to him, guiding his hand to a trash receptacle in the corner, into which he dropped a tattered Bible. And yet on that glorious day, his dearest appeared before him, a minute emerald forest. He looked upon her greenness and was reminded of things he thought were forever washed away: the chartreuse-backed frogs in his mother's yard, the algae floating gently on the lakes of his youth, the iridescent scales of bass as they swam by his strong legs, and the pine needles sprinkling the snow he walked through in yesteryear winters. Most of all, the paradise rising from the ground reminded Edward of the soft grass on which he had held his first love.

And she had been waiting for him all this time, he reasoned, to bead her petals with adoration and respect. Eagerness filled him as he counted down the hours until he could be with her again, images of her supple clovers caressing his gray beard. Together, in the nurturing soil hidden below their roots, they would proliferate. Their lovemaking would be an act the earth itself had blessed and given permission to take place. *But not yet, my dearest,* Edward thought. *We must be careful, because they are watching us always. We must keep our love hidden. Be vigilant, my sweetness.* He turned on his side to face the wall and clenched his eyes tighter.

Nothing could keep the old man from his dearest. When the buzzer sounded every morning and the white lights flooded his cell and the entire floor of the prison, Edward would struggle earnestly to his feet. Although the silence of the cell block was quickly poisoned with bitterness and sorrow, and he could hear the other men groaning and cursing the assaults on their ears and eyes, he was always ready, brimming with excitement. He would step feebly out of his cell when the steel doors slammed open, the only one smiling.

The herd of men would shuffle miserably to the roll-call line and then the mess hall, each man inwardly preparing for the wars of the day. For the inmate population operated like Balkanized states. The delicate balance between them was maintained by endless scuttles in the gladiator rounds of the prison yard and atop steel cafeteria tables. Like war clans, they battled ruthlessly over territory and influence.

But things were always different in the Great Room, an enormous glass box. There the populace became one. The men assembled under the watchful eyes of cameras that never grew sleepy, awaiting the signal. At length, a siren blasted through the silence, and the men poured into the maze of machines like thick liquid. The hum of the underground factory cocooned the inmates, their bone marrow, teeth, and eyelashes pulsating, keying to the vibrating flecks of granite under their feet. They drank deeply of the five-hour shifts, intoxicating themselves with the sweetness of rote activity and tedium. For the everlasting drone of the prison-corps hive was their only deliverance from the flesh burns of private purgatories.

Edward drew his frayed blanket under his chin and thought of darker days in the Great Room before the advent of his dearest, when his spirit was just a heap of crushed stone. He toiled in the same manner as the other men, with his mind folded into the titanium pegs of the contraptions. But now, as he assembled sneakers in the Great Room every day, he could behold his dearest with elegant subterfuge. He could watch her as she waved joyfully from across the wasteland room. Now he could raise his head above the choked air and witness her triumph in an open pit of hell.

The miracle that no one else noticed her glory was, Edward felt, an avowal of the holiness of their union. He was certain that one day, a brilliant bird of paradise would erupt from her tender breast, and together they would fly away. Day after day, the old man looked at his secret green piercing the cement. Defiant beauty! He wondered how long it would be before he could truly be with her, his blood chilling at the thought of peering into the crack and finding her gone without him.

But the voices of men were always interrupting his concentration in accomplishing this destiny. Like that squeaky-voiced, cross-eyed inmate who assembled sneakers for the bin next to him. He had wished Edward a "Happy Fucking New Year." Edward stared at him blankly, no longer sure what a New Year was. Indeed, as his dearest grew more beautiful and strong, especially over these past several months, he found it increasingly difficult to understand the concerns of men. For rot and ruin were the only measures of existence left to any of them. These were obsessions Edward had long since abandoned, fixations he knew led only to madness. *But my dearest has ended my decay*, the old man thought, grateful.

The Mummy felt his bladder empty, and a warm, comforting spot spread on his thin mattress. It would soon turn cold, but he would first enjoy the coziness. He settled into infantile contentment and lay waiting for the buzzer.

"Hey, old man."

Edward turned his head. So there was another voice, something there. "What do you want?" he barked, his dry and cracked voice piercing the silence. He was angry that his solitude was interrupted; his preparation for his dearest was disturbed. "What do you want?" he croaked, louder.

Horus did not expect the Mummy to respond so quickly. "I came to ask you some things, old man."

"The name's Edward. And there ain't no answers in here. Only questions." He could feel that the buzzer was less than three hours away, and he was growing nervous. "State your business. Quick."

"I been someplace," said Horus.

Edward turned toward Horus. He could just make out his floating figure in the shadows. He had seen ghosts before, the ones that lived in the corridors, but this one did not look like any of them. "Yeah? Well, I been a lot of places. They're all the same."

"No. I mean . . . a place," said Horus.

The Mummy flared a gray, toothless grin. "What about it? Used to go places too. Till I got tired."

At this, Horus was surprised. He floated nearer. "You mean you . . . traveled too? Is there a way out of here?"

Edward looked from Horus to the blank walls. "Only one way out. The Catacombs."

Horus was enthralled. So they did exist. The tunnels. The gypsum. He thought that the Catacombs were endless, that there was no way to go into them and come out to someplace else, until he saw that light. Here was someone who knew about them too. "Tell me what you know about the Catacombs."

The Mummy laughed. "Spent years in them. But I had to come out of there. I couldn't go back."

"Why?" asked Horus.

The Mummy sighed. "Saw that light. That was all right at first. Followed it and followed it. Took forever to get up on it. And then I heard my mama's voice. I tell you, I stepped through that light, and there she was, sitting out there on the oak stump in the yard just like when I was little. She looked at me like she saw me, knew me. And she looked at me like nothing ever happened. Like she had really raised me, and I had lived a good life. I had to get out of there. I had to turn back." The old man coughed and mumbled something bitterly.

Horus waited for Edward to go on.

"There's other things besides the Catacombs. Mind traveling. Had a hoot with that before I found my dearest. Used to walk into someone else's mind like I was walking through a front door. Oh, the things I saw!"

Horus floated down and hovered just above the Mummy. "So you read minds."

The old man nodded. "Traveled minds."

"You mean you talked to them inside their heads like we're talking now?"

Edward snickered. "What makes you think we really talking?"

Horus looked at the toilet. Pieces of tissue were stuck to the sides of the bowl. "You said there was a light."

"I did?"

"Yes. You said there was a light."

"Where?"

"In the Catacombs, you said."

"There was. But I don't know much about that."

"Well, it sounds like you do. What about it, Edward?"

The urine spot on the mattress had cooled, and Edward felt a chill in his bones. "I said I don't know much about it."

"Well, tell me what you do know."

Edward shrugged. "There was the light, and then there was my mama. That's what I know."

The buzzer was not far off now. The Mummy had been lost in the talk for a while, but now that the spot was cold, he remembered why he resented the interruption in the first place. "Go on now," he said irritably. "Leave me be. And anyway, it ain't none of my concern no more." He turned away stiffly, curling up and facing the wall. "Can't no good come out of them Catacombs no way—seeing what you can't stand to see—can't no good come of it. I remember my mama left me on that oak tree stump out in that yard when I was a bitty thing, and that was the last I saw her. That was the last I saw her until I traveled through them Catacombs and walked through that light and looked in. She looked at me like nothing ever happened, my mama. Like it was all just fine."

The old man sighed. "You going where there ain't no way back, boy. Now, get out of here—if you really here—and leave me be. Don't come back and ask me nothing about going nowhere. The only place we going is in the dirt."

Awakening

M *ineralized and sleek, the locusts grew larger in the richening soil below, until even the eagles marveled at the greenness mysteriously spreading across the plains . . .*

Horus stood at the Catacombs entrance, thinking of the light, but he did not remember how it came to be that he was there. The smell of myrrh and roses and death was heavy in the stillness. He looked into the pitch black, thinking of what the Mummy said, how he, too, saw the Catacombs and the faraway light within. "You going where there ain't no way back, son," he'd said. What could that mean?

Horus stood at the threshold for a long time, and he felt something slowly melting inside of him that had been frozen over, and he came to the edges of his mind to ponder what he himself had forbidden. Dare he think of the child? Because from the moment the police arrived at his house to arrest him, Horus knew that he could never think of what he and Brenda made together as a person. He knew that he would never know the child in sight or sound, from experience and memory. Rather, for him, the child would be a concept. Like love or hate or beauty, an amorphous thing forever intangible but there, always.

Horus looked into the mouth of darkness and entered the Catacombs. The moldy gypsum was soft on his palms as he felt his way to the deeper chambers. The still air parted like water as he walked. The smell of roses hung over him like a vast canopy. Hours passed, until he reached a slant. Downward, downward he walked, his feet tender against the rough passage. His head was pounding. The lower he descended, the thinner the air became, and he felt as if he might fall a final fall, as he saw his father do, but he had the thought that perhaps there was something he might find somewhere in the black too. And Jack Thompson's words rose once again from the ashes: *That's what I want my boy Horus to know. To remind him that he can be free anytime he wants.* Perhaps that was the promise beneath the promise his heart persuaded his mind to make. Jack Thompson wanted his boy to fly. He wanted him to soar away from the coffin, from the rage, from the fear. Sweat ran down Horus's face. Or was it tears? And he wondered if Jack Thompson knew that once a bird is caged, it no longer lives. That at the end of it all, a man might understand only the smallest things of his life. Or the biggest.

And against the warnings of the Mummy, Horus descended deeper still into the Catacombs. He walked on for what felt like days in the darkness, without even the firelight of shunned memories, until at last he came to another tunnel. And there in the passageway was the distant light. Excited, he moved forward, but the tunnel seemed to lengthen and lengthen, until he was near to fainting. The dust and muck that lined the other passageways was replaced with something slippery running down the walls.

But Horus went further into the mysterious Catacombs, giddy with the delirium of the thousand miles he trekked, until at last the passageway stopped moving. The light was just ahead! He could see it clearly nestled in the black space. He journeyed on. The air grew thinner and thinner, and he felt that he would never catch his breath. He swooned, his eyes rolling, but he walked on.

"Come here." Horus gasped at the light. He tried to regain his strength and focus. Could light be called like a child? Like a dog? He struggled forward, stumbling, overtaken now by the powerful smell of salt. He would reach it this time, he thought, lunging forward.

The pain and throbbing in his head stopped of their own accord. Each time he called out, the light seemed closer. He kept moving. He would not let his legs betray him. He would not concern himself with time or distance. There was only the light and his singular purpose of reaching it.

Horus was at last before it, and the light shimmered through the crack of the crypt stone like a blade. He thought again of the Mummy's warning. He smelled sea water. He moved closer to the crack in the stone (so much larger now that he was near) and stepped through, clamping his eyes shut against a sudden brightness all around him. He stepped forward onto what felt like soft, warm sand under his feet. Blasts of salt air filled his lungs. He breathed deeply, greedily. He opened his eyes and squinted up at a golden sun. Horus looked down, and the blue ocean spread before him. He looked into the great liquid and thought of morning glories and blue jays and coral reef and cerulean glass. In the burst of color and the ocean breeze, his heart pounded in his chest, and he was filled with unknowing and knowing. Horus looked out over the water.

And floating there was someone in a little boat.

PART III

Jewelry Box

Sephiri awoke to the hum of locusts buzzing in his ears. What happened? He didn't want to open his eyes and find out. He tried to sink back into the safety of slumber but was unable to do so. He stayed still on his back and did not move. To calm his nerves, he thought of an afternoon he spent with his friend the dolphin. They floated on the sea together on their backs with their eyes closed. The sun blazed warm above them . . .

"You know," said the dolphin, flicking water with his fins, "I've seen many Air children before, standing on the decks of ships and boats. I've even tried to swim up and say hello to them, but none seemed to understand my greeting. You're the only one."

Sephiri felt special and honored.

"And you know what?" continued the dolphin. "I hope you can stay for a very long time."

Sephiri opened his eyes and righted himself and looked at the dolphin, treading water. "What do you mean, *stay?*"

Realizing his carelessness too late, the dolphin squeezed his eyes tighter in the gentle breeze. He did not want to spoil their fun with the way of things. "I've always told you what I know, right, Sephiri?"

"Yes, you have."

"And don't you think we'll always be friends?"

"Sure, I do," said Sephiri. "But you didn't answer my question."

The dolphin sighed. "Well, certain things are not my place to say. I have to keep my place, you know. That's how I stay happy. That's how I keep our cheer."

Sephiri could respect that. He did not want the dolphin to risk his place by pressing the matter further. All things ought to stay in place, where they belonged.

The dolphin brightened. "But I know that we're friends now, and we'll be friends tomorrow, and we'll always be friends. There's only one you, and there will never be another so wonderful . . ."

Thinking back on that sunny afternoon conversation with the dolphin now, in a different place and too afraid to open his eyes, Sephiri felt ill at ease. He turned his head without opening his eyes and felt something cool and firm beneath his head—a pillow, he guessed. Then he remembered what it was like when he tried to fight off the sounds and hands and fingers. The Air people asking and telling. The sensation that someone was lifting his body and someone was putting him down. Things got worse when he realized that his room and place and space of being had been changed at the center. He was desperate to get back to the Obsidians. He tried everything to let the Air people know—screaming, biting, hitting, flailing, jumping. He had even thrown up a few times to pour out some of what was too much, but still they did not understand. He tried to make the journey to the Obsidians. But somehow, on his way out to the water, he lost his strength. He was all worn out.

That was when his head felt very light, as if it could lift right off his shoulders, and his eyes rolled up in his head. He fell back into the warm black, and it pulled down over him like a drawn shade, more impenetrable and opaque than even the darkness of the cube. The black clung to every limb of his body. Sometimes this happened when the Land of Air proved to be too much. Like when he had to get his immunization shots and he knocked the needle from the nurse's hand before being pinned down by two others. Or the time he wandered away at the car wash and slipped into the backseat of someone's station wagon. The big blue brushes and long tangles of cloth tresses terrorized him so, and he screamed for what felt like hours, until someone stopped the machine. So it was in this between state that he felt soothed, and he wanted to hide inside of it until the Air people went away. Time went by—he couldn't tell how much—and he thought that maybe it was safe to open his eyes.

His head was aching, and it was then that he remembered his screaming. His throat was scratchy and dry. Slowly, he opened his eyes. Above, there was the familiar track lighting. He was at the center, but the ceiling was different. There was a bright mural of a summer sky painted there. For a moment, he imagined that the great swarms of flying creatures he saw in his dreams were sweeping across the fluffy clouds in the mural. Then he realized that he was lying on the white sheets of a small bed that he did not recognize. He thought about screeching to clarify and settle his jumbled feelings, to take control of the alarm rising within him like tidewater, but his head and throat were hurting.

He sat up slowly and looked around. The room was different. The cerulean-blue carpet beneath his feet was bathed in a soft yellow light. The walls were all made of glass, and a disquieting feeling crept over him that he was inside a giant jewelry box like the one he saw on his mother's dresser. He could see what was inside of it, but the lid didn't open. Worse, he could feel that there was someone standing behind the glass looking in, but he did not look at the person. He did not want to see the questions in the person's eyes right now. The solace of the grandfather clock was not there, and he began to rock to the pendulum in his head for comfort, to keep rhythm and order. He moved cautiously, turned, and scooted to the edge of the bed. He rocked back, forth, back, forth . . . he was beginning to feel better. He was moving back and forth with the ticking of the clock, the tide of the ocean, the cycles of the moon.

But the room was different. He saw that there was a round play table made of light pine with a single chair in the center of the room. In the corner, to his great delight, was a bathtub, but it was not the bathtub he knew of turquoise water. He looked down and realized he was dressed in bathing trunks that he had never seen before. He tried to accept the difference of this place, feeling his apprehension grow. He tried to fight the need to climb to the top of the tallest mountain and scream, to write "NO" in the sky with his finger. He rocked again and listened to his heartbeat, felt his lungs fill with air. He could breathe, at least. He might live. He continued rocking until he calmed down enough to listen. He craned his neck toward the glass walls and listened for the familiar voice of his mother.

He did not want to look around too much, anticipating that he might see the ruffled smock of the attendant or the rimmed glasses of one of the doctors. He missed the known world of the Obsidians, the medicine cabinet, the coat closet. Sleep called strongly to him again. He fell back onto the little bed, took in the coolness of the sheets, and closed his eyes. Although the new place had not devoured him whole as he feared, he was not prepared for the scale of effort it would take to process it, to glean some sense of understanding and meaning.

To beckon sleep, he would not think of any of that now, lest he scream again, and he was too tired to get up and spin or flail or flap. He would not think of the things that were still a mystery, like that place he drew, the giant black box with the dark figures that hovered on the edges of it, the mountains that stood behind it, the flying creatures riding the wind. Before sinking deeper into the black, Sephiri listened once more for his mother's voice. He would not think about the fear he pushed aside when, from the corner of his eye, he did not see her large frame behind the glass. He did not want to look and confirm that she was not there.

Impressions

Brenda pulled her car into a two-hour parking space near the Takoma Park Autism Center. She did not want to stand out front and wait for Manden this time. At the last appointment, she'd had the distraction of Sephiri's restlessness and the chilliness of the morning. This time, she didn't have the energy to struggle with Sephiri with the added apprehension that there were yet new dimensions to his autism that she was about to discover. She had put him on the van instead.

Sometimes, in the quiet of the car when Brenda turned off the engine and held the steering wheel to steady her nerves, fear of the future crept into her heart. The routines, the silences, the fixations, the limitations, the extremities stretched out before her like a long road. They would grow older together. Sephiri would grow bigger and would become an even greater mystery. She would grow larger and frailer under the weight of everything. And she would exist with Sephiri in a rift of time where she would be there to take care of him, to stand by the gate he held locked to the world. These things Brenda knew but felt she could do nothing about. Like the sugar in her blood.

Alone at the dinner table the other day, Brenda ate a large pizza. She wanted brownies to go with it, but she was too tired to stop at another store. She was only able to get Sephiri to eat half of a peanut butter and jelly sandwich before he threw the rest on the floor. She offered him a small plate of baby carrots, of which he ate two. She peeled a banana and set it next to the remaining carrots. Sephiri paid it no mind and left the table to wander the house, and she gave up and sat down. There was ice cream in the freezer, but only a half-gallon was left, not enough to satisfy her. She went to the pantry to examine the shelves: raisins, spaghetti sauce, boxes of macaroni and cheese, pretzels, pancake mix, parboiled rice, caramel popcorn, taco shells, graham crackers, goobers, canned tomatoes, egg noodles, tuna fish, marshmallows, pickles, cookies, and potato chips. There was nothing she wanted.

Sephiri slipped upstairs and got hold of a bag of M&M's she had hidden in her dresser drawer. By the time she discovered him, he had eaten almost the entire bag and launched into a sugar-powered, two-hour tirade of running and screaming all about the house. Her every effort to calm him was met with more screaming. She could not reach him, and this recurrent failure killed her inside. Frustrated, she left him rolling around on the living-room floor to wash the pans that were sitting since the day before. At the kitchen sink, she sliced her finger with the paring knife in the dishwater, but she was not sure if it was an accident. The cut stung under the running tap, and she was secretly pleased at the pain. It distracted her from Sephiri's fit in the next room. It fed something inside of her. She watched the blood ribbon swirl down the drain, her mind emptying.

Sephiri threw up on the living-room carpet while she was straightening up the kitchen. In her despair at the mess, Brenda consoled herself with the thought of the box of apple pie in the freezer. But then she thought of the long preparation (sixty minutes in the oven or thirty-five minutes in the microwave). The microwave, broken since Sephiri stuffed it with the filling from a sofa pillow and turned it on, stared back at Brenda from the kitchen counter, shiny and untouched. She saw her largeness reflected in the gleaming door of the microwave oven and wondered how much more it would take to bury the origins and components of her ordeal, how deep the hole she was digging had to be.

If you want to be around for your son . . .

Brenda got out of the car and walked to the Autism Center entrance. As far as she could tell, Manden had not yet arrived. She pulled the door handle and walked into the building. As she stepped inside, she tried to prepare herself to hear how Sephiri suddenly could not stay awake. How he had entered yet another labyrinth that led to other dimensions. He was sleepy all the time. There were suggestions to get his hormone levels checked again by his pediatrician, to run another neurological diagnosis. But she had just taken him for all of that when she discovered he was holding his bowels. She had taken Sephiri to the doctor so many times in his short life to try to find the answer to a million questions. What was it that set off a particularly violent episode? Why didn't he sleep? Why was he biting? What triggered him to hide in closets? The possibilities were endless. Dairy products. Overexposure to light. Sensitivity to fabrics. Unfamiliar smells. Something swallowed that she had not known about. It could have been anything, but it was nothing anyone could figure out.

Brenda sighed and looked over her shoulder once more, but she did not see Manden. He would catch up with her, she thought. Or he would not come at all. She could not be angry with him either way. It was not his responsibility. Sephiri was not his obligation. Beyond the envelope every month (which Manden offered without her asking) and his name on forms where the father's name was to be listed, what else could she ask of him? She opened the door and walked slowly toward the office at the end of the hall. Back when she had been painting the portrait of a perfect family in her mind, she planned to have more than one child. She wanted a home filled with the laughter of many children. But she ended up with silence after all. Sephiri lived as if he was the only boy in the world, a singular being around which other beings were the same as furniture. And still, she had never seen her boy smile and had been robbed even of this one small gift of solace. She had only his stiffened body and soapstone face. Hugs were a foreign concept. Kisses did not exist. There were only attempts at schedules and routines to guide them through the thick fog of their lives. Days were made remarkable only by the occasions when Sephiri grabbed her hand and bit it.

Brenda arrived at the end of the hallway. At the office door, she was greeted by Sephiri's speech pathologist, Dr. Susan Watson. A tear in the young doctor's nylon stockings exposed her pink ankle beneath the strap of one of her Italian leather slingback shoes, rubbing it raw so that she limped slightly. Brenda followed her in.

"Good to see you again, Mrs. Thompson," said Dr. Watson as they headed to her office. She opened the door and motioned for Brenda to go in first. The walls were painted a warm yellow, with matching guest chairs. Powder-blue pillows and a paisley-print throw rug accented the inviting color scheme. Van Gogh's *Starry Night* hung on the wall.

"Is Manden Thompson coming as well?" Dr. Watson casually asked without looking at Brenda.

"He should be along soon," said Brenda.

The doctor offered a thin smile. "Why don't we get comfortable first?" she said, gesturing toward the chairs.

Brenda sat down.

Dr. Watson poured them each a cup of coffee from the little brewer she kept atop her file cabinet. "I felt we should talk in a more private setting. The other meeting was rather formal, no?"

"A little," said Brenda.

"Well, Sephiri is doing fine right now. He's awake. He had something to eat, and he's quiet."

Brenda knew that this could mean any number of things, from staring at the wall, to shaking his head violently, to pacing the room. A shadow descended on her when she thought of the fact that she was not up to seeing her boy in this state now, in that unreachable place.

"We haven't allowed him to get into the tub again since that last scare when he drifted off to sleep," the doctor continued. "And we still don't know to what degree the room change affected him or what exactly triggered his extreme tantrum. As you know, it was a bit rougher than we expected, enough that he passed out. We did have our pediatrician take a look at him, though, and she didn't find anything out of the ordinary." The doctor shook her head. "But as I told you on the telephone, Mrs. Thompson, his unusual sleeping is anything but ordinary."

Brenda thought of all the nights Sephiri startled her, when she opened her eyes and found him standing over her dresser or heard him creeping around the hallway and downstairs. Now, incredibly, he could not stay awake. She listened to the silence outside the office door. Manden had not yet arrived.

"Of course, we'll continue to run the usual checkups on him," Dr. Watson continued. "But at this point, I'd like to know if there is anything different at home, any small changes at all?"

Brenda's eyes glimmered. What was this woman trying to say? She was doing her best with Sephiri. Although it hadn't been enough, she had been giving it her all. Sephiri had always been consistently bizarre in his own little way. There wasn't anything unusual at home. But this new issue about his drowsiness and heavy sleeping, in addition to the locust drawings, set her nerves on edge. "No, Dr. Watson. I can't think of anything that's been different lately. Sephiri's sleeping patterns were never regular. With all the trouble I have had getting him to sleep—to stay asleep—I can't imagine anyone actually having trouble waking him up. I don't think either of us has ever slept for more than a few hours at a time since he was born."

The doctor looked at Brenda carefully. "What about Manden Thompson? Has anything changed in Sephiri's relationship with him?"

"What do you mean?" asked Brenda.

Dr. Watson took out a folder from her drawer and handed it to Brenda. "Sephiri drew this when he woke up this morning. Like the

other drawings, the level of detail and skill is astonishing. It could
have been done by an accomplished Impressionist. But this one is
incredible for a different reason."

Brenda stared at the drawing in disbelief. It was a beautiful
rendering of the ocean in pencil. Most shocking were the delicate
lines and shading. The currents and skeins of moving water skipped
across the white paper. There were white-capped waves, which
danced just above the surface, and hints of ocean spray stretched
from the tops of the frothy peaks like strings of silk. There was a
small fisherman's boat out on the water, and a figure sat in the boat
in stark relief against what looked like a pale, lonely sky. In the foreground was a lovely sea line, with etched groves of sand that disappeared into the tide in some places. Hermit crabs and sand dollars
were scattered about. There was a line of tiny turtles heading into
the sea. And standing on the shore was the watery silhouette of a
man waving to the figure in the distant boat.

The doctor shook her head in wonder. "It's very tender, don't
you think? Beautiful, really. Perhaps that is Sephiri in the boat. But
what strikes me the most is the man in the foreground. We've never
known Sephiri to draw a picture of someone before. Who do you
think it could be?"

Brenda said nothing and stared at the nebulous figure. Sephiri's
watercolor-like crayon strokes made the man appear as if he were
shrouded in smoke. She looked at the sketches of the water, whim-
sical and silent. It reminded her of a recurrent dream she used to
have about Horus in the early days of his imprisonment. In it, he
was on the Maryland shore, where they spent so many weekend
holidays. The sun was setting down on the crystal water, melting
like a great candle. She could see him as if she were floating above.
He was lying on the sand, the landscape butterscotch and tan in
the sunset. The tide was coming in. Slowly, the soft waves moved
closer and closer to him. His feet. His legs. His chest. He made no
attempt to move as the sand and silt filled the crevices of his body
like the fossil of some long-dead creature washed ashore. He lay

stiff and unblinking, staring upward. She did not know if he could see anything in the sky, if he could see her watching. The tide washed up higher still, covering his chest, then his shoulders. The water reached his neck, but still he did not move. The tide moved over his lips, then his nose.

In the dream, Brenda wanted to cry out to him, to warn him. But having no voice, no form of which she was aware, she could not do so. The water, black and sleek, moved over his motionless body, over the bridge of his nose, then his glasslike eyes. It covered the last of his head, and then there was nothing to see but the surface of the ocean. Brenda had that same dream many times, until the years slackened the flow to her subconscious. She did not dream that dream anymore.

Brenda looked at her son's drawing, at the wispy waves and the lonely boat floating on the horizon. His drawings had been the first glimpses she ever had of the interior of Sephiri's mind. She looked again at the shadowy figure. She had never gotten an indication that Sephiri noticed Manden in any meaningful way. He acted with Manden with the same indifference he had with everyone around him. People were objects, just outside his field of vision. Their voices were white noise to whatever Sephiri was listening to in his mind. Yet there was this drawing of a man. And what scared her more was what the man might represent. The law of God she felt she'd broken crept into her mind once more. She kept Sephiri a secret from Horus, and now her boy wanted a father, something she could not give him. And she was pained that there was no trace of her anywhere in Sephiri's drawings. To him, she was not there.

Brenda handed the drawing back to the young doctor and shook her head. She looked at the other empty chair in the office. Manden had decided not to come to the appointment, she guessed. He didn't have the strength for what she dealt with every day.

Bastille

anden Thompson sat behind the thick glass of the information booth of the Shady Grove subway stop. The rectangle-shaped countertop inside was piled with an assortment of items left by other Metro officers working other shifts: yellow notepads, stacks of old newspapers and magazines, radio equipment, a shoe box of watches, appointment books, bracelets, and scarves that passengers had dropped. His eyes had grown poor over the years from having to constantly strain in the dim tunnels, so that now he needed reading glasses even when he sat down with the newspaper in bright sunlight. There was a little locked box underneath the counter that held *Playboy* magazines, which everyone (the males, at least) from all shifts silently agreed would not be disclosed to the supervisor as long as the key was kept under the gray industrial floor mat. The cleaning crew knew about it, too, and the floor was always vacuumed and mopped and the key returned to its place. An inch-thick wall of bulletproof glass encased the booth, and there was a muzzle-like piece embedded in the glass to communicate using the intercom apparatus. An envelope-sized cut in the glass with a brass tray underneath allowed for the passage of small things like tickets, money, pens and pencils, maps. Curiously, it smelled always of hammered metal, spoiled milk, and vinegar, no matter how many times Manden sprayed it down with a can of disinfectant before he began his shift.

His stomach tightened around the grinding thought that he had not shown up to meet Brenda at the Autism Center but had gone to work instead. He planned to join her in the lightest sense but did not want to face the fact that he didn't have the fortitude, the will, to see about a boy he couldn't save, to behold another piece of his family that could not be salvaged. He was not up to sitting silently in the office next to Brenda while the doctor talked about eccentricities and treatments, with his voice lodged in his throat, with his thoughts caught in the loop of time.

At the last meeting he attended, there were the mysteries of the locust drawings and the strange building sketches, the structure that he knew (deep inside when he saw it) was a prison. But could it really have been Black Plains? Why would the boy draw such a thing? How could Sephiri know of a prison he had never seen? He himself had not wanted to think about its familiarity when he saw the sketch, so much like the photographs he saw of Black Plains—what that might mean. And beneath this denial was the thought that something else he was ill equipped to handle lay waiting. He did not want to feel again that there was nothing he could do, as he felt those days in Uncle Randy's basement. He couldn't look upon the blankness of Sephiri's face, so much like the blank innocence of his little brother when they were boys, when their childhood was still intact.

Manden felt numb, frozen in the ruins of a situation he was powerless against. And this gnawing awareness only deepened the disgrace pitted in his stomach when he thought of how he was now sitting in the booth instead of at the center. "If you can make it," Brenda said when she called to tell him that there were new concerns about Sephiri. The "observational study" had not gone well, as she feared. Sephiri wasn't able to adjust to the new room prepared for him. The tantrum he had worried even Dr. Watson, since, this time, her boy raged and grieved at new extreme heights, dry-heaving and banging his fists on the floor and on the glass walls until he passed out.

And now there was the sudden onset of excessive sleeping, which seemed to be induced by something, even though there were no known changes in his medications or diet. She wanted no part of any further study, Brenda said. She didn't care whether the drawings could mean that a savant ability had emerged, that Sephiri had somehow seen what was impossible to see. She didn't want to explore how he might respond to the special room they set up for him anymore. "This is my baby, and I don't want reaching Sephiri to mean that he'll suffer," she said. The speech pathologists were puzzled and had no answers. Brenda felt it no longer mattered. When Sephiri fainted from the shock of being moved to the new room— from whatever outrage had fueled his tantrum—it frightened her more than she expected. It made her fear that she had lost her boy forever. Now Sephiri's autism seemed to have been transformed into something else. "If you can make it," Brenda said again at the end, a soliloquy of desperation. She hung up in the pause before he had the chance to respond.

Manden fumbled with the notes and papers spread out on the booth counter. His hands needed something to do, something to make neat and orderly when his thoughts were in the jumbled chaos that seized him at that moment. A headline on the cover of the *Washington Post* caught his eye: "Police apprehend suspect accused of murder." Such captions reminded him of his brother, for he saw his face in every mug shot, heard his voice in every film clip. Manden had wanted the man responsible for their father's murder dead, too, although he hadn't been able to admit it until he heard that Horus was arrested. His little brother, the one he had never been able to protect. He should have tried harder to look out for him. He supposed that this was what brotherhood was all about.

And how was it that he could feel only shame in the fact that it was Horus who took action, who sought to avenge their father's murder and his memory, and he had not? Manden, the eldest son of the father, the next in line, and the one with "the empire in his heart," words that held like an iron bit in his mouth. He was not the prince of righteousness that Jack Thompson intended him to be. But what had been his inheritance, his dominion? At ten years old, he became the man of a house that no longer existed. And he had been paralyzed since the moment he heard the gunshots, for the sound had taken his will, and he had been unable to retrieve it. What was left was a half-finished jigsaw puzzle, with huge parts of the picture missing. Was it the shame of his inaction or the shame of his brother's action that took a bit of his ability to live with himself, year after year? He didn't know what could be done about that. And never knowing what to do about it had driven him to silence.

Manden reached to massage his aching back as he slouched in the booth chair. His radio was blaring, the dispatcher barking out the usual. His mind was heavy with tedium, and the hours stretched out before him like a bleak tunnel. The radio spit static as he half-listened to the dispatcher's voice dribble out in a long, garbled drone. "Jumper reported on track one . . . Red Line . . . fatality . . . crew dispatched at seven thirty-eight A.M. . . . . shut down track and reroute until eleven fourteen A.M. . . . . Code Purple, guys . . ."

"Damn," said Manden. He wasn't in the mood for carnage. Rage, maybe, but not death. Code Purple meant it wasn't a simple housekeeping job. The motherfucker hadn't hit the tracks in such a way that limbs could be recovered with ease after meeting steel: torso with head still attached off to the left, right foot fifteen yards down, forearm in groove between tracks. Code Purple meant squashed concord grapes. Blood and guts destined to add aggravation and delay to an already tiresome day.

Manden signed heavily, turning to a blond woman who was banging impatiently on the glass of his booth.

"I need to know if this is the line I ride to get to the Chevy Chase Pavilion!" the woman said. Shopping bags stuffed with tissue paper dangled from her pink forearms as she struggled with her coffee and cell phone.

Over the years, Manden had become a skilled lip-reader, and he understood what the woman said even through the thick glass. He looked at her blankly, thinking of the delays and what was probably headed his way from the shift supervisor.

The woman banged again. "Excuse me . . . man, is this the train to get to the Pavilion?" the woman repeated. Her face turned strawberry red as she glared through the glass at Manden.

He had become part of the scenery for tourists (whom Manden loathed with every cell in his body), and "man" was something they called him as they would call other objects they happened upon during their odyssey: "Look, Dan, there's a bench we can sit on while we wait for the tour bus." "Here is a parking space, and we won't even have to walk very far to the Lincoln Memorial." "That man will know if this is the train for the Pavilion."

It was not so much that Manden hated the job for which he was being paid. But when he did have to deal with people, it was the job's necessity that he not be human, not be a person, that he was viewed as (and required to be a part of) the scenery, that bothered him. He was asked by one of the passengers, for instance, to carry a bag and became a Pullman porter resurrected. A woman argued with him about the directions he gave her to the Watergate—how could someone like him know the quickest route to a place like that? "You speak very good English," a man once told him.

But on some occasions, like when there was a terrorist alert or a suspicious package was found on one of the platforms, Manden was transformed from "man" to "sir." The steely and unforgiving eyes of women became soft rivers, pleading and submissive. The rough, curse-ridden voices of men became low and edgy tremors. Manden had seen the phenomenon before and had learned that when people feel threatened, they huddle around the fire of imagined security. And just as quickly, when safety and normalcy seem restored, they throw caution onto the ground as a child would throw a pacifier. Fear was a delicious thing to Washingtonians, and they were electrified by something during citywide alerts and evacuations, chatting excitedly as they emerged from the subway tunnels, a grim delight in being a part of something horrible and media-worthy burning in their bellies.

And so the glass information booth, from which Manden administered small doses of power, was a fortress, bulletproof and impervious to injury and insult. And it was only when he was outside of the booth, like on the other days of the week, when he was on another post or special detail, that he was vulnerable. But he reminded himself that today he was working in his very own Bastille, and that the phlegm from small minds, insolent brats, and undeserving bastards would not hit him in the face but would instead splat squarely on the thick exterior glass walls of his booth and slowly roll down to never having been said or heard.

Manden looked at the woman with furrowed brows standing outside of the booth and zeroed in on the coffee she was holding. "You can't bring food or drinks into the nation's subway system, ma'am," he said.

The ground shook with an oncoming train, and the woman looked worriedly at the platform. "Did you hear me? I just need to know if this is the train or not!" she shouted.

Manden leaned casually into the small brown speaker and pressed the intercom. "Ma'am, you may not board the train with food or beverages. You'll have to dispose of that drink first."

Rowdy middle-school students rushed past the woman, jostling her and the shopping bags. In her efforts to avoid dropping her accoutrements, Manden thought she looked like one of those Chinese acrobats, contorting her limbs with nimble magnificence. Ball balanced on a finger. Candle balanced on a foot. Plate balanced on a head . . .

The dispatch radio snarled between loud jags of static, "Status Code Purple . . . jumper could not be identified . . . transit police . . . delays expected to extend . . ."

Outraged, the woman went to a nearby trash can, threw away her coffee, and stormed back to the booth. "Look, sir. I'm late meeting up with my group. Does this go to the Chevy Chase Pavilion or not? This *is* the information booth, isn't it?" Her eyes were moist with indignation.

Manden hit a button that opened a metal bar next to his booth, allowing her to pass. "Yes, this is the right train," he said in perfect monotone through the intercom. He watched the lady run to the platform in her high heels to catch the train, which had just arrived, missing it by seconds as the doors swished shut.

He had taken part in this sort of banal sport over the years to distract himself from the deepening chasms of his own psyche, from the apertures that were forming. Like the women with whom he'd broken things off when they got too close. Like the way the days months years ran together, indistinguishable by the markers that ruled the lives of others: holidays, anniversaries, graduations, birthdays. On his brother's birthday, Manden let the sun rise and fall and the moon rise and fall without acknowledging it. But he did not want to think of that now, because he would then have to think about Brenda and Sephiri, a tangle of confounding feelings that he could not unravel.

And so the petty, lowly exchanges with subway passengers were imperative interludes that suspended certain uncomfortable sensations and allowed him to escape (temporarily) the realization that even though it was Horus rotting in a cell, he and his brother were slowly vanishing together nonetheless. "I could quit this job," he would say to himself, but he would then have to face the fact that without his life in the tunnels, he did not know what his life would be.

The radio chattered on. "Cleanup crews will be reporting to section . . ." Manden reached across the booth counter to turn down the volume and caught a glimpse of his reflection in the polished glass. The procession of wasted years written on his face looked back at him. He looked away as he had a thousand times before, since in the tunnels beneath the city, there were other things to see.

Sometimes he would arrive at the subway entrance and stand at the top of the escalator, watching the steel steps march down to their destinies. Other times, when he worked the hours on toward midnight, he would come out of the booth, step to the edge where the yellow line was painted, and look into the still tunnels. He would lean over and peer into the cave and let the abyss wash over him, let the cold concrete and steel seep through him. There was a darkness so alive it was as if it wanted to open its mouth and speak but dare not. In the silence, the black shifted on its own. Shadows hung in the air, waiting for something to happen. What was it that gave him the feeling that something was approaching besides the trains?

Manden looked at the time on the cracked analog clock sitting amid the counter clutter. The meeting at the Autism Center was long over. Had there been a new treatment prescribed? He wondered if the observational study (which he was straining not to call an experiment that he had sanctioned with his silence) did more harm than good. Manden remembered the bag of marbles he gave Sephiri and wondered if they were already lost out in the street and long fallen into a drain or given away to some other child who might have taken a direct interest in them. Or were they in Sephiri's room somewhere, in the windowsill, like where he and Horus used to keep them?

It was a funny thing that the memory of marbles should plague him now. Such small pieces of glass filled with ribbons of color. But they held a world in them, and they were all he and Horus wanted to play with, all they talked about, when together they burned through the New York summer days of 1966. He remembered those precious times when it was just the three of them (he, Horus, and their father) outside of their apartment building. He and Horus shot marbles on the sidewalk, with Papa watching over them from the stoop, smiling and smoking a cigarette. Jack Thompson would point to the chalk line they drew in the middle of the game circle and say, "Make that line, boys! Whatever you do, make the scratch." July 21, 1966, started like every other day when school was out and childhood was in full swing, packed with daring and games, adventure and enterprise . . .

"Come on, Horus, shoot your Alley. We ain't got all day."

"I'ma do it when I'm ready, Manny."

"Told ya this one ain't easy, with your big head and don't know what you doin'. Should have used the shooter. You know we playin' for keepsies."

"Well, I'm almost eight years old, Manny, and I ain't losin' my mean, green Alley to no shooter."

"Well, you still seven years old right now, while you runnin' your mouth. It's 1966, and we ain't got all day."

Horus stared down at the brilliant green cat's eye marble nested in the hole made by his thumb and index fingers. His eyes looked as if they were piercing the round glass, and in the glare, he couldn't hear the sirens wailing somewhere in the neighboring streets or old ladies calling for their cats. He couldn't hear the doo-wop playing in the parked cars, the soft rap of young men laying it on thick to giggling girls. Horus couldn't hear the metal wheels of little girls roller-skating down the sidewalk. There had only been the marbles in his hand, the line, and the target . . .

Manden had seen that kind of concentration on Papa's face, too, when he was preparing for a meeting, one of his speeches, or an article he wanted released in the black newspapers. Manden would watch him go through his ritual of preparation (steps he thought as a child were the steps all men took in being men every morning). First, there was the quiet breakfast he shared with his wife at the table. Maria always fed her children first and waited to have breakfast with her husband. Then Jack Thompson did a silent shave in the mirror. With each stroke, there was always a contemplative pause, as if he was working something out in his mind and the movement of the straight razor helped to straighten out the thought. Then the methodical selection of shirt, tie, pants, and jacket, whether or not a vest should be included. Finally, the collection of books, notes, and papers neatly arranged on the dresser by his wife. Each page was taken in hand, absorbed, and returned to the pile. "Manden," Jack Thompson would call out after all of that, "bring me my cane."

As the eldest son, it was Manden's job to bring his father's dark wood cane, which he did not seem to need for walking but carried with him always when he was about, a third leg that supported his pride in himself, in the community he dreamed would one day exist. And every time Manden brought the cane, his father would quote from a book of African proverbs. Rain does not fall on one roof alone. One falsehood spoils a thousand truths. The ruin of a nation begins in the homes of its people. Then, offering a nod and a smile, Jack Thompson would depart . . .

Manden looked through the subway booth at a group of young boys roughhousing near the escalator. The boys, five or six teenagers in all, grew louder and formed a circle on the platform. The teenagers clapped and nodded to a sound it seemed that only they could hear. One boy, wearing a baseball cap turned to the back of his head and combat boots, entered the center of the circle and started dancing, contorting his body and popping his head and arms like a robot. He spun around, gyrating, his long, slender build moving like a rubber band. Passengers walked by quickly, holding bags closer, shifting direction to take the stairs. They paused in disgust or avoided eye contact altogether. The boys were oblivious to the crowd and the hostility, engrossed in the rapture of their world. A heavyset boy with a deep, booming voice began to rap:

Lil' man in the game to play
Ain't even got another day
In a fucked-up world
With a fucked-up hand
But he gonna play it quick
Cuz nobody gives a damn
Yeah he gonna play it quick
For he lose the chance to can
All them suckers in his way
Fuckers hatin' on his life
Tryin' to sink his battleship
Tryin' load him down with trife . . .

The boys grew louder and louder, laughing and stomping their booted feet on the ground. A short boy with a scarf around his head took a joint out of his pocket and lit it. Older women looked on and shook their heads. Businessmen and students with backpacks skirted the circle. Small children pointed. But nobody said anything to them.

Manden watched the boys play at shooting each other and sighed. He sighed because he would not have said anything, either. Even with the roughhousing, the dancing, and the loud profanity, he would not have said a word. But part of his job responsibility was to ensure that there was no smoking anywhere in the subway, let alone an illicit substance. He would have to approach them. He would have to attempt to put the fear in them that a grown man could put into a boy, and he knew that he did not have such power and they had never known such fear. He was not their father, they would remind him. And they would burn into him with the white heat of young, hateful eyes. And they would hate him for appearing as if he was trying to be their father, of reminding them of the fact that their fathers were not there. Or that men around them did not really want them in their lives. Like Uncle Randy. Manden knew this feeling. He grew up with it himself and carried it with him like a diamond that each day became harder and sharper. He knew that when he approached the boys with authority, they would not re- spect him any more than the other men who looked like him, those who glared at boys like them with hatred and disgust.

Manden left the booth and walked slowly toward the boys, his back throbbing. Some of the teenagers saw him coming, and their faces became masks of stone.

"There's no smoking here," said Manden. "And you all need to quiet down and move on."

The short boy with the joint took a long toke, pinched it out with his fingers, and stuck it behind his ear. "We ain't got to do a damned thing, Mr. Officer. How you know we ain't got somewhere important to be, toy cop?"

The other boys were electrified by this opening exchange, and Manden could feel their excitement, their heat. Their eyes all said: "I dare you."

Manden said, "You all have to go."

The tall rubber-band boy said, "You ain't none of my mama. Daddy, neither, wherever the fuck that niggah is. We ain't going nowhere."

Manden put his hands in his pockets and looked at the boy. Although he wanted to smack him across the face, he understood the boy's anger and disrespect. He understood the triggers and knew the boiling points as well as any alchemist, although his own fury had long ago been snuffed and cooled and hardened.

Passengers rushed by, eager to get to their next subway destinations. Manden looked at the teenagers, and they glared back at him through the brimstone of defiance and rage and helplessness. One of the teenagers said again, "Man, we ain't going nowhere." The others cackled and nodded in agreement.

Manden looked through them, into their frightened hearts and out to the dark and empty tunnel behind them. "Well, that's one thing you boys are right about," he said. "You ain't going nowhere."

He left them there and returned to the glass booth. Their laughter and jeers followed him in the stagnant trail of air, until he closed the door behind him and they hit against the glass. He let other thoughts empty from his mind. Because it was easier, Manden reasoned, looking away from the boys, much easier to watch the other creatures of the herd that passed hurriedly through the subterranean chambers of the D.C. Metro system. Peacocks flashed their wares, chirping loudly in the hopes that the world would see and hear all of the reasons they were special and valued. Silver-backed gorillas, angry and bitter from years of anger and bitterness, pounded their chests as they walked, daring any challengers. Packs of hyenas scavenged for easy prey, stiff competition for the snakes waiting in the shadows. But sometimes there was a lone elephant that had long ago lost touch with its own kind, watching the jungle

of creatures disapprovingly, despairing in the disappointing truth
that its own reality differed not from the others. Manden watched
the passengers go by. Had he become a lone elephant too?

On the radio, the dispatcher began again, and since Manden
heard his name this time, he could no longer ignore it with the
ease with which he had done most of the morning. "Dispatch to
Thompson. Come in . . . Thompson, what's your twenty?"

Manden snatched the radio, cursing under his breath. "This is
Thompson. I'm stationed at the information booth at the west entrance today. Come back." Manden waited for a response, grinding
his teeth. Nothing.

So except for the Code Purple, the day was ordinary. Still, a man
had ended his life earlier that morning. He had his reasons, thought
Manden, whatever they were. The man "jumped the fence," as
Manden and other guys working the subway sometimes joked
about during break times when there were other such incidents. But
after the chuckling died down, a coughing affliction always seemed
to take hold of them all, and death hung heavy in the air like a smog
that choked them the rest of the day. This no one ever discussed.

Manden again caught a glimpse of his own watery figure mirrored in the booth glass. He leaned against the counter, his back
aching. There was still that thing growing near his spine. He called
it a thing, since the chiropractors and radiologists had found nothing there, nothing wrong with him. On damp days and in moments
of uncertainty, he could feel the thing's presence more than ever.
It had started growing when he was sitting next to his mother all
those long hours in the pew at his father's funeral. She was holding
his hand tightly, until the numbness in his fingers traveled up his
arm. He felt the beginnings of the thing growing then, a hard kernel
that formed and pressed into the high-backed wood as his mother
swooned and the deacons shouted, a lodged pit that his spine had
since curved around. He could feel it always.

The sound of keys jingling the booth door interrupted Manden's
thoughts. His coworker, Piper, a red-headed man in his twenties,

let himself inside. His face held a pale green pallor. He nodded at Manden. "Going home, Thompson. They got somebody to relieve me, thank God. Sick to my stomach. I guess it was too much excitement for me today," he said.

"What?" asked Manden.

Piper covered his mouth with his hand, shaking his head. "I saw him."

"The jumper?"

Piper nodded. "Some of him, anyway. Coroner had pieces of him on a black plastic sheet on the platform." He covered his mouth again, as if staving off an urge to retch. "Did you know that it takes eighteen football fields for a train to come to full halt when it's traveling at top speed? I've seen a lot of things. You probably seen it all, but Lord Jesus."

Manden felt nothing. "Bad, huh?"

"You should have seen his hand, Thompson," said Piper. "I swear, I'll see it in my dreams tonight. Usually, they leave notes tucked in their pockets, you know? Or they spray-paint something. 'Fuck You.' 'I hate life.' 'Love Always.' You know, something. But this jumper had written one word on his damned palm. I had my flashlight, and I was scanning near the police line, and I saw it. On his palm, he wrote the word 'WHY,' with three question marks." Piper rubbed his stomach. "That's it. Just 'WHY.' It gave me the creeps. You know what I mean? For him to end his life and leave a one-word epilogue like that. To take himself out and leave only a question. I lost my breakfast right then. Spilled my guts, but I couldn't help it." Piper shook his head. "See you tomorrow," he said, and exited the booth.

Manden watched Piper walk away, thinking of the jumper. People ended their lives for a lot of reasons. Some of them didn't seem serious enough to commit suicide over. Others might have been understandable. Like losing your mind bit by bit. Like a slow death in a cell. He wondered if Horus had ever thought about ending his life. Manden looked into the darkness of the tunnels. It was between train arrival and departure, and there was no air blowing about.

And in spite of being inside the Bastille he had fashioned for himself, Manden could not keep the rushing thoughts from breaking through the walls of his mind. Was he any better than the jumper? He woke up every day and asked himself why he was here. He could think only of what he hadn't been able to save. But there was Brenda and Sephiri, both of whom he had let down today. Wasn't there still something worth trying for with them? Surely his brother's family was worth salvaging, but he didn't know if that was possible, and he didn't know how to find out. In those small, quiet moments, when Manden watched Sephiri staring or spinning or flailing, he wondered what he was waiting for. Maybe in his heart, he was waiting for some moment when the boy would somehow be different, when things were not what they were. So much of his life was still in conflict, still left blank. But he could not haunt the underbelly of the city forever, could he? He would have to face what he pretended did not exist at some point, for nothing was going away.

And it was then that Manden wondered what Jack Thompson would have thought about his boys now. The man who had brought Bed, Louisiana, to its knees when he was only nineteen, then went to New York to become the man he was to be. At least, that was the stuff of bedtime stories with their mother long ago. What would he think of his sons now? The one who lived beneath the Rocky Mountains. The one who dwelled in tunnels under the city. Jack Thompson's boys had fallen out of separate windows of the moving thing that their lives became. And his grandson, Sephiri, was floating in amniotic fluid, able to hear only his heartbeat and the muffled rumble of the world.

Manden looked into the dark tunnel. The blackness stared back at him. "We're all a long way from home," he said.

Leaping Spirits

*B**ed, Louisiana. Summer of 1940.*

The old men said that Jack Thompson had too much blood in his eye. And every time his grandmother Lucy Thompson looked at him, when she was fireside to his obstinate ways and brazen nature, she was proud of him and scared to death. At such moments, she would press her hands into her soft gray tufts, her eyes twinkling from a deep chocolate, almost wrinkleless face. "Look like my Nathan is still here," she would say, barely able to reach his shoulder to give him a pat. When she looked at Jack, she knew that his grandfather—her husband, Nathan—had returned. She was convinced of it. When Jack was born, she recorded the event on the limbs of the family tree sketched in the back of a heavy Bible, right next to their dead daughter's name, which was Annie Mae.

And when Lucy looked at young Jack Thompson's smile, the one that lit his face when he came back from the river with his sack loaded down with fish, she knew that Nathan, *her* Nathan, hadn't gone anywhere. No, he hadn't left at all after Baker and his boys hung him from that tree. After everyone had their fill of gore and rage, and the children went hoarse from cheering alongside their parents as he swung in the evening breeze, Nathan Thompson hadn't flown back to heaven like everyone thought. Lucy was sure of that now.

That day, her Nathan waited until the mob left. Then he untied himself and dropped to the ground. And Lucy understood now that it hadn't been safe for her Nathan to come by the barn where the women took her after she passed out, after she tried to fight off Simon Baker and his boys as they dragged her Nathan from the front porch and one butted her in the head with a rifle. The other women hid Lucy in the barn after that, out of sight, back there where the sows were suckling.

And when Lucy swept the porch before sunrise, she sometimes thought of the stories the old women used to tell her about the leaping spirits when she was a young girl. Those spirits that re-fused to move, having so much left to do and having so much they needed to right, they came back. "When a man dies badly, and he angry about movin' on, or if he got important things he want to finish first, his spirit leaps back across the gorge to the living," they said. And that was when she understood that Nathan had become a leaping spirit. Lucy was sure that was what her Nathan did. How else was it that she could turn over under her quilt at night and crack her eyes to see him sitting by her side? There he was, smiling, with the same smile her grandbaby Jack had now. Yes, Lucy was sure that Nathan decided to come back when they tightened the noose around his neck, when the perfume of magnolia blossoms filled the air like perfume. He decided then to return after they were all finished with him.

Lucy had worked it over many times in her mind. Jack's grand-father Nathan untied himself after he was lynched and dropped to the ground. Then he went for a long, long walk. He strolled through the poplar groves, bogs, and wispy mounds of Spanish moss, crossed the Pearl River, and headed back up the dirt road to her porch on the bright morning their daughter Annie Mae was dying as she was giving birth to Jack. He waited until she sighed her last breath. He waited until Jack's crown arrived at the threshold of her womb. He waited for Lucy to let go of their daughter's cold hand and grab hold of Jack by the head, then the shoulders, then the

arms. He waited until Lucy held little Jack in her arms, all bloody
and furious. And right after she wrapped Jack up tight in the quilt
that she spent all summer stitching for him, and he was all warm and
new, why, that's when her Nathan made the leap. Leaping spirits.
Yes, indeed. So when the strapping Jack Thompson, all of nineteen,
grinned at Lucy every time she handed him a glass of sweet tea,
when he cocked his head that certain way, she knew it was Nathan.

But it was the blood in his eyes that worried her. They were just
like Nathan's. The way those eyes stared down at someone, even if
he was taller. And here again, it seemed like those eyes glared down
from a watchtower Jack built somewhere in the sky. Her grandbaby
became an inert substance when people tried to make him bend. No
matter the request, his response was always the same if he thought
it ate at his manhood. "I ain't pickin' no cotton, and I ain't 'bout to
bale no hay," he would say.

And by Jack's nineteenth summer, the people of Bed, Louisiana, had more than enough of him. They complained of Jack's
sassy mouth, which they insisted would get him killed. "He won't
do right," they said. "Why can't the boy just do what he's told?"
they asked. To top all of this, when he was thirteen (and before
Lucy knew or could do anything about it), Jack became Bad Man
Hank's adopted son. He was his protégé in both dog fighting and
gun running. No one was bold enough to say anything to Bad Man
Hank, so they emptied their grievances out on Lucy's front porch
over iced tea and spoon biscuits. "The boy's *too* sure," the old men
warned from rocking chairs. He was too insistent, too questioning.
"It's a shame, the things he learnin' from Hank. And plus your boy
got that brass-runnin' mouth. Can't no good come of it," they said.

And even if the black people of Bed couldn't purchase anything
without first drawing up an account of debt, even if the water in the
creeks on their farms was diverted away from their crops, even if
the Bourbon family elite ruled the land like the hand of God, what
business was it of this hard-headed boy? People said that Jack was
"smelling himself," which was what some young bucks did when

the scent got too strong even for their own good and they took to stirring things up. And since Jack's father was never around, and his mother and grandfather were in the ground, they shook their heads and looked to his grandmother Lucy for an answer to the problem.

But when Jack announced that he was going to marry Delia, a slip of a girl whose family had been making furniture since the first slave quarters, the town of Bed sighed with relief. The area had long ago been christened Bed for the sturdy sleeping frames the girl's great-great-grandfather made, popular with many plantation families far and wide. Lucy rejoiced in the anticipation of a family simmering her grandson's temper down and clearing his eyes. She set about embroidering handkerchiefs and canning peaches for the harvest wedding. She smiled and told herself that her Nathan decided to sit on the porch with her this time around after all. She exulted in the thought that he had finally decided to leave the impossible task of altering evil alone.

And all of this might have been true if one of Simon Baker's sons hadn't touched Delia. When they came looking for Jack at the Pearl River and told him what happened to Delia, how Judd Baker waited for her as she crossed Boudreaux Field and unleashed himself, the blood in Jack's eyes deepened, and even the Pearl River flowed in currents of ruby before him.

Upon hearing about the rape, Lucy looked everywhere for her grandson. She arrived back at the house, praying he would be there but knowing that the laws of cause and effect had already been set in motion. She saw that the shotgun was missing from its brace above the front doorway frame, where it had been since the day of Nathan Thompson's hanging. Finally, some people came to tell her that Jack shot Judd Baker, that the sheriff had organized a manhunt for him, that she had better prepare herself for a funeral, because there would be nowhere he would be safe. "There's a history," one of the men said as he stood on Lucy's porch, barely able to look her in the eye. "He too much like his grandfather."

A deathly silence settled over them all as they stood on the rotting planks, as they thought of what happened to Lucy's husband, Nathan.

Another man began again. "Before your boy run off, I heard Simon Baker sayin' it's time for a repeatin' and none too soon." He gave Lucy a hard look then. "Jack's got too much of what they like to kill in him, Lucy. Can't you see that? It's him standin' up what make 'em cut him down. We all seen it before. I just hope we can get to him 'fore we got to put him in the ground." The women pleaded to Lucy with their eyes after this, unsure if they could handle one more. One more husband. One more lover. One more nephew. One more son. One more lynching in their lifetimes, in their memories, in their dreams.

After the people left, Lucy stared into the sky for a long time. Then she stood up and went to the kitchen to get a bucket. She was going to do what she saw her Gullah grandmother do, an ebony-toned matron from the Georgia Sea Islands. Lucy went out into the yard to the pump and filled the bucket with water. Then she took the bucket to the front porch and sat down in her chair next to it. She stared into the water and began to pray. She prayed that her Nathan would help Jack get away. The wind blew across her cheeks.

Lucy looked into the bucket. The water rippled.

She could hear Jack swimming swiftly across the Pearl River, his strong, young arms cutting through the current like blades. *Go!* She could hear his legs thrashing through the water lily and rattlesnake master and bounding across the pecan groves. *Run!* He was striding on past the state line. He was running on the wind. Away from the noose. Away from her.

Lucy looked into the bucket. The water rippled.

She could see Jack running up the black silhouettes of hills and through greenish blue pastures. She could hear him bounding and panting, his footfalls pounding the earth. And when the hot, swampy air around her dissipated to a cool northern breeze, she knew her grandbaby was safe at last.

Lucy looked into the bucket. The water was still.

But now Lucy knew something else. The ending of everything
was now laid out before her in a neat row: her buried children, her
murdered husband, her missing grandson. The wind blew across
her cheeks. "No more leapin'," she whispered, since it was clear
that everyone she loved had decided not to come back again. And
she was too tired to consider what the rest of the days on the porch
might be like alone. Lucy sat in her chair until the long shadows of
late afternoon vanished into the night, until the moon rose and fell,
until the flies came to cool themselves on her cold body, a refuge
from the blazing sun of the new day.

Scratch Line

Jack Thompson ran. He did not know where he might end up. He didn't have the time to think about what he did when he was running for his life through the flesh-cutting high grass, the path that his grandmother Lucy made for him in the water of the spirits. His reasons for running were clear. How it would change the course of his life was not. But he never, even for a second, thought about letting Judd Baker live (had he done it just for Delia or for his grandfather Nathan too?). And he knew—even as he stole food and hid under bridges at the Virginia border, even when he skirted the Capitol Building and the Washington Monument in the dark and joined the other cargo and stowaways on the ferry from New Jersey, he knew he would make the scratch. He would make the line, no matter what he met when he made it. He arrived in New York City in the fall of 1940. Busted but sure of himself nonetheless.

Scratch, as old Bad Man Hank used to call it, was when it came time to determine if a pit bull dog was brave enough, if he was willing to fight in spite of everything, if he could rise from the blood and the dust and the shouts like the champion he was born to be. "If he don't make the scratch, he's a damned cur," Hank would say. "Don't ever be a cur in nothing, boy," he would tell Jack. And it was from Hank that young Jack Thompson learned that there were worlds beneath the one in which they were forced to live. There were rules of governance that they themselves could decide. "A man's will can't go but one way," Hank would tell him. "Let it be of your own choosin'."

Back in 1934, young Jack was the only one allowed to stand next to Bad Man Hank. The "Bad" stood for the gun-running and moonshine businesses he conducted. Like the other men whom people discussed in hushed voices, Hank insisted on being his own man in his own way. Infamous Hank, dark as coffee, with his opulent three-button suits and hats bought with money from mysterious sources. "I'ma train you up," Hank told Jack. "Cuz you got that red fire in your eyes. I likes that. Don't ever lose it, boy. It'll help you see some thangs that you didn't know was there."

The pit bull dog was Hank's love. During important events like dog fights, Jack stood next to Hank, to the envy of men twice his age. Rich in several things, Hank owned many dogs, but his favorite was a dog named Toby, a buckskin-colored canine with a shiny, stout nose. He came to matches with much pageantry to watch his dog do battle. Many men placed their bets on Toby. One hot summer evening, when Jack was thirteen, when the insects in the air were louder than the humans, he stood with Hank and the other gentlemen dog fighters in the dirt round. There were old white men descended from old money. There were refined black bootleggers and gun-runners. They were all businessmen, and this was business. But they were also curators, protectors, and preservers of lines of canine aristocracy brought over from the gray cliffs and kelly-green pastures of Ireland. They were the keepers of the Colby, Heinzel, and Corvino blood lines that coursed through the veins of these dogs of the New World.

If a dog turned away, hesitated, or sat during a pit fight, a scratch was called by the referee. It was the great moment of truth. Each spectator held his breath. For this was the final test. This was the instant when the dog who showed any weakness had to make his choice. He had to answer a question. This was the moment the dog who tore into his challenger, splitting skin, crushing bone with his teeth, and blinking in the blood spatter, got to see if his opponent had the courage to continue the challenge.

And at such dog events, silence rolled in like a fog, and all were tense, eyeing the two dogs in the ring and their dog handlers down in the pit, one for each warrior. And the men knew that for the dogs, the scratch line in the center of the pit was the equator of the earth. Each dog was brought to the opposite side by its handler, panting and drooling, preparing for the moment from its point on the axis. Each looked at the other from the miles across the scratch line drawn down the middle. Each looked into the other's eyes as if to ask the only question that mattered: "Will you quit?"

Hank and young Jack watched Toby with apprehension that day. Toby had been the most injured in the pit fight, and Hank and Jack struggled to control their trepidation, to brace themselves against the bite holes in Toby's neck and the piece of his ear flapping in the breeze. They had seen this sort of carnage before but never grew immune to its gravity. The other dog, his fur white all over, with splotches of black here and there, bit into Toby's leg early in the match.

Jack heard the *crack crack crack* over the banter around him. He heard the sound of Toby's femur breaking. Toby shifted his weight under the stronger dog, trying to free himself from his vise grip. But Toby's opponent seemed to understand his strategy right away and pressed Toby to the ground, dislocating his shoulder. But Toby quickly shifted beneath him, and the other dog lost his bite hold. Toby struggled to his feet, staggering. But suddenly, Toby turned away, unexpected and so impossible. Hank's jaw dropped, and young Jack gasped, and the men around the pit chattered nervously.

"Scratch!" shouted the referee.

All of the men were motionless and thunderstruck. From the opposite side of the ring, the other dog stood still, as if daring Toby to challenge his throne again. Then, trembling with excitement, Toby lunged forward. In the hush of the pit round, it seemed that only wind and heartbeats could be heard. He pushed forward again and again, shaking his head as if to clear his vision. Toby hauled himself to the very edge of the scratch line, the dust trampled down by blood and spit and foam and urine under his body. The two inches across might have been like two miles, and the other dog was waiting for Toby still, daring him. Toby towed himself like a boat through a swamp, his broken limbs dragging behind him until he neared his destination, the towering, powerful leg of his opponent. And with the last bit of strength in all his body, Toby bit into the other dog's leg before collapsing in front of them all.

It took a few seconds for the men to emerge from their trances. Hank was the first. "That's enough," he said, climbing into the pit.

The owner of the winning dog, a tall red-headed man, looked on respectfully, reverently, at this ritual. And after a long silence, he said, "By God, what a warrior, Hank. He'll always be game. That's for sure." He wiped his forehead with a handkerchief as the other men nodded somberly in agreement, and there was talk around the ring:

"Never seen one go down like this."

"Gotta have some pups off this one."

"Hard as nails and dying harder."

But Bad Man Hank couldn't hear them, and he quietly held Toby, for he was not sure if the dog would survive this time. And no one knew the love Hank felt for him and the kindred sense he had; for like himself, the dog had many times looked death and destruction in the eye, as he himself had done in many business meetings, when the guns sat on one side of the table and the money on the other, and the men standing behind each pile dared the other to make a move. "The great pit bull got the heart of a lion," Hank said at last. Then, turning to young Jack, his eyes burning, he said, "Keep that fire you got, Jack, like my Toby." Neither of them knew that soon after that day, Hank would die in a gun shootout, and the blood in Jack's eyes would seal his fate.

And all of these things burned deeper into Jack Thompson's mind when he arrived in New York and walked the streets, stumbling in his worn shoes, his legs rubbery with fatigue. There was Lenox Avenue and Mount Olivet Baptist Church. There were little boys chasing each other around, loud and dirty. There were twin little girls, their chocolate faces like dolls cradled by their frilly yellow bonnets. They smiled at him, and he smiled back. He walked through mazes of drugstores, chop suey places, barbershops, and endless rows of tenement buildings with laundry hanging out of the windows, a great net that webbed the city. He passed a theater, and there was a poster of Daisy Richardson's legendary brown legs. Cab Calloway boo-wah boo-wah-ed in his ears. There were children, their eyes clogged with mucus, the toes poking out of their shoes, begging for money. There were women with ruined eyes and painted faces like those he saw in Louisiana juke joints and feeble men with the empty eyes of the fallen. So much was different and so much the same. And it was then that the seed of his desire to seek out something else of his own choosing, to change something around him, took root in his mind and grew.

Jack walked on. There were vendors and street hawkers, all of them bold and brash and smiling. As he walked by, one of them shouted, "Buy Eternity Tonic and live forever!" And he thought of his own mortality and what taking the life of someone else might mean, what his own death would have meant in the ring of time. And he had the thought (which came to him from a realm beyond understanding) that if he'd been killed, had Judd Baker's father or brothers caught him and hanged him as they planned, he could always come back. He could be killed and then return. Lives were like that. Spirits were like that. He knew this with great certainty when he saw his grandfather Nathan in the doorway once when he was sneaking home from Hank's place at dawn. The lamp on the table in the window illuminated his grandfather's face, so much like his own and yet so different in the way it shimmered like water. Nathan Thompson stood in the doorway holding his gun, as he had when the Klan tried to come for him, as he had on all the nights he protected his wife, Lucy, after his death. In the slow seconds, Jack opened his mouth to speak to the apparition, but in the moment he blinked and tried to ready his tongue, to ask his grandfather what it was like in the dimension in which he dwelled, he was gone.

All of that coursed through Jack Thompson's mind as he made his exodus from Bed, Louisiana, as he crossed the scratch line of 125th Street in New York City in 1940. The early part of what was being called World War II consumed the city's attention. But in the back alleys and bars and velvet-curtained rooms, people wondered and whispered, asking, "What world? Whose world?" Jack heard this back in Louisiana, too, when worn brown men talked about another war on the stoop of the town store, folding their newspapers and shaking their heads. "What world? Whose world?" they asked. One old man, who in 1919 played trumpets from the deck of the U.S.S. *Philippines* in the 803rd Pioneer Infantry Band in Brest, France, during the first World War, answered, "Don't nobody know, but it sho wasn't ours. Still ain't."

And standing near the door of a club on a trash-littered street, Jack again listened to the old black men wonder what all the fuss was about as the jazz poured out like a hot liquid over everything. He walked on, all the way to the edges of the city, where the Hudson River rippled in dark majesty, ebbing and flowing in brackish currents. There he cried for Delia (what would become of her now that he could never return, now that what happened to her had made her someone else?) and for his grandmother Lucy, who he felt in his blood was gone, for he could no longer hear her whisper in his ears or feel her hand pat his shoulder. And that was when he put it all away in a box in his mind: the memory of his grandfather Nathan's face, the look in Judd Baker's eyes when he shot him, the love of his grandmother Lucy, what once was his sweet Delia, and the father Bad Man Hank had been. Staring into the Hudson, he closed the box and dropped it into the river for eternal safekeeping.

Then Jack Thompson turned to face the city and breathe its ferociousness. He let the smoke-charged air fill him with the promise of another life, one he would craft out of concrete and steel. He listened to the city sing. The blues swirled with the sapphire sky, and Ethel Waters's voice floated through the air. He listened to the city cry, the creak and clank of empty ice boxes and plates, and the bitter grumblings of tired women. He looked at the waiting buildings. They loomed high above, shoving against one another in the crowded skyline, daring Jack Thompson to enter their company. He turned back to the Hudson River, in awe as he looked out beyond the currents reflected in the last rays of the vermillion sun and beyond that to the horizon.

Years later, as he died on the concrete of a basketball court in Harlem watching the clouds move across the sky, he would have that same feeling of wonder, possibility, and love for his wife, Maria, for his boys, Manden and Horus, for all that was and all that might have been. He would come to know the secret of all things dormant, of all things risen.

Red Folder

*A*s the water source beneath the surface slowly shrank and the vegetation soured, the locusts began to feel the pull of time . . .

In the early morning, Warden Stotsky arrived at his office and found a red folder on his desk. He knew a red folder meant that a prisoner, either through formal medical examination or random HIV blood check, had contracted something fatal, something that came to claim his wasted life. On the lip of the folder was a white label with the number 02763 printed in small letters.

Stotsky stared at the folder but did not open it. There were no second chances, only existing conditions. Rehabilitation had never been part of the equation. It was not his business to care whether his prisoners lived or died, only how, and the state of mind they came to hold at the end. For how else was he to measure the success of Black Plains—the measure of his own success—long aligned with life inside the prison? It was will against dominion.

He stood up and went to the cabinet that held all of the prisoner files and extracted the one belonging to Horus Thompson. Stotsky read a list of family members: Brenda Thompson (former wife), Manden Thompson (brother), Maria Thompson (deceased mother), Jack Thompson (deceased father). There were no children listed. There was an old police report from the 28th Precinct in New York, that read, "Jack Thompson: 45-year-old black male shot and killed at political rally. 197 Chester Avenue. Harlem. July 21, 1966."

The report went on for several pages. The inciting event was an escalating protest rally. Police moved in. A riot ensued. Jack Thompson was shot in the fray. There were no suspects, and no one had been arrested. There was an FBI report detail attached to a photograph of Jack Thompson that listed previous residencies, places of employment, locations frequented, speaking engagements. Under "Special Family History," it read, "Anti-American activities; Jack Thompson (father) affiliation with Communist groups, militant organizations, and inflammatory statements against the government in New York beginning approximately 1945."

Stotsky turned back to the front of the paper stack and stared at the mug shot of Horus Thompson. The piercing eyes, the whites looking as if made of alabaster, the pupils of the blackest coal, stared back at him. He had graduated from high school. Following that, he went into security work in the employment of the same company for more than ten years. He lived in a small apartment on Hawaii Avenue in Washington, D.C. There was a copy of a property deed that listed his name and Brenda Thompson. He had no prior police record. Not until he kidnapped and killed a retired police officer, Sam Teak.

So there in print was one life in one file. Now Stotsky felt ready to read about the rest of it. He reached for the red folder and opened it. His eyes raked over a medical report and settled on the summary: "Horus Thompson. Age 34. Male. Black. *Diagnosis*: Possible Advanced Multiple Myeloma, cancer of the blood plasma cells. Aggressive stages. Hypercalcemia detected. Abnormal levels of monoclonal (M) proteins found in blood and urine. High levels of beta-2 microglobulin and lower levels of albumin suggest poor prognosis. Possible accumulation of tumor cells beneath the skin. *Location*: Scalp/back of the head. Possible widespread malignancy in the bone marrow. *Suggested test:* Full pathology with bone-marrow aspiration and biopsy to establish extent of malignancy. *Suggested treatments*: Autologous stem-cell transplants and chemotherapy maintenance thereafter."

Stotsky closed the folder and leaned back in his chair. There would be no medical assistance or treatment, of course. Nor would 02763 be notified of his condition. He was already a dead man. That much had been certain—had been promised—since the day he entered Black Plains. There was no need to punctuate that knowledge with the contents of the red folder, Stotsky decided, as he had done before with other files, other lives. Horus Thompson's death would not sway the institution one way or another. In any case, there would be more Horus Thompsons, millions more.

But the warden sank deeper in his chair, trying to stem a growing agitation. Because to admit that he was troubled by Horus Thompson's medical report, that it bothered him that death could enable him to escape before he was finished with him, was a disconcerting sensation. He looked around his elegant office and wondered what he was really doing. He was not collecting debts to God, the devil, or society. He was only keeping inventory of the dying and the dead. He was merely the ferryman, trapped on an enormous barge of cement and monitors and steel and fear, floating without end from one current to the next. Each folder in his filing cabinet held a story, each inmate with different beginnings, variant middles, but all with the same end. Sometimes he thought about the finality of this and wondered if he, too, was lost, adrift on the raft. A pain streaked the warden's chest as he stared at the red folder on his desk. And that familiar nameless quandary showed its face to him, as it always did on such occasions as this, when he looked from the windows of his castle and cursed the rule of time.

Strangers

Sephiri felt as if he hadn't been to the Obsidians, the great black rocks that rose from the ocean, for a long time, and he was distressed by the fact that the route was no longer clear in his mind. How could he lose his way there? And he wondered how it was that he could remember how many seconds it took for the swishing sound in the toilet to stop after flushing or the symbols on the license plates of cars but not this. He was stricken by a panic that he might never see the dolphin or the Great Octopus again. There would be no one to answer his questions. In his usual way (screaming, kicking, biting, flailing, silence), he tried to tell the Air people about his concerns, but they did not understand. They put him in that different room, with the different ceiling and floor and things inside. They changed his space—changed his position on the planet—so that he could no longer remember the exact route to his friends, his world. And if that were possible, then wasn't everything in danger of disappearing? The sanctity of the medicine cabinet, the precision of time, even himself?

All of this plunged Sephiri into a great depression, and sleep lay upon his chest like a heavy stone from under which he could not rise. He thought he heard his mother's voice, that familiar sound in his ears as he lay in a haze of grief for his lost room, his lost place, his lost way, but he could no longer be sure. He lost track of time in the long, drowsy stupors that came one after the other.

Sephiri even lost his boat for a time. He wandered the shore looking for it, until fatigue caused him to sit down, and he fell asleep near a sea turtle's egg nest burrowed in the sand. The eggs hatched and crawled into the crashing waves as he slept. Some survived to meet their destinies. Others were picked off by waiting gulls and folded back into the cycle of birth and destruction. He awoke to find the boat washed up on the shore and was filled with relief. It was just as he'd left it. It had not suffered some happening on the high seas, as he'd feared. And it was a great balm to Sephiri to know that the boat, at least, would never leave him. That even if he were never to find the Obsidians again, the boat, at least, would hold him safe. The World of Water, his world, had righted the axis again.

He longed for the iridescent coral reef, the serenades of the whales, the bright scope of the anglerfish that escorted him through the black water of the deep. He got into the boat and sailed aimlessly out on the surface, looking. But he could find nothing. Worst of all, out there in the lonely expanse, he missed the cheer of his friend the dolphin, who never allowed him to drift into unhappiness. Where could he be? His friend was gone, and he had the sinking feeling that the other inhabitants of the World of Water were somehow gone, since even as he floated in their life force, he could not find a single sign of them. He looked up at the lonely sun. It looked back at him with indifference, with inconsequence, like the beings of Air who were deaf to his language, lost to its meaning.

Meaning and messages. Sephiri wondered what of these the locusts brought. Those mysterious beings that somehow found the way across the two worlds to visit his dreams. He thought of how they swarmed about his head and on the pages of his drawings, their amber bellies glowing in the darkness of incredible landscapes. Where were those places? Sephiri looked over the water, bleak in its everlasting flatness, not a sign of the Obsidians as far as his eyes could see. And he despaired at the thought of never knowing what happened to his world, as he had never known about so many other things. Bitter tears ran down his face.

Sephiri looked over the side of the boat into the water. He saw his shifting face reflected and wondered if it would be better to be absent—not there—like the empty side of his mother's closet. And a longing to be free of the two disconnected worlds grew inside of him. In the Land of Air, he was merely a visitor who could neither speak the language nor understand the customs. In the World of Water, down in the deep, he had neither gills nor buoyancy enough to stay. He slid down into the lap of the boat and cradled his knees to his chest, listening to the tired thump of his heart. The soft slosh of the water against the sides accompanied his whimpers. He sank further still and settled on the bottom, his body pressed against the warm, splintered wood. The cloudless sky lay over him like a billowing sheet, thin and silent.

He felt an urge to cry out to his mother. Could she hear him? More disturbing was the fear that there could be no comfort between them, even if his sorrow could reach through dimension to her. There had never been a common language between them. In those seconds of exhaustion when she clutched him in the coat closet, when he rose and fell with the heaves of her chest and listened to her sob, there was no way to tell her that he did not want her to cry, that it was OK. And she possessed no language to allay his fears. Not like the dolphin or the Great Octopus. Not like the order of the medicine cabinet or the perfection of the grandfather clock. Sephiri looked up at the boundless sky. He had lost the way to the Obsidians. He couldn't find his way back to the shore.

He drifted into whatever stasis exists beyond sleep but before death. Then he awoke to the sound of waves. At once, he was aware that he had been drifting for a very long time, but something felt different. His eyes were crusted over with dried tears and the salt air. Slowly, he opened them.

The sun burned behind a huge white cloud. He sat up and looked around. The little boat that carried him was now beached on the shore. But he did not recognize this one. It was not like the other shore from which he had disembarked so many times before. The sand was not tan but white. There was no trace of the sea turtle nests or the geometric patterns of the sand crabs. But now, incredibly, there was a man standing in the shallow water near the boat. He was tall and lanky. His eyebrows, his lashes, and the tufts of his hair were caked in salt. His dark skin was ashen and hung over his frame as if on a hanger. He wore thin gray clothing that was torn about his arms and ankles. But his eyes were clear and sad and kind. Sephiri stared in confusion and disbelief. What world did this man come from? He was mesmerized but not frightened. And he stared as the man waded toward him in the shallow water, climbed into the boat, and sat down without a word.

The tide came in as if it had been ordered to do so, and the two of them floated out to sea. They sailed in silence for a long time, neither of them saying anything. The man did not look at him and stared out over the water. And when the sun (which never set but moved only across the sky) had repositioned, it began.

"How did you get here?" Sephiri asked.

In the wake of the child's voice, the man thought that there was something familiar about it, like a song heard somewhere before, but he could not identify it with any certainty. "I don't know," said the man, not taking his eyes off the water. His head, to his surprise and relief, had stopped throbbing. "I followed the light, and here I am."

Sephiri was shocked that the man could understand him. But he was more shocked at the mention of the light. He thought of the light he knew from the coat closet. "You know about that too?"

"Yes," said the man, dipping his hand over the side into the water and letting it run through his fingers. He did this over and over. Intermittently, he stopped to look at the sky, then went back to dipping into the water. At last, the man turned and looked at Sephiri. "Yes," he said again.

Sephiri was thinking that there was something familiar about the man's face. He thought he looked like the man in that picture he'd found in the duct vent. Maybe he had come from the picture world, wherever that was. "In the other world, I saw the light in the coat closet. I tried to follow it, but I got tired. I got lost in the dark."

The man looked deeper into the boy's face and thought that something was recognizable about it but did not know what it was. "Me too," he said. "But I kept coming. Now I'm here."

Sephiri wondered if this man could help him find his way to the Obsidians.

They floated on.

"Do you know about the Obsidians, the three great black mountains in the ocean?" asked Sephiri.

The man shook his head.

Sephiri was disappointed. "Well, my friends are there. It's a wonderful place. I looked and looked, but I can't find them anymore." And he was newly pained by the possibility that the creatures of the deep and the lair at the bottom of the ocean had somehow vanished. He thought of all the lovely afternoons floating on his back with the dolphin and fought back tears.

After a while, the man said, "Sometimes we lose things we can never get back, and sometimes we find something that we didn't know was there." The man smiled.

Sephiri shook his head as he stared at the man's smiling mouth, the grayish teeth. "I don't like this place anymore," he said, his stomach knotting. He looked out at the water. "This was my world. But now there's nothing here." Sephiri looked back at the man. "Where do you come from?"

"I come from a place where everything is gone," said the man.

Sephiri warmed to him a little. "Really?"

"Yes. Everything is gone. Color is gone. Light and dark are gone, at different times, but one or the other is always gone. Everyone I loved and hated is gone. The past is gone. The future too."

Sephiri tried to imagine such a place. In the Land of Air, there was the problem of too much being there.

"Is there anyone you love in the place where you come from?"

asked the man, thinking of diamond-encrusted skies and a woman who was chiseled into sculpture. In his mind, he could see her face, the licorice locks that framed doe eyes, the dark berry lips. But he could not remember her name.

"What do you mean?" asked the boy.

"Is there anyone you love there? Anyone who loves you back?" He looked into the boy's tender face.

Sephiri was not sure what that meant. Love. Maybe it was the order of the medicine cabinet, the way the long words on the boxes never changed. He looked out at the empty water and wondered if missing something was love. Sephiri looked at the man, confounded.

The man's mind was a swirl, and some thoughts were vanishing forever, and others were surfacing to stay. He thought of the Mummy who would not go back through the Catacombs. *We ain't going nowhere but in the dirt.* He looked at the moving sea. "You can always go back, you know," said the man.

Sephiri balked at the idea of going back without finding the Obsidians again. He didn't want to feel as if he was giving up on his friends. But he was not sure if floating around looking for them was better.

The boy and the man sailed on silently.

At length, the man leaned back in the boat. "I've seen and learned a lot of things in the place I was before. And now that I'm here, I know that things can be different. You have to choose the world you want before you can live in it, don't you think?" He looked up at the bright sun.

"I guess so," said Sephiri.

"Maybe we can get back to the shore," said the man.

"I don't know the way anymore," said Sephiri.

"Well, how did you do it before?"

"Do what?"

"When you came out here and went to the Obsidians place, how did you get back?"

Sephiri had never really thought about how he got back to the shore. Or out to the three great black rocks. He just knew the way out to sea, to his friends, and he knew the way back. But just before he did go back, there always seemed to be something from the other world that interrupted him or called him or . . . something. Now everything was quiet.

"I don't want to talk about that right now," said Sephiri. "Tell me about where you were before this place."

Thinking of the cell, the man did not want to answer. He did not want to revisit, even for a moment, that place where he once was. That place that wanted to put him to death. There were so many other important things to remember, now that he was free to do so. Now that he had put away the rest. "There's nothing more to say about that other place. But I'll tell you about something else."

Sephiri listened with great interest. "Yeah?"

"Sure," said the man. "When I was walking and walking through the path to get here, it was the first time I actually believed that I could see my way through."

Sephiri thought about the distant light he saw in the long, meandering passages of the coat closet. He had tried so hard to make it to the light. "I was in a dark place like that. There was this light, and I tried to get to it, but I was too tired."

The man nodded. "I know how you feel. The longer I traveled, the farther away the light was. But after a long, long time, after I couldn't feel my legs hurt or my head pound anymore, I thought only of reaching the light and making my way out of the dark. That's what drove me here. You might have made it, if you had kept going."

The boy thought about that. This was his greatest fear. Being lost and not finding his way forward or back. When something was moved, like his things in his cubby box in the playroom, like any of the toys beside his bed, or like the room itself as they had done at the center, he felt his path was threatened.

The man sat up and looked closer at the child's face. As he

looked into the boy's eyes, something in them spoke to him of a long-ago time. "Do you like marbles?" the man asked suddenly. The question came to him as if he had waited all his life to ask it.

Sephiri was surprised that the man was familiar with such a thing. He thought about the bag of marbles that the man who sat on the dangerous couch had given him. They were a wonder, and he enjoyed them very much. Each a perfect sphere of glass. Each encased with some smidgen of colorful magic in the center. He lined them neatly down the center of the upstairs hallway, then lined them up along his windowsill over and over. In the evening, when they were lit with the last of the day's bluish light, they looked like stars. "I do like marbles," Sephiri said. "I like to line them up on the windowsill when the sky starts to get dark. They look just like the faraway balls in the sky."

The man looked at the boy, and more things faded while others became clear. "I used to be really good at shooting them with someone," said the man. And here he tried to remember Manden's face but could not. "That was a long time ago. Do you shoot them too?"

The boy shook his head. "No, but I like to make lines with them."

"Yeah? I used to hold it just like this." The man curled an ashen index finger under and around his arched thumb. And he wondered why he could remember these things and forget others. "I used to park my favorite cat's eye—it had this mean green streak straight down the center—right here in this finger pocket. Then I'd look along this imaginary line in my head, you know, a line that went from my mind to my hand to my target. Then I would just will it there. I would just will it to happen. You know what I mean?"

Sephiri did not know what to say. He had never thought of willing something before. He was not sure if he had willed the World of Water or if it had always been there. He was not sure if the Land of Air could be willed into something else. He knew only what was and how he felt it should be.

"I'll bet you could do it, if you tried," said the man.

The boy looked at the sea foam scattered about. "If I went back there, do you think I will see you again?"

The man watched the current move to and fro. While they talked, the boat had floated back toward the white, sandy shore. He thought about the song sound in the boy's voice and the something that looked back at him from the child's eyes. "Yes. I'll meet you here at this shore," he said, pointing.

"What will we do?"

"Oh, I don't know. We can ask each other questions." And one question surfaced in the froth of the man's mind, and his heart answered it: *Yes, this is the child.*

"Really?"

The man was filled with the wonder of his thoughts. "Yes. But only the ones worth finding the answers to. Only the ones worth asking."

The boy looked out over the water. The dolphin hadn't come, and the ocean would no longer take him to the Obsidians. This world had abandoned him. "No one understands me in the other place."

"But we understand each other here, don't we?" The man smiled.

Sephiri stared at the smile, feeling doubtful. "But that's because we're in this place."

"Maybe it's because you wanted to hear me, and I wanted to hear you."

Sephiri thought of what the Great Octopus said about a voice waiting and wondered if it were really true and why this man could understand him but his mother could not. "I tried for a long time to get my mother to hear and understand me, but she doesn't," he said.

The man nodded, and a solution to the boy's problem came to him without having to think about it. "You could try with your heart."

"With my heart?" The boy looked around at the empty world.

There was only the sound of the wind and the water. He looked back at the man. "What's your name?"

The man was silent for a long time. More things faded while others became clear. "The thing I was called . . . It seems like the longer I've been here, the more I'm forgetting those kinds of things. But I don't think that's something to worry about. What's important is who you are." And here the man remembered the words "I am dead to you" but could not remember what they meant together.

"But how can you forget who you are?" asked Sephiri.

"You'll remember for me, won't you? The important parts of me. Besides, the only thing left I know that's real is my voice. And you."

"Me too. But inside," said the boy.

"Me too. Deep down inside," said the man.

"My name is Sephiri."

"I know."

"Oh . . . but how?"

The man looked intently at the boy. "I knew you before you were born."

Sephiri was filled with wonder. He looked back at the shore.

The man pointed to the low, rolling sand mounds. "It's OK to go back sometimes, you know. Sometimes that's the way through."

They floated on and landed in the shallow waters of the shore. They sat together in the boat and looked at the dunes. The tide came in again, and Sephiri knew that the boat would soon float out again. He thought of the warm bed in his room. His stomach churned with hunger at the thought of a peanut butter and jelly sandwich. And there was the smell of coconut oil and cinnamon. Always. These were guilty comforts, and Sephiri was not proud that he had stopped to consider them in the midst of such a time of uncertainty. But maybe if he tried . . .

Sephiri got out of the boat and stood in the shallow water. He turned to the man. "But where will you go?" he asked.

"I don't know," said the man, and he was not bothered by the thought.

Sephiri looked at the horizon. "There is a line," he said, pointing to the beyond. "The Great Octopus once told me about it. He said it marks the beginning and ending of all things."

"What is it like?" asked the man.

Sephiri shrugged. "The anglerfish are the only ones who have gotten close enough to guess. The dolphin told me the others were afraid. They said it's like a great mirror that goes on forever."

"A mirror?"

"At least, that's what they said it looks like. But they didn't want to get too close."

"Oh," said the man, staring at the horizon. There was a distant humming sound. There was a sudden breeze, and the ocean ebbed and flowed.

The waves grew higher and chilled Sephiri's shins. "Will you go there?" he asked.

"Perhaps," said the man.

"But what if you can't find the shore again? This place is a big place."

"Call to me, and I'll follow your voice."

"You'll hear me?"

"I promise."

And so the boy turned to go, and the man watched him walk over the sand and disappear.

Promises

*T*he locust eggs continued incubating and birthing, and each new clan
tunneled its way to the surface, prepared to live and die in this way,
generation after generation . . .

Horus watched his son vanish from his sight, and it was a long
time that he sat in the boat staring at the place where the little one
had been standing just a moment ago. He was filled with an inde-
scribable joy and longing. He distilled the sound of the boy's voice
and imprinted the little brown eyes, pensive and wide, into his soul.
These he would never forget. And he would remember the shore,
this shore, always.

The tide rose higher still, and the boat headed out without being
directed to do so. The sun once again moved across the sky. Horus
sailed out on the water toward the line that the boy spoke of. Time
melted into the waves. One moment was a day. One day was a lifetime. He lay down on his back in the little boat and looked up. The
billowing sky lowered over him like a veil of chiffon, and it looked
as if it was close enough to touch. He reached his hand up and felt
the cool slip of atmosphere.

And then from afar, the locusts appeared. Horus heard them
first, then he saw them in their countless multitudes roll closer and
closer, a swarming, boiling mass. At last, they arrived above his head
and hovered there. With their unremitting hum, the locusts spoke

to him of the time of change, when today becomes yesterday and tomorrow becomes what is to be. They spoke of a universal law: life is a series of choices, and time is a series of lives. And when Horus had taken in all there was to take, when he absorbed the truth, both a poison and a cure, the locusts dispersed and were gone.

He sailed on.

The rays of the yellow sun warmed his head. He watched it move once more across the sky. One moment was a day. One day was a lifetime. Then he came to a place where the boat stopped of its own accord. Horus inched his head to the lip of the boat's side and looked down. Bright shimmering light rose from something below, blinding him. He sat up and leaned over the side of the boat for a closer look. There, reflected in a great mirror, he saw his face and his hunched back and his battered head. More of his memory faded, and other things became clear.

Horus looked deeper at his face in the water. "I promise," he said to the reflection. "I promise to come back again, to start again." And when he blinked in the awesome gleam, he saw a hawk, magnificent with plumes of black and gold. He would take this form, his heart decided. He would soar the sky. He would land on the shore when called by the boy that is him and not him. He would wait for the time when he could fly again.

Disappearing Acts

*C*rowded deep in the earth, the locusts rubbed against one another and signaled exodus. And even the dormant incubating nymphs knew that they could no longer remain there . . .

Jimmy Eckert rode the elevator down to his lair. As he descended, the silence poured into him like a thick oil, filling his throat and plugging his ears. The kind of quiet he had grown accustomed to was a salve to the gratings his ears endured on the outside. The special silence in the Secured Housing Unit was something he learned to welcome, even miss, for he had neither patience nor use for the sounds of men outside of Black Plains, busy with futility, loud in nothingness.

The rodents made a special kind of noise that mixed with the silence, which he carefully observed for abnormalities. In fact, it was those times when the rodents were more talkative than usual that concerned him. Sometimes they even talked to themselves in different voices. He'd heard them before, among the sounds of the fallen. It was as if each changed voice was not just another voice but another person. Different personalities inside of a mind. There was this one rodent who spoke anxiously of his family being dead. Of course they were dead. He had killed them all. But the rodent had somehow blocked all of that out and talked only of a man in the

232

shadows who was trying to do him harm, who was responsible for the atrocities to his family.

Jimmy Eckert learned as a boy that so many things happened for so few reasons, too few to matter. It was love, hate, redemption, revenge, or fate. There were infinite combinations, but the ingredients were always the same. Still, this rodent would chant over and over about how he had tried to protect his family, but now the shadow man was after him. The rodent's "friends" assured him, according to the rants he'd taken to just before they had to use the stun gun on him and put him in restraints, that they would help him, that they wouldn't let him down. His friends would accompany him when the time came to kill the man in the shadows. They would meet him at his end and help him understand what his life had been. "They haven't made it yet," he would say at the end of his ravings. "But they'll be here."

One day, when Jimmy Eckert looked through the slot of his door, he smelled something fouler than usual. Something dead. When he opened the door, he found the rodent on the ground next to the toilet. Staring at the body, Eckert wondered if he died in his hallucination, with the different parts of his self, his hated life, bleeding out of him. The inmate had smeared feces all over the cell and all over his body, before whatever happened had happened. This was not too great a shock to Jimmy Eckert, since he had seen more than one phantasm, and the worst that dreams could create. But what sent tremors through him was the look of the dead man. Bluish-gray and mouth agape, he looked like a different person. His hair was blond, not brown. The fingers were long and contorted in the pose of death, not the stubby nubs they had been before. Jimmy Eckert stared at the body, unable to move. And there again came the difficult questions with difficult answers. Who was this dead rodent on the floor, and whom had he been guarding all of this time? The prisoners could not walk through walls of concrete and doors of steel, he reminded himself. There were coercions and restraints. There were bars and locks. Gravity pulled them toward the core of the earth. Time held their minds in a vise. They were flesh and bone. And yet this dead man was not the man he had been guarding.

Years later, when Jimmy Eckert could stand to go to edges of his mind and think of it, for it frightened him, he wondered if the dead man he saw that day had been the man in the shadows that the inmate spoke about. And he wondered if the rodent had become the shadow man and then killed him or if it was the other way around. And he wondered how many pieces someone could split himself into, if a man could really break apart—one man into many—on and on in infinite patterns, with cells splitting down into more cells, then atoms, then nuclei, then . . . oblivion. These were the peculiar questions, the rare mysteries born of the Black Plains realm. These were the things that none of the guards discussed, that no one dared speak of. Warden Stotsky called such things pure fantasy but never ordered further explanation. The silence and the frost settled over everything once more, and time made it all seem distant and imagined.

Jimmy Eckert was thinking of the shadow man when the elevator touched down on the lower level, like feet on the lush carpet of a funeral parlor. He reminded himself that Black Plains could be like rust on the mind, eating at it slowly. The shadow man was a phantom of what this place could do to both the guarded and the guards. His thoughts were not to be trusted. His eyes were not to be believed.

That was why Eckert liked making up his chants, his special poetry. It kept him anchored to the despair he believed he did control, to that which could never be changed, a liniment for his angst. The small masterpieces described a certain kind of truth, one he alone inflicted on the rodents, one he alone authored. The chants empowered him, and he used the poisonous words to erect a prison within a prison. To remind the rodents that there were levels of existence that they would have to be prepared to deal with at his hands. He had conceived of a new chant for Horus Thompson, something more they could share in the long stretches of time to come. The words appeared to him so clearly when he was driving down the two-lane road to the facility for the day's shift:

When the sun has stopped burning
When the wind has stopped blowing
When the earth has stopped turning
And the world is dust and ash
I will be there . . .

The elevator doors hissed open, and Jimmy Eckert walked down the corridor. As always, each door of the Secured Housing Unit stood at attention, saluting him. The fluorescent lights were made brighter only by what was hidden in the darkness. The rodents were braced, as usual, for the worst. And the worst would be theirs, forever. Jimmy Eckert walked slowly by each door and listened. He could hear some whimpers, some cries. He could hear whispering, manic rants, and euphoric screams of madness. But he did not hear a sound from behind Horus Thompson's door, as was most often the case. And Jimmy Eckert relished the thought that the rodent would be in a mood to match his chant, to consider ceaseless misery once again, to partake in the acrimony that Black Plains, that fate, had forced them all to share.

Jimmy Eckert approached Horus Thompson's door as he had a thousand times, as he would do a thousand more. He opened it and found the cell empty.

The Bath

In the bathroom, Brenda bathed her child in the deep, claw-foot tub. The surrounding white porcelain, the tiles, the chrome, the sound of trickling water were together cathartic, and the bathroom itself, with its buttery lighting and dark blue rugs, was at that moment a sanctuary for them both. Pouring bathwater over Sephiri's shoulders with the little wooden ladle made each dip seem a libation. On the wall was a framed Kenyan proverb Brenda had purchased from an antiques shop years ago. "Absence makes the heart forget," it read. She bought it hoping that it was true only in the largest sense, that absence only made the heart forget the sadness that had been there, not the brightness of what was and could have been. In the elegant calm, she forgot her swollen ankles and strained eyes and sat on the ledge of the tub. She lathered the soap into big white puffs and slathered it gently on Sephiri like meringue. He did not balk and was silent, as he sometimes was during this evening ritual. She, too, was quiet, emptying her mind of her troubles.

She had stayed home with Sephiri all this past week. The long sleeping bouts at the center scared her, and she needed to watch him go to sleep and watch him wake up. To her relief, it seemed that over the past few days, the fog that had gripped him lifted, and he returned to his habit of sleeping three or four hours at a time.

Sephiri curled his back, and Brenda again ladled more warm water over his shoulders. He murmured something soft and unintelligible, as he sometimes did. It reminded her of the cooing sounds he made when he was an infant, his head a downy crown, a ball of plump preciousness smelling of fresh cotton and powder. She used to snuggle him close to her, both of them curled together on the bed. That had been a time when they didn't need words between them. And it struck her that she had been grieving not only for Horus but also for the child she thought Sephiri would be.

Brenda listened to the sound of the slow leak from the tub faucet, the steady metronome of drops into the sudsy water, and let her hand rest in it. She could feel her sugary, pulsing blood, challenging her to live on her own behalf. And she knew at last that it was time to lay it all down. That the sugar had become too heavy a burden even for her to carry any longer.

More than that, she regretted that in her quest to see what might be going on in her boy's mind, she had set aside the greatest part of the truth. She alone was his mother. No matter what studies were tried or what medications taken, no matter how many articles she read or how much professional advice she received, she alone would be the one to dry Sephiri's tears. Her son had been the shape and make of her life, and she could not imagine what form it might have taken without him.

And now all Brenda wanted was her baby. To hold him, even if he fretted and hung from her arms like a doll. She wanted to pull him close to her, so close that he might soak up all of the love and comfort she wanted to offer him. Sephiri, the hidden treasure that meant his name, that had always been most precious to her, was in this little boy's frame, somewhere. And she was ashamed to admit that in the secret garden of her hopes, she had been engaged in this business of trying to fix Sephiri, as if he were a broken toy. And staring into the bathwater, she thought of all the pain and strife that gripped the world, that had befallen herself and all she loved, and she wondered if it was everyone else who was broken, and if children like Sephiri were messengers of the silence that needed to replace the noise. And it was then that she felt it was time to ask God an important question, which was this: *If I accept Sephiri as he has been given to me, might we then find our way to each other?*

Humming now, Brenda poured more water over Sephiri's sleek back and watched it run down in smooth rivulets. A mother's love. It had no limit, a story with no end. This much she knew. She would wait for Sephiri in the labyrinth of their life together. She would listen for him and move ever nearer.

Sephiri listened to his mother hum and cradled his knees in his arms, his bowed head nestled in them. What she could not have known, even if he could find a way to tell her, was that there was a man who rescued him from confusion, who helped him get back to the shelter of this moment with her, the stranger in the World of Water, who was now, for reasons he could not explain, familiar. The man who was at first not there but then there. And Sephiri could not tell his mother that when he was out in the open water, adrift in a world even he no longer recognized, when he bowed his head and cried, he thought of her. Not as a talking person of Air, but as an entity of safeness, a place of harbor, and he had longed for her then, as he longed for her now. He wanted always to know that her presence was near, of which he had been aware since the day he was born. But there were no words in the Land of Air or the World of Water for such feelings, no vowels or consonants wide enough to hold what she meant to him.

Sephiri lowered his knees into the water and lifted his head to look at the emerald green of the mouthwash bottle sitting on the sink.

Brenda beheld him. Always Horus was there looking back—in Sephiri's eyes, in the jawline, in the dimpled chin. He was there always in the little face, an echo of the man she wanted to save from the world, from himself. And there was no language for what filled her, for what had grown into fullness since Sephiri's existence began. And so she let her heart speak, and listened for the slightest sound from his. And when her eyes captured a flitting moment of his direct gaze, her heart said, *I love you, Sephiri.*

And ever so slightly, so much so that Brenda almost missed it, Sephiri smiled.

Acknowledgments

I've learned in writing this book that there is real magic in relentless effort, vision, and people who believe in your work. I would like to acknowledge and thank my husband, who for many years was my only fan, coach, and reader in the world. I thank my three incredibly patient and hopeful children who tolerated the hours and silence it took for me to write this book. I am deeply appreciative of my editor Malaika Adero for hearing me in the dark and understanding much from a great distance. My heartfelt thanks go to Annie Cameron and parents of autistic children everywhere fighting the good fight every day. I am grateful for the support of the wonderful Wilkes University MFA community: Robert Mooney for his literary hawk eyes in reviewing my work in its primordial stages and seeing it through to the end; Nancy McKinley for her priceless encouragement of all my efforts; Norris Church Mailer for that twinkle in her eye when she handed me a scholarship; Kaylie Jones, Jeff Talarigo, Jan Quackenbush, Christine Gelineau, and Ross Klavan for cheering me in the ring; David Poyer and Lenore Hart for their steadfast advice; Bonnie Culver and J. Michael Lennon for opening academic and literary doors on my behalf; and Rashidah Ismaili Abubakr for the living history she shared with me. I greatly appreciate the unwavering international support of Steve Moran of the Willesden Herald in the United Kingdom,

Suzanne Kamata of the Yomimono Journal in Japan, David Fraser of *Ascent Aspirations Magazine* in Canada, Santosh Kumar of the *Taj Mahal Review*, and Gloria Mindock of *The Istanbul Review*. I thank the PEN/Bellwether Prize, the Dana Awards, and Johnny Temple of Akashic Books for recognizing the early promise of this work. Finally, I honor those unnamed individuals who have inspired me with their light and refusal to quit.